Unspoken Pursuit

Unspoken Pursuit

KELLY AUL

Printed in the United States of America

ISBN   978-0692904787

Dress made by Matti's Millinery & Costumes

Making Your Costume Dreams Come True!
www.mattionline.com

Purebooks

"Blessed are the pure in heart for they shall see God."

Matthew 5:8

Purebooks artwork by Jessica Benson

BOOKS *by* KELLY AUL

Special thanks to:

Maggie Aul, Natalie Aul, Hannah Wagner, Matti Wangerin, Jessica Benson, and Patti Kelly

I give all the glory to my Heavenly Father, my Lord and Savior, Jesus Christ, and the precious leading of the Holy Spirit.

PSALM 18

"I will love thee, O LORD, my strength.

The LORD is my rock, and my fortress, and my deliverer; my God, my strength, in whom I will trust; my buckler, and the horn of my salvation, and my high tower.

I will call upon the LORD, who is worthy to be praised: so shall I be saved from mine enemies.

The sorrows of death compassed me, and the floods of ungodly men made me afraid.

The sorrows of hell compassed me about: the snares of death prevented me.

In my distress I called upon the LORD, and cried unto my God: he heard my voice out of his temple, and my cry came before him, even into his ears.

Then the earth shook and trembled; the foundations also of the hills moved and were shaken, because he was wroth.

There went up a smoke out of his nostrils, and fire out of his mouth devoured: coals were kindled by it.

He bowed the heavens also, and came down: and darkness was under his feet.

And he rode upon a cherub, and did fly: yea, he did fly upon the wings of the wind......

He sent from above, he took me, he drew me out of many waters.

He delivered me from my strong enemy, and from them which hated me: for they were too strong for me.

They prevented me in the day of my calamity: but the LORD was my stay.

He brought me forth also into a large place; he delivered me, because he delighted in me.......

For thou wilt light my candle: the LORD my God will enlighten my darkness.

For by thee I have run through a troop; and by my God have I leaped over a wall.

As for God, his way is perfect: the word of the LORD is tried: he is a buckler to all those that trust in him.

For who is God save the LORD? or who is a rock save our God?

It is God that girdeth me with strength, and maketh my way perfect.

He maketh my feet like hinds' feet, and setteth me upon my high places."

Unspoken Pursuit

PROLOGUE

London   1836

*H*aven ran for her life. Fear rose up in her until it was so great, she struggled to breathe. She willed her legs to move faster, but deep down, she knew she was no match for whoever was after her on horseback. They would surely be upon her at any moment.

Don't look back! It will only slow you down. Keep going! You have to find a place to hide. Haven's panic urged her onward, through the dark and dingy streets. There was no doubt other unsavory characters in that part of London to fear besides the ones after her.

"Oi! What's your hurry, pretty lass!" Sure enough, a spindly old man spewed as Haven rushed by. The frightful act distracted her for only a second. That was all it took for her to stumble over her filthy skirt. She tripped and fell to the damp ground. Her hands and knees burned from her attempts to catch herself on the cobblestone. She swiftly glanced behind her. Over her wild heartbeat, she could hear possibly more than one horse beating the street with their hooves at a fierce rate. Was she caught? Was her brief fall the end of her? Haven didn't care to wait around to find out. She lifted herself to her feet. Her lungs ached from already running so far. Where could she go? Where could she hide?

Why...why did I have to leave when I knew it wasn't safe? Regrets flashed through her mind. *But there's no time for that!* Her pursuers would round the corner any minute! Haven picked up her skirts and hurried down the narrow street. *Where can I go?* The alarming question followed her every gasp. She tried her best to watch where she was going and at the same time desperately searching for a place to hide. There, out of the corner of her eye, a dark side street came into view. Though she doubted it would provide a quick hideaway that would cause her to disappear completely, it was her only choice. She slid to a halt, almost falling in the process for the street was fairly wet, and dashed into the other street. She didn't have time to think of the possible dangers that dwelt in the shadows. Her only focus was the people after her.

The horses sounded closer and closer. When they raced down the very street she had just stood in, Haven drew back against the cold, brick building and tried to calm her gasping breaths.

Please don't let them see me! She hoped against hope as she glanced up at the dreary clouds that covered the moon. It was then that the horses passed by the street where she stood. She pressed in further against the building and into the shadows. She felt as if she might faint as she froze. Haven didn't look but heard the horses bound down the street and to the next block. She breathed a sigh of relief, however, deep down she knew she wasn't safe quite yet. There was still a substantial distance between her and her safe abode.

"Miss?" The low voice behind her made her jump. She peered down the alley where the mysterious voice came from, but it was completely dark. "Miss Romiley?" A man stepped out of the shadows as he said her name. He moved slowly, trying not to frighten her in fear that she might bolt.

"Who—" Haven began to ask when she realized what he held. It belonged to her. He slowly held the book out to her, freely offering her to take it. Haven gazed at it. When she glanced back up at the man's face, she finally recognized who he was. He had seemed nice enough upon first observation, but she didn't know for sure if he could be trusted. She remained guarded just as the sound of horses echoed again.

Oh no! It can't be them! Instead of taking the book, she spun around. She had to get out of there and find another—

"This is yours," the man spoke, swiftly drawing her attention back to him.

"Did you read it?" she hurriedly asked. The man lowered his gaze to the book in his hand. He struggled with a reply. This only caused Haven's panic, which had returned when she heard the horses growing closer. She didn't have time to wait any longer! *Doesn't he know there's someone after me?* "I must hurry. Did you read it?" she urged sharply. She again turned to glance behind her swiftly. The faint sounds were growing louder.

"I uh…that is…." the man stammered. It now appeared that it was painful for him to let it out.

"Well?" Haven took one step back, getting ready to make her escape!

"You're going to die," he blurted at last. He almost winced as he said it. Haven looked at him intently, trying to take in what he'd just stated. The man seemed relieved now that he'd gotten the heavy truth off of him.

"I know," Haven suddenly replied in assurance. The man's mouth dropped open. It was the very last thing he thought she would say in response to such devastating words. The calmness and almost determined tone in her voice baffled him above all else.

"What? Wha—" he was cut off by the sound of a loud neigh from the street.

"Hurry!" Haven breathed, "We must hurry!"

PART

I

"Then they cried unto the Lord in their trouble, and he saved them out of their distresses. He brought them out of the darkness and the shadow of death, and brake their bands in sunder."

Psalm 107:13-14

CHAPTER ONE

April 2, 1835

 love you," a soft voice whispered in her ear. Her eyes shot open. It was so real, so familiar, that it caused her heart to flutter. The young woman sat up and glanced around the small room with a hopeful smile.

"Derek?" The minute she said his name, a pang of grief hit her. She longed to keep living this unreality, yet the actuality of the matter smothered her. Deep sorrow swept over her as her heart ached with a boundless void.

She lay back once again and began to sob into her pillow. Her shoulders shook for some time before she turned and gazed at the low ceiling through blurred vision.

"Haven?" a muffled voice called her name. "Haven, are you awake?" Haven gasped and wiped her face. The door soon opened and her younger sister entered. "Why are you still in bed? Hurry up and get dressed! We don't have much time before we set sail."

"I know, I know," Haven rubbed her eyes in frustration. Her voice still wavered with emotion. Her sister noticed it immediately.

"Have you been crying again?" she neared the bed, but Haven wouldn't answer. "Mother sent me to fetch you. We need to get a few things in town before the long journey. Now get up!" she urged.

"I'm not going. I'll wait here," she replied in a melancholy tone.

"You're going to regret it. Three months is a long time to be cooped up on this ship. This is your last chance to get off," Haven's sister took her hand in one last attempt and tugged.

"Lillian, stop...I'm not going," Haven whined as her sister huffed.

"You're hopeless." With that, Lillian left. Haven listened to her stomp down the narrow hall in the hull of the ship and call for their mother.

"Oh, here we go," she moaned.

In no time at all, the door to her cabin burst open. Haven's mother marched inside with Lillian at her heels.

"What's this I hear that you're still in bed?" When she saw it was indeed true, she came to a halt and put her hands on her hips. "Haven, I told you what time you needed to be ready. We don't have much time. If you get up this instant, you might—"

"I'm staying here," Haven declared stubbornly and met her mother's gaze head on. She could tell she was more than irritated with her. Isabelle said nothing right away as she thought of what should be done. She finally turned to Lillian.

"Dear, please allow us a moment alone." Lillian flashed her sister a wry smile, telling her she was in for it now. She then silently left.

Haven didn't care in the least. Her family, especially her mother, couldn't make her do anything. In Haven's mind, Isabelle was nothing more than a flibbertigibbet. They used to be close, but ever since Derek's death, they couldn't seem to understand one another. All they did now was clash.

"You need to get up…now."

"No. Why is it so imperative that I go? Just leave me alone for once." Haven's harshness stung as she said it, but she was tired of doing this, day in and day out.

"Alright. I'll be frank with you," Isabelle spewed, "You need to stop this nonsense. It's time you grow up and start conducting yourself like a lady. This pathetic act has gone on long enough."

"Act? You think this is an act?" Haven sat up angrily and slammed her fist on the bed. "How can you possibly think this is a farce? My heart is broken!"

"This grieving has been long enough. You have a responsibility now…to this family."

"I don't care about any of it in the least."

"You don't, do you. Don't you care your father's business is in ruins? This arrangement is our only hope," Isabelle informed in all seriousness.

"Surely it's not as bad as you suggest."

"Well you don't know everything then, do you? Your father is in denial about it and too proud to ever let on to his two ungrateful daughters. If we wish to remain at this status, this is the only way to stay off of the streets. It's high time to put away your selfishness and go through with this. Mr. Wentworth has taken a liking to you. His interest and proposal is a godsend. We can't pass up this opportunity."

"I know! How many times must you tell me?" Haven shouted. "Can't you see how hard this is for me? And that I'm trying? It's just so soon after," she choked. *Why am I even trying to get this across to her? Mother wouldn't understand, nor does she want to.* Haven glanced down. How could she share her heart and tell her mother the truth? *She would surely think I'm crazy.* The pain was still too near. The man she had loved was all too real yet. She could still hear him whisper in her ear, feel his hand holding hers.

"Why won't you see reason? You are not happy to marry Mr. Wentworth, yet you aren't happy right now. What is it you want?"

"I want peace!" Haven cried. She wanted to say so much more to her mother, but her emotions wouldn't allow it.

"Well, you are sadly mistaken. There isn't a guaranty of peace in life…quite the opposite in fact. You must come to realize this," Isabelle responded without an ounce of compassion. "We are about to cross the ocean for you to marry Mr. Wentworth and start a new life for all of us. Dry your tears, swallow your pride, and get over this!" she heartlessly demanded then left the room, closing the door behind her. Haven's hands were clenched in rage against the sheets of her bed. She reached for the glass lamp on the nightstand and threw it at the door. It shattered loudly as she buried her face in her pillow and cried.

CHAPTER TWO

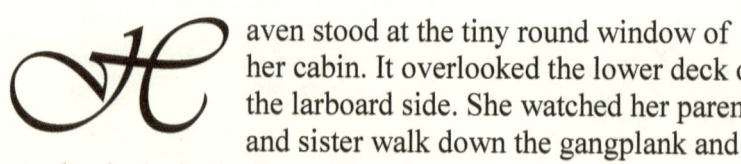 aven stood at the tiny round window of her cabin. It overlooked the lower deck on the larboard side. She watched her parents and sister walk down the gangplank and onto the docks in the Port of London.

"How I despise them. They don't care a thing about me," she mumbled angrily to herself. "Are you still with me?" she asked the empty room but was only given silence in return. Haven wiped her damp face. "Please talk to me! I need you!" she turned back to look at the rest of her cabin and set eyes on a dashing young man, sitting in the only armchair. He wore a casual blue waistcoat over a white shirt and sat back comfortably as if nothing was out of the ordinary. He met Haven's gaze with his soft brown eyes and smiled lovingly.

Haven wasn't shaken or surprised by his presence for it frequently happened ever since the tragedy.

"Derek, I miss you so much. Everything was perfect before," she moved to her bed and sat down on the edge of it, across from where Derek sat. "When you stole a kiss," she sighed sorrowfully, "It was the last time we were together before…when there was peace."

"I'm still with you. Every time you think of me, I'm here," he replied calmly with assurance.

"What am I supposed to do? I feel ill every time I think of what's about to happen. I can't marry Mr. Wentworth when I'm still in love with you," Haven painfully explained. Derek grinned at her confession. His deep brown eyes made her blush.

"Then don't," he shrugged and stated simply.

"What do you mean, don't? It's the only way to save my family from the poorhouse. And what is my alternative? Look at me…I can't go on like this," her voice wavered, and she began to cry again. "What should I do?"

"Haven, deep down you know what you need to do."

"No, I don't!" Haven glanced away from him for a swift moment. When she looked back, he was gone. She stared longingly at the chair. She thought deeply about what he'd said. Determination came over her, and suddenly, Haven stood to her feet with purpose. She now knew what Derek meant. She grabbed her purse and rushed out of her cabin.

Minutes later, Haven carefully peered out of the door of her parent's cabin. It was located across the hall of her room. She made sure the coast was clear then stepped out into the hall with a sigh of relief for her plan had been carried out successfully. She quietly closed the door then turned and ran right into someone. Both women gasped in surprise.

"Cecil? What do you want?" Haven nervously asked her ladies maid.

"Beg your pardon, miss. I was just coming to see if you needed anything."

"No, I'm fine. I'm going for a quick walk on deck, that's all," Haven lied.

"Shall I fetch your parasol?"

"No," she replied, irritated. She had to get her nosy maid away from her! "Just go and…prepare my lunch. Then wait for me in the dining room."

"Yes, miss." Cecil flitted away at once.

I'll be glad to be rid of her as well. She always makes me nervous with her fretful and jabbering ways. Haven watched the ladies maid make her way down the hall. She waited until she was out of sight before hurrying back to her own cabin to gather her things.

CHAPTER THREE

'm free! I never have to put up with my family again! Haven strolled down the street, feeling as if she was floating. The salty breeze tugged at her violet cloak and skirt, along with her upswept hair, secured under her hat. *I never have to see Cecil or the blubbering Mr. Wentworth again. I can do whatever I want! I'll show them…I'll show them I don't need their fortune or dowry. I can make it just fine on my own.* It was then that a thought struck her. *Why I'm in London! It's where the—* Her musings were cut short when a man accidentally tipped over an entire cart of fish right in front of her.

"Sorry, miss," he began to pick up the mess by reaching for a herring that had fallen on top of her silk boots.

"It's alright," she replied yet covered her nose with her handkerchief to block the foul smell. "Can you tell me how far it is to the Theater Royal?"

"Theater Royal?" he appeared surprised, "Well that's a long way off." He went back to gathering the fish as if it was the end of it. However, when he noticed Haven didn't move, he glanced up at her. She still awaited his answer. "Oh, uh...." The man stood up straight," It's several miles that way," he pointed west."Thank you. Oh, is there a hackney coach I can hire nearby to take me there?" The man burst out laughing at Haven's second question. It wasn't long before he realized she was serious.

"There's hardly a hackney that comes all the way out here, miss, especially at this time of day. Unless hired by someone of high society," he continued to chuckle. Haven wasn't amused in the least. Being laughed at was something she loathed.

"Fine, I'll walk," she huffed and she picked up her bag once again, mumbling further under her breath.

"If ya keep going that way, you'll eventually find a hackney, miss," the man hollered after her as she marched away. She ignored his snide tone and continued onward.

Haven walked and walked, down one grimy street and to the next. At times, the smell was almost too much. The east side of London, surrounding the harbor, left much to be desired. She had only been to London twice during the Season, but those times were only spent at social events in the more pleasurable part of the city. Haven had never been near the poorer side, much less on foot. She took in her surroundings with wonder at how people lived. Children ran and played among the waste and filth, while their mother's hung out the laundry, making the best of the cramped quarters. The small, rundown row houses lined the streets.

Haven couldn't help but recall her mother's words about how close they were to being forced to live with the same status. The joy she felt from her newly found freedom was beginning to wane at the gloomy thoughts. She tried her best to push them aside although, the longer she walked, Haven slowly began to realize it might not have been such a good idea traveling alone.

Maybe I should have brought Cecil along after all. Haven took in two foul characters pass by. They leered at her shamelessly. She tried her best to ignore them at all costs as she quickened her pace a bit. *No, it's a good thing she's not here,* Haven thought otherwise. *Cecil would surely be frightened out of her mind like she is about everything. She would most likely faint.*

Haven's feet began to ache badly.

How far is it? She glanced up at the sky. The sun was lowering swiftly. *What will I do when it gets dark?* She asked herself. Her determination had been so great, albeit, with each passing moment, it was starting to fade, along with her vigor. *Should I turn back?* Doubts rose up in her mind when Haven rounded the corner and heard music. The pleasant sound caused all apprehension in her to vanish, and in its place, curiosity stirred. She followed the music down another block until there was a break in the row houses and the buildings grew more sparse. There her gaze fell upon a man strumming a mandolin. A young boy stood beside him, playing the fiddle. A woman, Haven guessed was around her age, danced while tapping a tambourine against her swaying skirt. Haven watched in wonder at the free spirited young woman. Her dark eyes and skin were dazzling. She was barefoot and her long black hair flowed freely. Though she'd never seen any before now, Haven had always thought the gypsies were romantic. She could never understand why they were hated by so many. They fascinated her.

Haven took in the colorful, round wagons behind the group. It looked as if several Romani families were camped out in the grassy area. Some of which were selling their trinkets and wares such as baskets and furniture. There were a few small signs offering their fortune reading services also.

Haven slowly approached. She could tell they were aware of her presence, but it didn't faze their song one bit. She did notice an older woman get up from her place by the baskets and reached her hand towards Haven.

"Your palm, miss?" she asked in a thick accent and raspy tone. Haven silently obliged and gave the lady her hand. She intently watched her study her hand. The woman was inches shorter than Haven and had deep wrinkles from years of hard work and being in the sun without a bonnet. Her greying black hair was pulled back with a colorful scarf tied around it. She wore a dark dress with a yellow scarf tucked into the waist and a bright shawl over her shoulders. Haven tried not to stare at the woman's dirty bare feet.

"A good zign. I zee happiness in love. But you look at your past and childhood vith a cautious and fearful outlook. You've had sadness."

"That is true," Haven admitted. The woman let go of her hand and took a step back. She then took in the young lady from top to bottom.

"Vat is a beautiful young rakli like you doink in ziss part of de city alone? Runnink avay maybe?"

"I'm on my way to the Theater Royal. I sing opera, you see," Haven stated hurridly. She was tired of being treated like a child. "It is not vise for you to be travelink diss far alone," she admonished.

"Yes, well…." At this point, Haven had had enough, "I better be on my way then."

"Vait…did you say de Zeater Royal?"

"Yes."

"I know one of de men in charge there."

"You do?"

"Yes. And it's still very far. You vill never make it before dark. If you have no oder plans, you could stay the night here," the woman offered. Haven glanced at the gypsy village behind the woman in uncertainty. Although, what was her alternative?

"I have plenty of room in my vagon."

"Are you certain?"

"Yes, yes. My nav is Sabina Dooriya."

"Nav?" Haven asked in confusion.

"My name," Sabina smiled.

"Oh," Haven met her smile with her own. "I'm Haven Romiley." They shook hands. Sabina didn't let go straight away. Instead, she quietly groaned.

"Zat is more clear to me now," she opened Haven's hand, palm up.

"What?" Haven was hopelessly enthralled.

"I almost missed it," Sabina went on, causing the young woman's curiosity to stir with anticipation. "Diss line here…you vill be met with much fame. Diss must be the Zeater Royal, vere you are headed."

"Truly?" Haven gasped with delight. Sabina finally let go just as a young man stepped up behind her and caught Haven's attention. He was very skinny with long black hair that touched his shoulders. It covered his face as if on purpose, for he appeared quite introverted and shy. Sabina must have noticed Haven looking past her and also turned to see who it was.

"Oh, dis is my son, Jessekiah."

"Hello," Haven greeted. He only nodded in return. She had to strain to see past his hair to find his warm eyes. There was a kindness in them.

"Jesse, dis rakli is stayink viss us tonight," Sabina stated. Haven watched him smile slightly, revealing severely crooked teeth. She could tell he was trying to hide it.

"I know he's not much to look at…." Sabina turned back to Haven and spoke as if her son had already left but she suddenly stopped herself. Haven guessed she merely realized he was still present. Her presumption swiftly turned to confusion the way Sabina gazed at her. "But he's very smart. He's a very talented craftsman," she finished. Then, instead of standing right in front of Jessekiah, she stepped back a bit and smiled at him. She put her hand on his arm. Haven couldn't understand the abrupt change in Sabina's behavior.

"Jesse, I told her dere would be plenty of room in our vagon because you like sleepink under de chere."

"Y-y-yes," he stammered, causing his mother's smile to waver.

"Chere means de stars," Sabina put in quickly, trying to cut him off. "Alright son, za za," she shooed the gawking Jessekiah, "Hurry up with ya. You must move your thinks from the vagon."

CHAPTER FOUR

April 4, 1835

*M*erril finished up sweeping the steps in front of the clinic. She turned to go back inside when she stopped. She squinted down the street where a young man was walking.

Garrett? No, it couldn't be him today. Merril went back and forth in her mind and continued to watch the man intently. As soon as he came closer and the sun fell upon his honey brown hair and scholarly apparel, she sighed in satisfaction. *It surely is him!* She would know him anywhere. His broad build and tall stature stood out. He walked at a leisurely pace, saying hello and giving a quick nod to almost all he passed by. He'd always had a kind way about him. It showed through his stunning hazel eyes and the moment he smiled to anyone he met, Garrett would unintentionally win them over with his charming personality.

"Garrett, my boy!" Merril couldn't wait for him any longer and rushed to meet him. When he saw her coming his way, Garrett quickened his steps. He met her with open arms. "We weren't expecting you until Sunday!" Merril explained in excitement. She soon pulled away slightly to look up at him.

"I wanted to surprise you," Garrett replied. His warm smile did not disappoint. He offered his arm to her as they slowly made their way back to the clinic. The two-story brick building was sandwiched between two others. It wasn't much to look at but it had been dutifully kept up.

Merril did not remove her gaze from her only son.
"Why, you look weary. Is everything alright? Are you feeling well?"

"I'm fine," he simply said, but Merril knew better by the way he hesitated. He was hiding something. Garrett quickly caught on to her suspicion. "Really…I'm alright," he urged. They entered the clinic then went to the very back of the old building. The humble clinic they owned doubled as their own home. There was a kitchen and a sitting room with two bedrooms upstairs. It was small but they were fortunate. All of the surrounding families were far poorer and their homes no more than a one room shanty.

"Are you hungry at all?" she asked after Garrett sat down at the table in the corner of the tiny kitchen.

"No thank you," he sighed and sat back. Merril took the seat next to him.

"There's no use trying to keep anything from me. What's troubling you, son?" she patted his hand with concern.

"No…I suppose not. Well, to be honest…I don't know if I'm meant to be a doctor," he leaned forward and rested his head on his arm.

"Your studies aren't going well?" Apprehension began to rise up within her. At that very moment, they heard someone come through the front door. It wasn't long before Stanford walked into the kitchen.

"Well, you're home early," he greeted rather coldly. "How are your studies going?" Stanford bluntly asked before Garrett had a chance to greet his father.

"As a matter of fact," Garrett's first inclination was to hide the truth to please his father. Yet, what was the point?

I've never been good enough for him. Why should I continue to act like everything is fine? I've done that for far too long for nothing. "It's not going well at all," he finally blurted.

"You must not be trying hard enough."

"Trying hard enough? It's been nearly two years! It's been nothing but a struggle since the very first day. It doesn't come naturally for me like it does you."

"It's a choice I made…that is all. You must make it as well. You must continue on with my practice." Stanford remained standing and crossed his arms over his chest. He was a dedicated doctor who had followed in his father's footsteps, and Merril was a midwife. The clinic had been in their family for generations and Garrett was next. Both of Garrett's parents thrived in helping people of squalor, never requiring anything in return. They felt it was their family's calling from God. The poor that resided in the east part of London were neglected, with no one to care for them, other than the dangerous factories and workhouses. The conditions there were far worse.

"I don't know if I can," Garrett replied hopelessly and lowered his gaze to his lap.

"What will happen if you don't? Who will take care of all these people in our area?"

"Stanford," Merril tried to intervene.

"You know I speak the truth. No one else will care for them," he briefly turned to her and finished angrily.

"Why must this weigh so heavily on me?"

"It's your duty!" Stanford stated in a sharp, demanding tone. Garrett couldn't take it anymore.

"I didn't ask for this," he swiftly got to his feet.

"You didn't have to. It's a God given talent as well as a responsibility!" His father was relentless.

"Well, it's not mine!" Garrett shouted louder than he meant to and stormed out of the room. Stanford and Merril froze until the front door slammed shut.

"I just don't understand that boy...never have," he sighed and plopped into the third chair at the table for it was lunchtime.

"You're too hard on him. He only wants to please you," his wife spoke up.

"Merril, doesn't he realize what his education is costing us? We're using every penny of our savings to see that he becomes a licensed physician."

"He doesn't see things as we do. Perhaps...we should tell him."

"What? No!" Stanford argued.

"Why not?"

"Do you want him to leave for good? He'll despise us. Now, I've worked long and hard today. I only wish to relax, have a bite, and not talk any more about it." When it was apparent that he was finished and had his mind set, Merril stood to prepare lunch.

He possibly despises us already, she thought.

CHAPTER FIVE

April 7, 1835

P ut it through here, then pull it all the vay through," Sabina sat closely to Haven, teaching her how to weave a basket. Haven tightly held the thin strand from a willow tree used to construct it and concentrated on keeping the weaving taut. All of a sudden, it slipped from her fingers and all of her hard work loosened. It was ruined.

"Oh, I give up!" Haven huffed and pounded her fist on her lap in frustration. "I'm not good at this at all…nor do I have the patience for it," she quickly got to her feet.

"I just takes time, dear," Sabina stated. Haven slowed upon hearing this. She had been with Sabina and her son for five days now, and she was getting more than a little anxious to be on her way. She mentioned the theater to the woman many times, in different ways, but never really got a straight answer. Though Sabina and the other gypsies were very kind and accepting of her, Haven was growing weary of the holdup. She had to be on her way to become famous.

She turned back and looked at Sabina. She was already at work finishing the basket Haven had failed to make. Her hands moved swiftly and effortlessly. It was obviously second nature to her.

"Uh…Sabina," Haven began. The older woman glanced up at her while her hands continued. "Please don't take this wrongly. You have been more than welcoming to me and I greatly appreciate your help…but, I was hoping you could accompany me to the Theater Royal and introduce me to someone there…as you said you would." There, she'd finally said it. This was the most direct and straightforward Haven had been in her several mentionings of the matter. She gazed steadily on Sabina, waiting for a reply. The older woman glanced back down at the basket.

"Are dese all done?" At that moment, another woman came over from her stand, holding two baskets of her own.

"Yes," Sabina replied. "Haven, can you help take dese and put dem under the vagon?" she managed to change the subject entirely.

"I suppose," Haven sighed and bent over and picked up an armful. On her way to the wagon, her skirt got caught on a piece of wood from a nearby worktable. As soon as she felt it tug, she stopped. She glanced behind her just as Jessekiah appeared. He smiled at Haven's odd predicament of having her arms completely full and caught.

"Oh, um…," Haven said awkwardly. Jessekiah silently stepped up to the table and gently pulled the fabric until it was free. "Thank you." He still said nothing but only met her gaze. His large eyes, partially covered by his hair, were filled with amusement and pleasure. It was apparent that he was taken with her. Everyone knew it, including Haven.

She was about to continue on her way when Jessekiah rushed in front of her and put his hands out.

"I'll h-h-he—"

"Thank you," Haven put in when she saw him struggle with his words. She could tell he was very angry with himself and embarrassed by the way he blushed. This only added to her desire to leave the gypsies and be on her way.

That night, Haven made her way into the wagon. She walked under the rounded ceiling, passed the tiny stove, two built in seats, and a cedar chest of drawers. Sabina's bunk was at the rear of the caravan with a curtain for privacy. Haven's was kitty-corner to it, near the stove. It was quite cramped but at the same time, very cozy. It was better than Haven's cabin on the ship before she fled. She pushed the curtain to the side with one hand and held up the lantern in the other. The light revealed her small bunk. Her few belongings were at the foot of it in her carpetbag. She stored her clothing in the drawers underneath the bunk.

Perhaps I can find a hackney coach a few blocks closer to the theater, Haven thought. It was slowly dawning on her that Sabina wasn't ever going to bring her there.

"This delay wasn't part of my plan," she mumbled to herself.

After Haven set the lantern down, she went for her bag. *I must find a jeweler somehow, so I can trade before I can purchase a hackney.* She dug to the very bottom of the bag until a she felt the beading on the outside of a small reticule. She pulled it out then loosened the drawstring. Haven swiftly glanced behind her to make sure she was alone. She knelt on the bed and pulled the curtain closed behind her. She then carefully poured out the contents onto her bed, on top of the brightly colored quilt. Necklaces of sapphire and emerald, along with matching bracelets and rings, etched with clear diamonds, sparkled in the candlelight. Haven took in each exquisite one, reminding her of all the times her mother wore them at different social occasions.

Before leaving the ship, Haven had slipped into her parent's cabin and taken the precious jewels. They were her mother's best. Haven took them as a means of money for her new start. She often wondered which her mother missed more, her or the jewelry?

This will surely be enough for several hackneys in addition to a few gowns and a place to stay, she thought as she moved her fingers across the items on her bed. *Just as soon as I can find a jeweler.*

She picked up the last necklace when she noticed something. *Wait, where is the diamond one?* She instantly grabbed the reticule and tipped it again, in case the piece was still inside. Nothing. *I know I took that one also!* Haven gasped. It had been the biggest and probably worth the most of all the other pieces. The thought slowly came to her. *Sabina! Would she have taken it?* Haven glanced behind her, *Or perhaps her son? Is this why she doesn't want me to leave? Is this the reason why she's been so generous?* "I've been far too trusting," she breathed and tried to come up with what to do as fear washed over her. Was there no one she could trust? The safety she had felt from the kindness of the gypsies was gone and in its place, speculation and distrust.

"I have to get away from here! Until then, I'll have to keep my wits about me." Haven opened her purse then stopped. Instead of putting the jewelry back inside, she reached inside the large bag once again and pulled out a stocking. She quickly went about putting each piece all the way inside it securely.

CHAPTER SIX

April 8, 1835

Haven emerged from the wagon the next morning. She found Sabina building a small fire nearby. "Mornink," the older woman greeted once she caught sight of Haven climbing down the narrow steps to the yellow wagon.

"Sabina, we must talk." Haven couldn't be sure, but she thought she saw Sabina stiffen a little at this.

"Yes, dear. Is somethink wrong?"

"Well no…I mean yes," Haven stumbled over her words. Practicing what she wanted to say inside the wagon was one thing but facing Sabina was another matter. If truth be told, she was a bit intimidated of the older woman and the powers she believed her to have.

"What I mean to say is...."

"You are unhappy vith me," Sabina finished. This made Haven all the more uneasy.

"No, I just...It's time that I be on my way. To the theater, I mean. You have been more than generous." Once she stopped blundering on, she fell quiet and nervously waited for a response.

"I know you tink I've been stallink dese past days and perhaps I have done it a little. I'll be honest, I've been watchink you very closely since you've come to us."

"Really?" Haven's distress quickly turned to confusion. "Why?"

"To see if you vere ready," Sabina set down the stick she used to stoke the fire and met the young woman's gaze for the first time. She briefly paused to let her smooth words sink in for she knew fully well she had stirred Haven's curiosity.

"Ready? Ready for what?" Haven was hopelessly enraptured.

"I have somethink for you. Follow me."

Sabina led the way into the wagon and came to a halt at a cabinet above the front door. The most amazing thing Haven discovered about the gypsy wagon was how much storage there was in the most unlikely places. Sabina stood up on the tips of her toes and opened the small door to it. Haven tried to see what it was over her shoulder. It appeared to be a book of some kind. After she wiped off the layer of dust in its cover, Sabina turned to face her. It was indeed a book but it had no title. It looked like an heirloom yet in almost perfect condition.

"What is it?" Haven asked when she handed it to her.

"Dis is a journal. But no ordinary one," Sabina answered. Haven inspected it closer and discovered an inscription etched in the hard leather cover. It was in another language so she couldn't make it out. She then saw that a pen was placed on the side of the binding, held in place by a small leather strap.

"Use dis pen and write in it…all of your hopes and dreams. Vatever is written vill come to pass." Haven was immediately skeptical.

Is she merely trying to sway me from what she is truly up to?

"You don't believe me, do you?" She was again taken back by Sabina's preciseness. "It's a long tradition in our Romani vays," she continued.

"Thank you," Haven finally said, still a little curious, yet her trust in the woman was growing less and less with each passing day. She took the journal nonetheless.

"Make sure you write in it." Sabina moved closer to her and placed her hand on Haven's arm, looking up at her earnestly. Haven searched her gaze for deception but found none.

Was I too quick to assume she stole from me? Maybe I did forget to take the bracelet from my mother's jewelry.

"I vant you to succeed in your dreams of singink at de Theater Royal," Sabina smiled, causing Haven's defenses to come down.

"Dya!" Just then, Jessekiah opened the door quickly and very nearly plowed right into the two women. When he saw that they had been talking and he'd interrupted, he blushed. "Oh, I-I-I'm sor—"

"Vat is it, Jesse?" Sabina swiftly cut in when he began to stutter. Jessekiah removed his gaze from Haven and looked down in embarrassment.

"Dere's some-someone here. Day need you…your services," he quietly explained slowly to get the words out.

"Alright." Sabina took her leave and passed by her son on the way out. Haven and Jessekiah were now left alone, which seemed to happen more and more often, almost intentionally. Things grew uncomfortable rather quickly for Haven. He said nothing and only stared at her, smiling slightly.

"Well, I suppose I should go and help…with something,"

Haven blurted and started for the door as well. When she neared him, he didn't move. She had to scoot closely beside him to leave.

CHAPTER SEVEN

April 15, 1835

t's your last night with us, son. Did you enjoy your short break?" Merril struck up a conversation as she turned from the hot stove to set the last plate of food on the table. She removed her white apron then took her own seat to join them.

"Yes. It was nice to get away," Garrett replied and began to eat. He momentarily glanced at his father, who ate in silence.

"Are you looking forward to going back?" His mother asked again. Garrett saw her look at Stanford as well. She appeared saddened by the fact that her husband put no effort into their son's last night before returning to medical school for a long while.

"I suppose," Garrett sighed. He didn't try to hide his displeasure.

They both fell silent for some time. Stanford took a moment to wipe his face with his napkin before he finally spoke.

"When I was going through college, I never went home on my breaks. I chose to stay and use those times to catch up on my studies." Garrett put his fork down on his plate and glared at his father. There was no missing the insinuation in his voice.

"Stanford, please," Merril began. She couldn't bear to see them quarrel again.

"No mother. Why not let him speak his mind." Garrett sat back in his chair. "Go ahead and tell me what a failure and disappointment I am." This made Stanford finally stop eating and glance at him.

"If you only tried a little harder, you wouldn't be."

"Stanford, don't do this…not on his last night with us." Garrett was about to stand in his anger when they all heard the bell, above the door to the clinic entrance, ring.

"Doctor! Doctor!" Stanford instantly stood at the man's panicked call. He rushed out of the kitchen to the front. "There's been an accident and my son—" Merril and Garrett didn't hear any more for Stanford and the man hurried out of the door.

"Don't pay any mind to what your father said. He just…just…." Merril had made excuses for him for so long she was running out. What could she tell him this time? *Other than the truth.* She took in Garrett's sorrowful expression as he waited for her to finish. *I can't tell him. I can't!* She fearfully thought. *Stanford is right. He might never forgive us!* "I know he doesn't mean it," Merril eventually blurted. She tried to cover up her distress. "He loves you."

"I want to believe it. I did once," Garrett scooted his chair back from the table. "Yet he does mean it…every word. I don't see a reason to come home any longer when all I face is his disapproval," he stood to his feet and started to leave to go and gather his things.

"Wait, don't go," Merril quickly got up to follow. When Garrett turned to her, she found tears in his eyes.

"I'll write to you," he replied. That was it. Merril now knew she had no other options left. She would risk his anger and possibly never seeing him again, for if she kept the secret any longer, she would surely lose him forever.

"Wait, please. Come back and sit down…I beg of you." She was already growing emotional at the thought of what she was about to tell him. *Stop this! How are you going to get all of this out if you start blubbering!* She scolded herself. "Please, come and sit," she urged until Garrett obliged and returned to the table. Merril took his hand.

"I have…," she fought back the tears the moment she opened her mouth.

"Mother, what is it?" Garrett quickly became concerned at seeing her cry. Normally, she was anything but sad. "I'm sorry for upsetting you so."

"No, it's not that. I have to tell you something. You must hear me out before saying anything. Promise me."

"Alright." Although Garrett was now very curious, he didn't know if he really wanted to find out what was causing his mother to be so troubled.

"There's something you don't know. It happened long ago," she shifted uncomfortably before taking a deep breath. "One evening several years ago, I was riding home from helping deliver a babe. It was near the more wealthy part of London. I heard a shriek. I then turned to see a woman, very large in the family way, in front of a grand townhouse. She slipped and had fallen on the front steps. I wanted to see if she was all right but instead, I find she was in labor. I helped her all during the night, but I knew something was wrong. Your father came to help in the wee hours the next morning. The babe finally came yet it wasn't breathing." Merril stopped to take a breath when she saw a confused look flash across

Garrett's face. There was no turning back now. She forced herself to go on. "The woman's husband sent for another, more well-known doctor but no one would come. They were…well, looked down on because she was Irish and her husband, English. We took the babe and started for home. This was when a miracle happened. He started to breathe. He was still very much in danger of not making it and had to have special care day and night."

Garrett wanted to ask what this event had to do with anything, albeit he held his tongue. Why was she telling him all of this?

"Dear," Merril squeezed his hand and became even more serious. "You must listen to me carefully. Stanford and I never…. We could never have children of our own," she paused to allow the truth of the matter to sink in.
"What are you saying?" Garrett's brow furrowed.
"We were persuaded that it was a sign from above."
"What?" his voice grew louder.
"There were many times we thought you wouldn't survive the night. You received medical attention from us. Something you wouldn't have gotten with them," she tried to explain calmly.
"You mean to tell me…they are my true parents?" Garrett pulled his hand away from her grasp. "Who are they? What are their names?"
"Can't you see you would have died? You are our son. There's no doubt about it."
"Their names!" he jumped up so quickly, Merril gasped. He had never shouted at her before. She shut her eyes momentarily before breathing the names that were forever etched in her mind.
"Reid Lennox. His wife is Ave…Ava…Eibhleann."
"Wait…Reid Lennox…isn't he the Marquess of Kerrick…the man who got the Irish into parliament?" All

46

Merril could do was nod. "That's why no other doctor would help them?" he finished putting it together before his mother also got to her feet. "Why would you do such a thing and never tell me?"

"I wanted to tell you so you would understand the reason behind the differences between you and Stanford. So you would—"

"I understand now…very clearly! Everything I've ever known is a lie," Garrett spun around and stomped out of the house. Merril didn't know what to think, other than being overwrought with guilt and so much regret. One thing was certain. Stanford had been correct. Garrett did indeed hate them.

Everything would be different. I surely wouldn't be struggling with this doctor business. Garrett walked the streets like a man with a purpose. *How could they think this was a sign from God? To take someone else's child? To keep this horrendous secret all these years?*

He didn't stop until he went all the way to the west part of London and to the block filled with the townhouses owned by the high society and members of nobility. By now, it was growing dark and the men were out lighting the tall lanterns on the street.

"Excuse me," Garrett spoke to the one nearest him. "Do you know which house is owned by Lord Kerrich?"

"I believe it's the one on the end of the block next to this one," the man replied. "Don't know if he's there now. They don't usually stay more than they have to…seein' how they don't have many friends around here."

"Thank you."

Garrett began again. He couldn't rest now. Not without going to it, though he didn't know what he would do once he arrived. He continued for two more blocks with a mission he knew not of until he finally came upon the tall townhouse. It was even grander than the ones beside it. The light grey brick was etched with intricate carvings around the bay windows. Two white columns on either side framed the entrance.

Garrett was taken back by the enormity of its size, one he could only hope to ever live in. Seeing it made the truth hit him hard all the more, knowing what could have been his. He tried to contemplate the vast difference one decision had made over his life.

Garrett ascended the stairs very slowly as if in a daze. He never removed his gaze from the front of the house. He almost regretted coming, now that he'd taken in the wealth portrayed from the building for he was helpless to change his fate. He was now even angrier.

My parents not only lied to me but also stole all of this from me…the wondrous life I should have had.

Garrett had no intentions of knocking on the door.

None of this would be happening right now…I wouldn't have to strive to please father with this doctor nonsense. All my life of working hard for every single thing…I could have been carefree. All I've ever known is a lie…and for what? For an alleged sign from heaven? He stood there fuming for some time.

Since there was nothing more to be done, Garrett turned to leave. He stepped onto the sidewalk when the door opened behind him and a butler peered outside.

"May I help you, sir?"

"Oh…um…." Garrett spun around in surprise and tried to come up with something to say. "Are the…lord and lady home?" Now that he was so close, he couldn't help but at least ask.

"I'm afraid not. They are currently residing at their estate in Ireland."

Estate? Of course! Garrett thought. "Thank you anyway," he assayed to be as polite as he could. With that, the butler shut the door, and Garrett was on his way.

I should have never come. It would have been better not to find this out at all.

He began walking again but this time, aimlessly. The more he thought about it, the more Garrett started to make sense of his situation. He also always wondered why his parents were considerably older when he was born and why he never really resembled them. Growing up, he never felt as if he belonged to his family. Even now, as an adult, he still felt austere and far off. He somehow always thought if he discovered the reason why it would make everything easier for him.

How wrong I was! Garrett mused as he sauntered to the end of the block. Finding out the truth made it all the worse and revealed to him, not only did he not fit in with the Blakeslee's, he could never find a place among his true family. He felt completely lost.

CHAPTER EIGHT

May 4, 1835

May 4, 1835

I want to make my way in this world without the help of my parents. I'll show them that I can make it on my own. I don't need them!

aven stopped writing when she realized she was growing upset and in turn, writing a little too vigorously, flipping through the journal before closing it, she was amazed to see nearly half of the book was full already.

She looked up from where she sat outside, under the shade of Sabina's wagon. Three children were running and playing within the camp. Their giggles and squeals made Haven smile. However, a passing thought caused it to fade.

Yes, I'll surely show my family that I can make it on my own by staying at a gypsy camp of all places! What am I still doing here? Sabina's ploy had worked. For the first time, Haven realized the reason why the woman had given her the mystical journal. It was merely to make Haven forget. *Why, it has been nearly a month since! How could I be fooled so easily?* Haven slammed the book shut and stood. She marched into the wagon and to her bunk. She approached it and was going to pick up her bag but stopped abruptly when she got a closer look. *That's not where I left it!* Haven knew exactly what was going on here and did not plan to waste any more time. She picked the bag up then threw a few more of her things into it.

I'll not stay here with these thieves for one more second! She huffed and started to leave until she passed the small side window. Sabina was busy cooking supper over the open fire. Jessekiah was assisting her in building it bigger by adding a few more logs. It dawned on Haven just then what time of the day it was.

It will be dark soon. I probably won't get far...and how will I get past them, so they don't try to stop me? She stood in indecision and continued to watch the mother and son.

"You fool! Now you've made de fire too big! You vill surely burn de stew," Sabina spewed and slapped Jessekiah on the shoulder. He didn't flinch for he was well used to being treated in such a way.

I'll wait until morning before they wake. Then I will leave!

Haven's eyes shot open at the first sign of morning. She could hear the birds chirping from the open window on the other side of the room. She had decided not to change the night before, so she was still fully dressed and ready for a quick escape.

Haven pushed the blankets aside, got to her feet, then lifted up her pillow, where she'd hidden her bag. She didn't want any more of her mother's jewelry stolen. She tiptoed through the wagon as quietly as possible with the creaky floor. Her breath caught in her throat when she heard Sabina stir on her bunk, behind the drawn curtain.

I made it out unseen! Haven stepped onto the grass. She glanced at the smoke coming from the fire that was only smoldering now, before moving her gaze to Jessekiah, who slept on the ground beside it. Haven only had a little further to go before she was out of the camp and on her way to the theater. She didn't care anymore if she had to walk the entire way.

Jessekiah rolled over when he heard someone walking through the grass. He opened his eyes and saw Haven headed in the direction away from the camp. Her almost whitish blonde hair that he adored was easy to spot.

"Dya...dya," Jessekiah stood over Sabina's bed and whispered. "Dya, wake up!" Sabina suddenly startled awake, sat up, and hit her head on the shelf above her.

"Oh my," she gasped loudly. Vat do you vant? You're goink to be de death of me yet, you worthless boy!" She quickly found her voice and spitefully stated. "Go avay and let dis old voman sleep."

"But...Ha-h—"

"But vat? Come on!" Sabina pressured him, which only caused him to stammer more.

"She-she," Jessekiah was growing red in his frustration with himself. He clenched his fists and raised them to either side of his head.

"Oh, you are so daft!" Sabina huffed cruelly.

"Hav-h—" he tried one last time before his temper boiled over. "Haven left!" he shouted furiously and slammed his fist against the small round table beside his mother's bed. The unlit lamp on top of it fell onto the floor and immediately shattered.

"Now look vat you've done!" Sabina stopped when she realized what her son had said. "Vait...she left? Vere did she go?" Instead of trying to speak again, Jessekiah pointed in the direction she had gone.

CHAPTER NINE

aven's feet ached. She tried her best to keep her mind off of it, but it was growing harder with every step. She kept her eyes peeled for any hackneys or jewelry shops, even for tinkers who might be willing to trade but there was nothing, only street, after filthy street. She couldn't help but wonder if her so-called gypsy friends would follow her, once they found out she was gone. Haven pushed the uneasy thought aside and forced herself to go on.

I must be getting close by now! She gazed up at the sun that was directly above her. *Perhaps lunchtime?* She guessed, although she hardly knew. Growing up, she was much too distracted with other things than to care about the direction of the sun.

Because she was so focused on getting to the theater, Haven didn't look back at the bustling people and other noises behind her. That is until; she heard a wagon approaching her from behind. It sounded like it was getting closer at a fast pace. Haven turned to see Jessekiah and his mother driving a wagon. It wasn't their round abode, but a flatbed wagon.

Oh no! She quickly returned her gaze in front of her and quickened her walking. *I will not be swayed...no matter what they say!*

"Haven dear, vait a moment!" Sabina called out, her voice cheerful. The wagon pulled up beside Haven. Still, she wouldn't look at them.

They have a small wagon. Why couldn't they have used it to take me to the theater? This just proves Sabina has lied to me all along, in several different ways. Haven's anger rose.

"Please, it's very important!"

"Oh really?" Haven finally stopped so Jessekiah pulled the reigns to come to a halt as well. "You have a wagon? Why didn't you—"

"Vat was the name of de ship your family is on?" Sabina abruptly asked and climbed down from the wagon. She walked around the horse to the young woman.

"The Harrowgate. Why?" Haven asked suspiciously.

"One of the men returned to the camp from making a trip to the harbor," Sabina took Haven's hand. "The Harrowgate never arrived in Boston." Haven's anger vanished and fear washed over her instead.

"What?"

"It vent down in a storm…with no survivors," Sabina informed solemnly. Haven gasped at the horrendous words.

"What? No…no!" she began to weep loudly. Her knees gave way in her grief. Before she sank to the ground, Sabina pulled her close and into a motherly embrace. The young woman cried against her. Amidst her deep sorrow, Haven saw Jessekiah jump down from the wagon, through blurred vision. He silently put his hand on her shoulder.

"Come now. Come viss us," Sabina gently admonished. Haven willingly obliged. She cared nothing about the theater now. Her guilt, shock, and distress was all she could feel. It weighed down on her so greatly, she felt smothered. Breathing under such sorrow was difficult.

Haven felt Jessekaih place his arm around her now as they walked her to the back of the wagon. Normally, the act could be seen as merely a caring gesture. However, she knew he didn't see it that way. To him, it meant much more. Once inside, they drove back to the gypsy camp, though she hardly noticed.

The moment they arrived, Haven jumped down before Jessekiah had a chance to help her. She rushed into to the large wagon and to her bed. She fell upon it as her tears overtook her in torrents.

I should have never left the ship. I should have been on it…I should have died with them! Sorrowful thoughts inundated until her head pounded and her throat grew sore.

CHAPTER TEN

May 10, 1835

erril entered through the clinic entrance. She hurriedly glanced around, looking for her husband, but he was nowhere to be found. *Oh good. He must have been called out to one of his patients.* She rushed to their quaint sitting room then tore open the letter she held. The curtains were drawn, so it made the room a little dim. Merril held the letter close to see it better.

Dearest Mother,

Tears sprung in her eyes, blurring her vision. She was touched that Garrett still referred to her as his mother.

Dearest Mother,

I regret my rash actions when I saw you last. I'm sorry I left without saying goodbye. I was just overwrought with learning the truth. I will be away for some time. I have a lot to think about but I wanted to tell you, so you won't worry.

Garrett

There wasn't a sincerely or yours truly at the end of the letter. He simply signed his name at the bottom of the page.

Merril wiped her eyes with her handkerchief.

"What is the matter?" She had been so caught up with her son's letter she didn't hear Stanford walk in. Merril didn't know how to respond. She couldn't lie to him. All he would need to do was take the letter from her.

There's no use hiding it from him.

"Merril," Stanford set down the medicine bottles he held and went to her side. "Tell me what's going on. Why are you crying?"

"Well," she sniffed. "Before Garrett returned to college, I...told him. I told him the truth," Merril watched Stanford's reaction. He was crestfallen. He didn't say anything at first but only sighed. He removed his hat, revealing his grey receding hair, and then his wool coat. Stanford sat down on the chair across from her.

"What did he say?" he finally asked.

"He reacted just how you said he would," she solemnly replied then held up the letter. "He said he would be gone for some time."

"Why did you tell him?"

"He was unhappy and I thought we owed it to him to tell him the truth. Garrett needed to know the reason why he's so frustrated in trying to do what you want," Merril spoke plainly; something she'd wanted to do for a long time.

"Frustrated?" Stanford swiftly met her serious gaze as if the notion had never entered his mind. "Garrett is not frustrated. And if he is, it's only because he's indolent. He doesn't realize the work it takes to—"

"Stanford, when will you see he's not like you!" Merril angrily spoke up. She couldn't take it anymore. "He's not like you and never will be. No matter how much you try. I told Garrett the truth so he would be released from trying to fit in your shadow." She started to leave the room when he spoke.

"And how well did that work? It didn't. He now loathes us both and will never trust us again." His spiteful words stung. As much as she didn't want to hear it, what he said was the truth. Merril continued on her way before he could see her tears begin to fall.

CHAPTER ELEVEN

September 9, 1835

aven ran through the crowded Port of London. Thick dark clouds, laden with rain, filled the sky. Haven wore a ghostly white satin dress with a matching feather in her hat. It was as if she stood on the side, watching the scene unfold before her.

"Wait…stop! Wait for me!" she screamed and rushed onto

the dock that led to a ship. Harrowgate was crudely painted on the starboard side of the ship in faded blue letters.

Heavy raindrops began to fall, drenching her in seconds.

"Wait...stop!" Haven reached the edge of the dock but the ship was already floating away without her. She was too late. Her family left without her.

"Come back!" Haven sat up swiftly and shouted. She soon realized where she actually was and that it was only a horrible dream. She quickly peeked through the curtain of her bunk, to see if Sabina had awakened from the noise. Haven was relieved to see her bunk already empty.

Sabina must be cooking breakfast. Haven wiped her eyes and tried to calm down. Four months had passed since learning the devastating news of her family's death. The shock was beginning to wear off but the pain around her heart remained. There was heaviness over her that never left, in addition to constantly feeling numb. She stayed in her room day after day for she couldn't find any reason to leave. She scarcely left her bed of late. If it weren't for Sabina, Haven would have refused to eat entirely. The older woman would come three times a day with food and have to talk her into eating.

Haven lay back down against her pillow as she began to tremble from weeping. She couldn't go on like this anymore. The sorrow was too deep. A few minutes passed before she sat up. She pulled herself out of bed and trudged to the washbasin, on top of the chest of drawers, when her foot caught on the strap of her bag, causing her to trip. This simple act made her huff in anger. She grabbed the bag and flung it against the wall. Several things fell out in the process, but Haven didn't care. She finished washing her tear streaked face. When she turned to go back to her bunk, she glanced down at the floor where she spotted the journal Sabina had given her.

"Write all your dreams inside of it and dey vill come to

pass," Haven recalled her words.

Dreams? What dreams? She asked herself. She had no dreams or aspirations any longer. They had all but disappeared. She now realized what was truly important. The people who cared for her was what mattered most.

"What have I done, Derek?" she spoke aloud. She waited for an answer but heard none. "Derek…are you there?" she whispered sorrowfully. Still nothing. She had never felt more alone. *First Derek…now my entire family. I have nothing more to live for,* Haven picked up the journal, opened it to the place where she'd left off last, and carelessly wrote the date at the top.

September 9, 1835

Haven stared at the blank page. There was only one desire she had left...one thing at the forefront of her mind. She took the pen in hand.

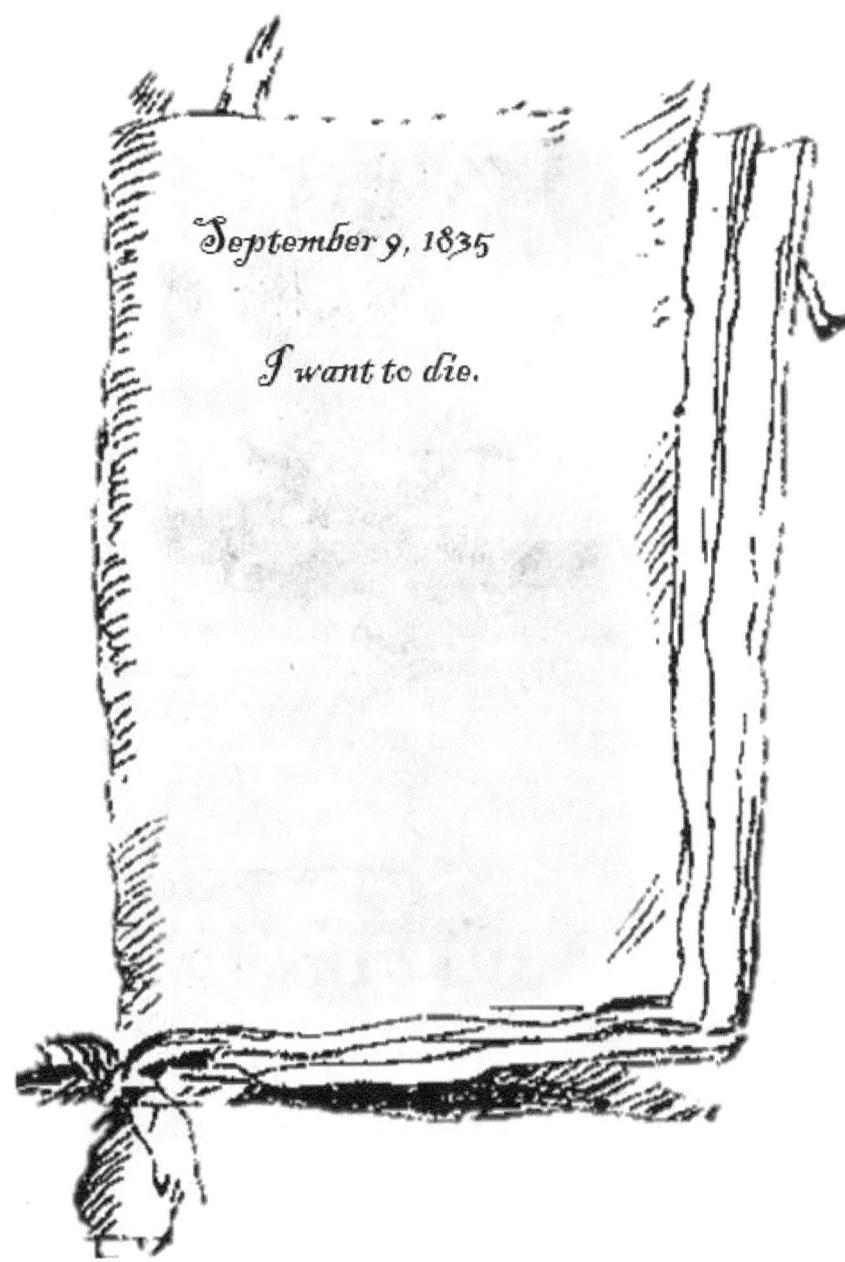

September 9, 1835

I want to die.

She wrote the simple statement before breaking down
again. It wasn't long before anger rose up in her. Without
shutting the book, she cast it to the floor. She then returned to
her bed and buried her face in the pillow.

Nearly two hours later, Sabina finished making breakfast
and put together a tray to bring to Haven. She walked into the
wagon and immediately saw a few of Haven's things laying on
the floor along with the carpet bag. Sabina took a few more
steps in when she stepped on something. She glanced down
and was surprised to find it was the journal she'd given Haven.
It was laying open on the floor. Sabina set down the tray of
food on the seat then carefully bent over to pick it up, without
tipping the tray. Instead of closing the book, she brought it
closer to see it more clearly. It was opened to the last place
Haven had written. She read the very short entry then moved
her gaze to the curtain to Haven's bunk. Sabina crept up to it
and peered inside

Sabina had frequently looked in the journal to see what
was written. It was filled with mostly foolish dreams and goals
of an idealistic young girl. However, now there was finally
something of interest, something that could change everything
if need be.

Sabina quietly shut the journal and set in against the
wooden base of the built-in bunk. She turned to leave as a tiny
smile formed on her face, one of satisfaction.

CHAPTER TWELVE

September 11, 1835

essekiah, vake up boy!" Sabina shook her son's shoulder until he slowly opened his eyes. He didn't say anything but pushed the hair out of his eyes and looked up at her in question.

"I'm goink to the market with Besnik. You must stay here and make sure de rakli doesn't leave."

"H-how?" Jessekiah rubbed his eyes and asked in a groggy

voice.

"Just figure somethink out. Vat ever you do, don't let her leave!" Sabina demanded harshly before she walked away. Jessekiah sat up and watched his mother climb into a shoddy wagon with Besnik and ride away. He then swiftly glanced at the wagon where Haven still slept. Since he had to keep guard and couldn't go back to sleep, he reached for a stick and went to work stoking the ashes in the fire next to him.

Haven opened her eyes and rolled over onto her back. The bright sun shined through the opening of the curtain. The beautiful day made no difference to her. She was still in the dark haze, much like an unending nightmare. She very slowly sat up and pulled open the curtain, only to see all of her belongings strewn out on the floor from when she threw her bag.

Haven got out of bed and knelt down to put her items back inside when she gasped. Among her belongings, Haven counted one lonely necklace and two bracelets.

There were more than twenty-five pieces when I left the ship! She desperately scanned the floor in case she missed any. Anger sparked in her as the realization dawned on her anew. She had guessed many times, but there was no denying the truth. It was clearly before her.

Sabina has been busy these past weeks! The urgency she had felt, before learning of the tragedy, came on her again in full force. She had to get out of there and quick before she was utterly penniless. Haven didn't know how much she would even get for the three pieces she had left.

I might already be penniless! How could I have been so trusting and ignorant?

Haven finished putting everything back inside the bag then got up. In no time at all, she got dressed and packed her clothes into the carpet bag as well. She really had no idea what she would say to Sabina if questioned, nor how to escape. She was much too outraged to come up with one. All she knew was, she was going to leave for the last time and would not be stopped no matter what.

After she marched through the wagon to the door, she emerged and looked around the humble camp but Sabina was nowhere to be found.

Jessekiah sat next to the fire, stoking it with a long stick. The moment he saw her he stumbled to his feet. When he took in her grey cloak and hat, it gained his attention all the more. She appeared to be going somewhere. The past few months, he hadn't seen Haven much. She always stayed cooped up in the wagon. The rare times she did come outside, her light hair was unkempt, as was her attire. Nevertheless, Jessekiah still thought she was the most beautiful woman he had ever seen.

Haven climbed down the narrow steps just as he approached. "Do you know where your mother is?" she asked and instantly grew uncomfortable. It was the way he stared at her unwaveringly. Jessekiah shook his head no. *That's odd,* Haven thought. She had never seen Sabina leave. *Thankfully, Jessekiah isn't much of a threat to keep me from leaving. He'll probably only gawk at me like he always does.*

"Well, I will be back shortly," she lied and started for the road.

"You c-can-can't leave." Jessekiah surprised her and spoke up. Now Haven didn't know what to say.

"Oh...well, I'm just going for a short walk. I need to think." Surely he would say no more. In fact, this was the most she had heard him say at one time. Haven turned to go when the unthinkable happened. Jessekiah caught her by the wrist. Haven gasped and shot her gaze up at him.

"Please, yo-y-you must stay here," he lowered his voice and said each word slowly, almost slurred so he wouldn't stutter. His deep brown eyes pleaded. Haven had never seen him like this.

"Let go of me," she demanded calmly and clearly, though inside, she was very frightened. When he wouldn't heed her, she pulled away to try and break free. Jessekiah only tightened his hold. Before Haven had a chance to scream, he yanked her toward him. Her back was now against him as he held her waist with one arm and covered her mouth with the other. Haven couldn't believe the strength he had for how lanky and skinny he appeared.

Jessekiah carried and dragged the struggling woman to the wagon. He had the most trouble getting her through the door for Haven reached for anything she could get her hands on. She grabbed onto the side of the door, yet Jessekiah eventually got her inside. Once there, he thrust Haven further in which made her stumble over her skirt and onto the floor. He swiftly shut the door and locked it.

"Why are you doing this?" Haven cried and got to her feet just as Jessekiah turned to face her.

"Why are you t-tr-tryink to le-leave?" he asked out of breath. Haven hesitated in her reply. Would he believe her if she told the truth and said it was because Sabina was stealing from her? Was Jessekiah in on it? Haven would have never suspected him until today. She tried her best to choose her words carefully but it was difficult to focus through her panic.

"I just have to get away from here! I can't stay here any

longer. I must be on my way." The more she ranted on, the
more upset she became. "You can't make me stay!" her voice
wavered with emotion. "You can't keep me locked in here!"
Haven darted toward the door even though Jessekiah stood
between her and the only escape. She put her fists up in front
of her to try and fight him but she was no match for him. He
held her arms back firmly until she stopped struggling. Haven
dared to look at him. There wasn't any fierceness on his
countenance. It made it all the more unbelievable that he was
holding her captive.

Why is he doing this? This can't be happening! It just
didn't seem real. Strangely enough, Jessekiah still held her
forearms even though she wasn't attempting to pull away
anymore.

"Please don't g-go. Don't t-t-try to leave," he spoke
quietly, almost caringly. Haven was more bewildered than
ever. "I love you," Jessekiah suddenly confessed. It was the
very last thing she thought he would say. Haven was
completely dumbfounded, to say the least, albeit she'd had her
suspicions for a long time. She merely presumed it was a
simple infatuation. This news didn't make her feel any better
about the situation she found herself in, in fact, this made
matters worse. This couldn't go on any longer.

"Di-di-did you hear me?"

"I don't…return your feelings," Haven said it matter-of-
factly, without any harshness to let him down gently. Although
she didn't know for sure, he seemed so much younger than she.
In a way, she felt badly for him and his pathetic predicament.
Before the words were out of her mouth, Jessekiah pulled away
from her like a wounded animal. He rubbed his face with his
hand as he grew red and began to shift back and forth from leg
to leg. It was as if he was trying to process this. Haven didn't
know what to do or say. Her eyes were fixed on the door
constantly but she didn't dare move. Jessekiah's strange

behavior was unpredictable and he still stood between her and the exit.

"It's b-b-because I'm stupid...I'm worthless!" Jessekiah bellowed, growing angrier with every word.

"No—" Haven started to say when Jessekiah lunged forward and into her face.

"Yes it is!" he shouted so loud it made her flinch. The young man pressed his clenched fist against his forehead. "I'm g-good for n-nothink!" his stuttering made his temper rise. "My s-speech...everythink I d-do-do!" his voice was growing louder. He furiously labored to say each word. "No one c-could l-lo-l...." he was stuck on the single word and that's what did it. His temper overflowed and he lost all control. "Love me!" he finally growled and grabbed a side table. He threw it across the tiny room. In a flurry of rage, Jessekiah picked up anything within reach and threw it as hard as he could.

Haven shrieked and cowered into the corner to stay out of danger. She had never seen anyone act like this.

"I'm sorry!" she cried and held her arms in front of her to shield herself from the flying glass and furniture. Jessekiah would soon run out of things to throw and kick. What would happen to her then? He was slowly making his way closer. Haven feared for her life.

"I hate myself! I'm go-go-good for nothing. Just like s-she says!" he continued his breathless rant. Haven knew he referred to his mother. Sabina was always telling him so.

He threw the last lamp across the room. It shattered when it hit the wall. He now stood in front of Haven, who still held herself tightly against the wall. Jessekiah stopped moving. He was out of breath and finally saw the damage he had done. He then moved his intense gaze to Haven. Shame washed over him all at once when he saw how frightened she was. Jessekiah couldn't bear to look at her tremble. He turned away and sat down on the only chair he hadn't thrown. He leaned over and hid his face by resting his head on his arm.

When it appeared his fury was finished, Haven stood up straight but very slowly. Unfortunately, he was still blocking the door. Now, however, Haven was a little less focused on getting away. A glimmer of compassion aroused in her. She carefully inched closer to him.

Is he crying? She wondered but couldn't tell for sure. She felt rather sorry for him and the abuse he'd grown up with.

"Why do you stay here?" Haven got up the courage to ask. Seeing him broken like this made her less afraid of him. Jessekiah quickly looked up at her, bewildered. The absurd thought had never crossed his mind. Sabina had told him how mindless and worthless he was and why he could never make it without her so many times, it was ingrained in him.

Haven watched him think over her words.

"You're not what your mother says you are." Boldness came over her when she saw how her words affected him. A very faint light glistened in his eyes as he slowly looked up. "Can't you see she's only using you and telling you lies so that she can keep you here? That's why I must leave. I must be free of Sabina and so do you." Haven tried to choose her words carefully. Though she wanted to tell him he needed to leave, she didn't want to arouse anything in him that might make him believe she cared for him as he did for her.

"This is why...." Haven hesitated for fear of making him mad again. "You can't keep me here," she stated pleadingly. Her hopes were put out as Jessekiah stood up.

Oh no! What have I done? Her breath caught in her throat at what he might do. He moved past her to the door. Haven finally sighed with relief when he unlocked the door then opened it. Jessekiah held the door wide open then turned to look at Haven. He didn't say anything as she gingerly slipped by him.

Jessekiah watched her from the door. Before going to the street, Haven picked up the bag she had dropped when she'd been dragged inside. She didn't so much as look back once she reached the main street. She was free!

CHAPTER THIRTEEN

t wasn't long before Sabina returned from the market. Jessekiah was busy building some furniture. He caught sight of his mother right away and watched her go inside the wagon. He knew it was only a matter of seconds before she would discover what had happened.

Sure enough, Sabina threw open the door. She frantically looked around the Romani camp but didn't see Haven anywhere. She found her son, however. He was hammering away as if nothing was amiss. Sabina marched over to him.

"Boy, quit that poundink!" she demanded. Jessekiah heeded and met her angry gaze. "Where is Haven?" When he didn't answer, Sabina knew the answer well enough. "You let her leave? I told you not to! I should have never left. You're much too simple to be left here alone!" She threw her hands up in the air. "Worthless...completely worthless...," she started in English but then continued her ranting in Romani. Jessekiah lowered his gaze, wincing as every spiteful word hit him. Each one stung. He then recalled Haven's words.

Maybe she was right after all.

"Did de rakli say anythink before she left?" Sabina asked but her son wouldn't answer. Her eyes narrowed as she stepped up to him and reached up to pinch his ear. "Tell me now!" she shouted and dug her nails in tighter until Jessekiah pulled away.

"She said she ha-had to g-g-get away from here...from y-you."

"She must be headed to de Theater Royal," Sabina mumbled to herself.

"Haven said somethink else too," Jessekiah spoke up again.

"Vell, spit it out, boy!" she huffed impatiently when he hesitated.

"She t-told me I should d-d-do the same."

"Vat? That's preposterous! You can't leave. You wouldn't make it for one minute without me," she laughed, though Jessekiah still stared at her. Sabina saw how serious he was. "How many times have I told you? Dere is a heavy curse on you. That's why you can't speak right. I'm de only one who can protect you from it. Now go and get de vagon from—"

"The only curse and-d-darkness on me is v-vat you've put

on me," Jessekiah cut in. Sabina had never heard him speak to her this way before, with a resentful tone.

"Vat?" He set down the hammer on the halfway finished chair. He then turned to the street. "Vat are you doink?" Sabina asked again. Jessekiah completely ignored her and kept going.

"You vill die without me! You'll see!" she shouted after him in one last attempt.

CHAPTER FOURTEEN

Garrett opened the door to his dormitory and found his father standing before him. Stanford was the very last person he thought would ever be knocking on his door. He looked older somehow as if he'd aged several years. His shoulders were slumped beneath his black wool coat.

"I know you weren't expecting me," Stanford stated

awkwardly when Garrett remained silent. Garrett didn't let on but if truth be told, he was shocked. He didn't think he would ever be worthy enough to have his father leave his precious patients and travel that far just to see him.

Something must surely be wrong. What if it's an emergency? Is Mother alright? Garrett began to question himself.

"Your mother told me what she discussed with you. I...." Stanford stumbled along. "I apologize for treating you with disrespect. I was wrong." Now Garrett was all the more astonished, almost to the point of panic.

There is no doubt something is terribly wrong! "Is Mother alright?" he blurted.

"Yes, yes. She's fine. We received word that her brother has passed away suddenly. He was the only family she had left." Stanford explained. "The reason I've come is because I need your help. Merril wants to go to the wake so badly...but I can't leave my patients." Garrett was starting to understand. This sounded more like his father. His first priority was his practice and always would be. Nevertheless, Garrett knew he had to help. He felt like he needed to make things right with Merril at least.

"All right. I'll come," he agreed.

CHAPTER FIFTEEN

aven walked and walked, once in a while glancing behind her to make sure she wasn't being followed. By now her feet were beyond throbbing and were nearly numb. Many times she was tempted to sit down and remove her high heeled shoes to give her feet a rest but decided against it. She was almost too afraid to see her sore feet. She'd made it much further than her last attempt in leaving the gypsies. Perhaps her plan had worked. She was indeed free at long last.

With every passing hour, apprehension began to take hold in her. Before leaving the Gypsy camp, Haven had never considered the notion of not being good enough to perform at the Theater Royal.

What if they don't like me? What will I do then? Where will I go? She thought. Just then, Haven glanced up and caught sight of the very grand building. It seemed to stand taller than the others around it.

The theater! She sighed with relief at the sight of it. The grand entrance was breathtaking. She had been to an opera there two times before, so she easily recognized it. That was how the dream had begun in her to one day sing on the stage herself.

Haven pushed her concerns aside and quickened her pace. She walked onto the colonnade and took in the enormous marble columns on either side of her. She soon reached the regal porch and to the tall double doors. She took a deep breath and tried the door. It opened! Haven meekly stepped into the empty entrance hall. She took in the colorful marble floor and majestic paintings on the white walls in awe. The lobby was a circular gallery, filled with statues of famous poets and actors. The very center was the grand staircase that led to the boxes on the upper stories. The two entrances to the auditorium were located on either side of the stairs.

Haven's gaze was soon drawn upward to a wondrous golden colored dome. She thought it looked much like a royal crown. All of a sudden, a noise made her jump. Haven glanced behind her but no one was there. There it was again. This time, however, it went on for a while. It was a faint, almost haunting noise like someone singing. It slowly grew louder.

Oh, silly me! Of course, Haven smiled when she

recognized it as indeed someone singing. She could even pick up some of the words of the song. *They must be rehearsing!* She reasoned as excitement and nervousness washed over her all at once. Was this her chance?

It has to be! This could very well be the one and only time to prove myself.

Haven walked over to the partially open door to the auditorium and meekly went inside. She was again astonished by the magnitude of the room. It was a horseshoe shape with three tiers of boxes, besides two more galleries. Two columns supported the richly gilt arch above the stage of great extent. Haven had guessed correctly. They were in the middle of rehearsals, with two women standing on the stage. One was at the very front of it. There were also two men sitting in the audience. One of which was talking loudly to the woman on stage. The only other person in the room was that of the orchestra.

"The end of the chorus could use a little work. Try it again, dear." Haven made her way down the red-carpeted aisle, building up her courage as she went. The mere size of the auditorium was rather intimidating. The orchestra began playing the intro but when the woman was supposed to start singing, she caught sight of Haven and missed her queue.

"Lindsay…." The man, Haven guessed to be the one in charge, spoke up. When he saw that Lindsay was looking at the aisle, he also turned to look. The moment he saw Haven, he marveled at her beauty. He'd never seen a woman with such a fair complexion that almost resembled a porcelain china doll, nor her light blonde hair. He got to his feet as Haven arrived at the his row.

"My, you are a pretty one," he stated. "Who might you be?" He quickly made his way to the aisle.

"I am Haven Romiley, sir. I apologize for interrupting."

"No need to apologize. This is my assistant, Malcolm

Barstow," he motioned to the other man but never removed his curious gaze from her. "I'm Trenton Martel, director of this theater," he made a large gesture as he spoke, showing off the magnificent auditorium. Instead of taking in the grand room, Haven's nerves got the better of her. She merely smiled weakly. In truth, she was trying to assess the man to determine if he was open to allowing her to audition. He appeared like a very knowledgeable businessman of medium build. Haven thought him quite handsome. His grey eyes sparkled as if he had a brilliant idea up his sleeve. His assistant was very serious and seemed only interested in business. She guessed he was several years older than Trenton.

"How may I be of assistance, my dear?" Trenton asked in a charming way. Haven couldn't help but smile, albeit, it did little to abate her anxiety.

"I am hoping to get a chance to audition for you," she tried to hide the nervous waver in her voice and put on a gallant front.

"Why yes...." Trenton replied a bit hesitantly. He seemed to take another look at her to size her up in a way. Haven grew warm under his scrutiny. "How about right now?" Haven's eyes widened at this abrupt proposition.

"Really?" she gasped before she could stop herself.

"Is that alright?" Trenton boldly put his hand on her shoulder.

"Oh yes. I'm ready," she swiftly recovered her shock and self-consciously reached up to make sure her hair was in place.

Trenton turned to the woman on stage.

"Take a short break, ladies. We are going to have an impromptu audition," he casually ordered. Haven couldn't miss the disgruntled look on the face of the woman, who had been singing. She angrily moved aside as Haven climbed the steps to the stage. Her legs felt numb and wobbly.

"I must apologize for the way I'm dressed. I didn't have—
" Haven began to ramble on when she came to a halt in the middle of the vast stage as the two men went back to their seats.

"Nonsense. You look fine. Don't worry, my dear. What would you like to sing for us?" Trenton asked.

"'Sveglio il mio amore' from Salomoni's 'Il Giglio tra le Spine.'"

"The Lily Among Thorns?" Trenton said, almost quizzically. The song she chose was from a simple, yet beautiful and prominent opera of a love story. It had been quite famous in years past and was still fairly well-known, but had very nearly been forgotten. "Interesting choice. Very well, carry on."

Haven looked out to the vast empty seats and gulped. This was it. Her chance had come. She couldn't let her nervousness stop her now. She took a deep breath as the orchestra began.

"Chi è colei che sale dal deserto, appoggiata al suo diletto? Ho sollevato te sotto il melo, dove tua madre t'ha partorito: eccola ti ha tratto che t'ha partorito."

She knew the song well, in fact, it was her most favorite. Because of this, she could sing it with full confidence. Haven became so consumed with the deeply moving words; she closed her eyes and was entirely encompassed by it.

"Mettimi come sigillo sul tuo cuore, come sigillo sul tuo braccio: l'amore è forte come la morte; la gelosia è crudele

*come la tomba: i carboni ne sono brace di fuoco, la quale ha
una fiamma più veemente."*

Haven instantly captivated Trenton. The innocence and
pleasantness in her voice were like none other he had ever
heard before. She sang each word clearly, almost effortlessly,
and was so caught up in the story she was portraying, it
brought all who listened into it as well. He had heard the song,
'Awake, my Love' before but never sung like this. Haven
brought a newness and different view to the song. It was as if
she was singing her own story right then and there.

*"Le grandi acque non potrebbero spegnere l'amore, né i
fiumi travolgerlo: se uno desse tutte le ricchezze della sua casa
in cambio dell'amore, sarebbe del tutto disprezzato."*

Haven finished the song and didn't open her eyes until the
music ended. Silence followed for everyone was far too much
in awe to speak. Trenton finally stood and clapped
enthusiastically. He was quickly joined by Malcolm and the
other ladies present, everyone but Lindsay. Haven could see
out of the corner of her eye the woman only stood stiffly with
her arms crossed.

"Well done! Well done indeed!" Trenton made his way to
the aisle once again. "Come here, my dear girl. That was
nothing short of angelic."

"Truly?" Haven smiled from ear to ear.

"Yes. I never lie about this sort of thing. You must stay and
join us here at the theater. I have just the part in mind for you."

Haven blinked at Trenton's offer. It was a dream come true! Part of her hoped she was hearing him correctly.

"There is nothing I desire more than to sing here," she confessed giddily.

"Splendid. Let's go to my office to discuss the details, shall we?" Trenton eagerly offered his arm to her, as Malcom prepared to follow.

"Carry on without me for a while!" Trenton called back to the women and orchestra before they made their way out of the auditorium.

"Do you reside here in London?" Trenton couldn't help but ask before they even arrived at his office.

"Well, that's just it," Haven slowed to a stop. Trenton stopped as well. "I've fallen on hard times of late." As much as she feared this would change his mind about her, Haven had to tell him. He would find out sooner or later anyway. "I uh…I don't have anywhere to stay and to be honest; I have very little money…"

"Say no more," Trenton raised his hand.

Oh no…that's it then. I've lost my only chance and will never again sing here. A million thoughts flew through her mind.

"All of that matters very little to me," Trenton grasped both of her hands, "You have a voice like none other. I am quite certain you can make it here. In fact, I know you can. I own a townhouse nearby and the other singers, all the women that is, live there. I should say, a handful of them do. Our cast is very large. Anyway, you'll stay with them. You won't have a care in the world there. Why, I can have a dressmaker there by tomorrow morning," Trenton came to an abrupt halt when he noticed Malcolm looking at him strangely. That was when he realized he was rambling on in his excitement. He nodded at his assistant, telling him he knew what he was doing.

"You are too kind," Haven spoke up softly, though inside, she was soaring. This was all too good to be true!

"Malcolm, I changed my mind. We don't need any other information at my office. Take Miss Romiley to the townhouse now so she can get settled. I'll come and check on you later to make sure you have everything you need."

"Yes, sir," Malcolm replied, incredulous. Trenton then turned to look at Haven.

"Is this arrangement acceptable with you?"

"I hardly know what to say. Thank you so much!"

"No, thank you for coming to audition," Trenton grinned in his alluring way.

CHAPTER SIXTEEN

aven made her way down the stairs in the lavish townhouse and to the dining room. Most of the rooms she had seen thus far, were decorated with feminine themes such as pastel and floral colors and décor. She had just gotten settled in her new room and had been told dinner would be served at six o'clock sharp.

She walked through the foyer and almost entered the dining room when she heard the front door open. Five ladies walked in, talking and laughing. Haven quickly recognized two of them from the stage at the theater.

As soon as Lindsay spotted Haven, she stopped. Her eyes narrowed as their gaze met. Other than the scowl on her face, Haven thought the woman was quite beautiful. She had reddish blonde hair and very light blue eyes that were almost piercing.

"Well if it isn't the angel," Lindsay chuckled. She then turned to the others. "You missed it, but she swooped in for an audition today," she informed mockingly. The others eyed Haven. That is, until the one, who stood nearest the door, walked around the ladies and toward Haven.

"I was there and I thought you sang beautifully," the woman offered her hand kindly, "I'm Wren. Welcome!"

"Thank you. I'm Haven Romiley." They shook hands. "The rude one over there is Lindsay Adair. Don't pay her any attention." Lindsay snorted at Wren's remark and marched passed them into the dining room.

"This is Maribelle, Christine, Ann, and Bernice," Wren made the introductions. They each walked by as well, but at least nodded and said a quick hello along the way.

Dinner was quite awkward for Haven, albeit she tried to make the best of it. The food was wonderful. It was all the more special for she hadn't had fine dining for a very long time.

"Have you been involved in any theater before this one?" Wren struck up the conversation to lighten the mood.

"Actually no, but it has always been my dream to one day sing at the Theater Royal ever since coming to an opera long ago," Haven replied and smiled.

"Do you have family here?"

"Uh…no," Haven glanced down at her lap.

"I've never heard of anyone being accepted after auditioning with only one song," Christine put in between bites. Her tone was more skeptical than happy for her.

"Just so you're aware, because you got in so easily, doesn't mean you are better than any of us," Lindsay stated smugly. "We have all worked hard to get to where we are today."

"Oh Lindsay," Wren cut in and sighed.

"Well, it's true!" No one spoke for the remainder of the meal.

It couldn't have ended soon enough. The maid started taking their plates when the butler walked in.

"Miss Romiley, Mr. Martel awaits to speak to you in the foyer." Haven got up and followed him to the entryway.

"Miss Romiley, sir," the butler announced then quietly left. Trenton turned to her as a smile formed on his face. It made Haven's heart flutter.

"Miss Romiley, did you get all settled in?" he asked.

"Yes."

"Is everything satisfactory?"

"Oh yes! Everything is wonderful. Thank you again." Haven put all the appreciation she could in her voice. She meant every word.

"Would you care to take a walk with me? It's such a pleasant evening."

"I would be delighted," Haven's face grew warm at his offer. She was thrilled that he asked. In truth, she was beginning to think he wasn't just being gratuitous any longer but perhaps it was something more.

They walked several blocks and slowly started to talk. Haven was having such a wonderful time during their conversation that she lost track of how many blocks they'd passed. She was swiftly growing to like Trenton. He was sophisticated and very charming. They talked about everything from different operas and theaters they had attended to dreams of the future.

"When did you first know you wanted to be in an opera?" Trenton asked when their pace began to slow. "I had vocal lessons growing up. I always enjoyed it. It wasn't until Derek—" Haven hesitated for a moment. She hadn't been able to speak about Derek without breaking down completely. Yet, something was different somehow. A pang of sorrow came over her at the mention of his name but it was lesser than ever before. She quickly looked at Trenton to find him waiting for her to continue. "He was my fiancé…he passed away…anyway, he urged me to pursue the opera because he said I have a gift for it."

"He was right. You most definitely have a gift," Trenton came to a halt and met her gaze. Haven smiled and blushed at his compliment. "You could say that I also have a gift. It's a gift of recognizing a success and a beautiful one at that," he slowly took her hand, lifted it to his lips, and kissed it. Haven froze as a tingling feeling rushed through her, all the way down to her toes.

"There's more to you than any other. I would like very much if you would sign a contract to stay at Theater Royal."

Haven tried to pull herself together to reply.

"Yes, I will!"

"There's just one little thing."

"What?"

"It takes dedication and commitment to sing here…and certain favors…that would be expected of you," Trenton took a step back to let what he'd said sink in and to await her answer.

"I'll do whatever it takes," Haven answered straight away in determination.

"Excellent. Miss Haven Romiley, you are about to be famous!"

Haven closed the door and sighed dreamily. Trenton saw her back to the townhouse right before sunset. She floated up the stairs and started down the hall to her room when one of the doors opened. Lindsay emerged from her own room, wearing her nightgown and purple robe.

"Might I have a word with you?" she asked coldly.

"Yes," Haven swiftly came back to reality as Lindsay approached. "I'm glad for this chance to talk," Haven began before Lindsay could. Her smugness didn't scare or intimidate her in the least. She had Trenton's favor and it was the only thing that mattered.

"We started off on the wrong foot and since I'll be staying, I would like for us to be friends," Haven smiled wryly.

"So Trenton is having you sign a contract?" Lindsay asked and sounded disappointed.

"Yes, he has," Haven lifted her head higher.

"Let me be honest with you," Lindsay took Haven's arm

and pulled her to the corner of the hall to be more private. "This isn't the first time Trenton has followed a whim."

"A whim?"

"It happens all the time. He'll soon see you're nothing special."

"Excuse me?" I don't—"

"I want to be very clear. I have worked hard to get to where I am and I'll not let you swoop in and steal it from me. Do you hear me? There are no shortcuts no matter who takes interest in you. I know what you are doing and I'll not stand by and do nothing," Lindsay said in her face.

"Well it's not up to you, is it?" Haven slowly pushed her away and calmly stepped back. "I don't plan to take any shortcuts. You're not the only one who is going to work hard. I'm going to do whatever it takes." With that, Haven sauntered to her room. She didn't look back to see Lindsay's furious reaction. If she didn't want to be friends that was just fine with Haven. She had tried.

I will not be intimidated or stopped from obtaining my dream, Haven said to herself as she shut the door. *If Miss Adair wants a competition...then so be it. This is only going to make me work all the harder to show myself worthy.*

CHAPTER SEVENTEEN

September 13, 1835

*C*his is the last of it," Garrett lifted the last carpetbag onto the back of the buggy and secured it.

"Thank you again for your help, dear," Merril stepped up and briefly embraced him.

"Have a safe trip," he replied. Merril then glanced at her husband, who stood on the other side of the buggy. She stared at him until he finally looked at her. She gave him a look, compelling him to say something to Garrett as well. Stanford sighed and dutifully made his way around the buggy to Garrett.

"Thank you, son. My bag is on the counter near the door in case an emergency arises. And you know where the medications are…and the key."

"Yes," Garrett assured. He understood Stanford's discomfort in leaving. He had never seen his father leave his patients. It was like a mother leaving her only child for the first time.

"We should only be gone for a few days. This way you won't get too behind in your studies."

"Oh, I'm not worried about that any—" Garrett blurted without thinking but caught himself. However, it wasn't soon enough.

"What? What were you saying?" Stanford asked.

Me and my blundering mouth! Garrett silently scolded himself. *Well, he's bound to know sooner or later.* "You might as well know…as soon as you return, I'm leaving medical school." There, he said it. Garrett looked steadily at his father. He knew very well what he would say.

"What?" Stanford asked, clearly stunned. Merril also appeared startled but honestly wasn't surprised by it.

"How can you just quit?"

"I see no more point in trying to be something I'm not, now that I know the truth."

"That doesn't change anything," Stanford argued.

"Doesn't change anything? It changes everything!" Garrett's voice grew louder. "I'm not like you. I don't have the talent you do. It comes easy for you but not me."

"It's never been easy. It takes determination. You've never been determined to do anything," Stanford's face and neck turned red. "You know what? Maybe you do speak the truth. Perhaps you aren't like me. I'm not a quitter like you are."

"Stanford!" Merril cried.

"Well, at least I'm not a liar!" Garrett shouted back and stepped toward the house. "My entire life has been a lie…because of both of you!" The frustration that had been building in Garrett exploded. "I could have been part of a different family. I could have been a Marquis!" his words pierced Stanford and Merril to the heart. It even pained Garrett when he saw their crestfallen faces. This made him soften a bit.

"I've agreed to help you and I thank you for paying my way all this time," he spoke slowly, carefully choosing each word. "I plan to pay you back…but I can't live this lie any longer." While Garrett might have calmed a little, Stanford was angrier than ever. He huffed as he climbed into the buggy.

"Fine! Do whatever you want. Throw away your life…you ungrateful…," he stopped himself from finishing his sentence. "You will see what it's like to live the truth then as you like. See what it's like to make your own way…alone!" After Merril sat down next to him, wiping her eyes, Stanford took the reins in his hands and they were off.

Garrett marched into the house. He was again furious! He felt like he might burst. He paced the room to find something to kick or throw. He finally stopped at the examination table and leaned his hands against it with a heavy sigh. Several small medicine bottles were sitting on the edge. The minute Garrett caught sight of it; it seemed to spark his anger. He instantly shoved them off, sending them shattering to the floor. Just then there was a knock at the door.

"Doctor Blakeslee! Doctor Blakeslee!" a woman cried. Garrett's teeth clenched in anger and frustration but went to the door nevertheless. He opened it to find a woman, probably in her mid-forties.

"Where is Doctor Blakeslee?" she wrung her hands anxiously.

"He's not here but I can help you. I'm his...son."

"Oh, well my father ran out of the medicine for his heart! He's having one of his attacks," she ranted.

"Come in. I'll get you what he needs," Garrett opened the door for her to enter.

"Oh, thank you! The apothecary is too far away and I don't think they're open this early in the morning," the woman continued nonstop as she followed. "I ran over here has fast as I could. He's in a terrible way! I must hurry back with his medicine."

"Yes, yes," Garrett went over to the cabinet as his father had instructed and picked up the correct bottle. He poured some of the thick amber liquid into a smaller glass bottle then handed it to the woman. "Here you go."

"Thank you again!" she rushed out of the door.

For the remainder of the day, Garrett busied himself with working on some much-needed repairs throughout his parent's home and shoddy clinic. Once his anger had subsided, he realized he had to do something to keep his mind off things.

He didn't notice the time until the sun began to go down and it grew dark while he was fixing a broken cabinet door. He stopped to light a lantern when he heard something. It sounded like whimpering in the distance. It was getting louder then he heard a familiar voice.

"Mr. Blakeslee!" It was the same woman earlier. This

time, however, she wasn't merely calling out but screaming!

"Mr. Blakeslee! Help!" she wailed.

Garrett ran to the front door at the unsettling sound. He opened the door just as the woman reached out to grasp the door handle.

"My father...something is wrong! He can't breathe...he's grown worse...much worse!" she stated out of breath and was hysterical. Garrett understood most of what she was telling him. He immediately grabbed Stanford's black bag and followed her. They ran the entire way to the woman's father.

"When did he start growing worse?" Garrett asked as they entered the tiny row house.

"A short while after I got home and had him take the medicine you gave me."

The house was quiet. The woman led the way to the cramped bedroom. Garrett entered and gazed at an elderly man, lying on the bed. His chest heaved up and down as he struggled for each breath. The low, gurgling, and wheezing coming from him made the hair on the back of Garrett's neck, stand on end.

"Father, the doctor's son is here," the woman went to her father's side as Garrett set down the black medical bag. He opened it and searched for the stethoscope.

"Here's the medicine you gave me," she handed the bottle to Garrett. It was nearly empty now.

"Father? Father?" the woman cried but the man wouldn't respond. "What's wrong?" she helplessly turned to Garrett. Garrett stopped searching through the bag and lowered his gaze to the man. All of a sudden, the man took a big, raspy breath then exhaled loudly. Garrett waited for him to inhale, but he never did. The deathly gurgling noise stopped as well.

"Father?" the woman called to him with panic in her voice. "Father no!" she cried loudly.

Garrett leaned over the bed and reached out to search for a pulse on the man's neck. There was nothing. He was gone. The woman watched him closely through blurred vision. She must have seen Garrett's downtrodden look to realize what had just happened.

"No! He can't be dead. He can't!" she fell over her father's chest and wept.

This was too much to Garrett. He stumbled out of the bedroom and out of the house. He didn't care that he'd left Stanford's bag behind. He had to get back to the clinic! He had to see for himself.

Once there, Garrett rushed through the door and to the medicine cabinet. He carelessly fumbled through the differently labeled bottles until he froze. He found it. He found the bottle that contained the medicine he'd given the woman. With a shaking hand, Garrett pulled it out of the cabinet and into the dim light. To his horror, it wasn't medicine for the heart at all. It was completely different and highly potent.

The bottle slipped from his grasp in his shock and hit the floor.

I killed him. That man is dead because of me! A cold sweat washed over him, along with a fearful dread. *I was so angry I wasn't thinking clearly.* Garrett clumsily stepped backwards until he hit the wall behind him. He had to do something. *It won't be long until word spreads. Father will surely lose everything...because of me!*

A strong urgency suddenly rose up inside of him. *I have to get out of here!* Before Garrett could grab any of his belongings, he hurried out of the clinic under the dark, foggy sky.

PART

II

"I call heaven and earth to record this day against you, that I have set before you life and death, blessing and cursing: therefore choose life."

Deuteronomy 30:19

CHAPTER EIGHTEEN

April 9, 1836

P lease allow me, Miss Romiley," a perfect stranger rushed up to the door that Haven was about to open, and pulled it open for her. In the past year, Haven's name had become very well known in all of London. She was famous. She had starred in only three operas when people began to adore her. Trenton was correct. Haven was making him rich. Seemingly, all of Haven's dreams were coming true.

The man at the wide marble counter glanced up to help her when he smiled.

"Oh, Miss Romiley! Welcome," he greeted, excited to have such a prominent young woman in his restaurant. "Please, follow me. Mr. Martel is right this way."

As Haven followed, she could hear happy whispers and gasps from the people she passed by. They were more than delighted to get a glimpse of her.

"My dear!" Trenton exclaimed the moment he saw her and quickly stood. He stepped over to the other side of the table to pull her seat out for her.

"Hello, Trenton. How are you?" Haven asked as he gently pushed her chair in and she was seated.

"Much better now that you are here," he replied and was seated as well. "Did you see the paper this morning?" Trenton held up the very newspaper he was referring to.

"No, I didn't."

"Well, you must hear the latest. It's on the front page, mind you. 'Since starring in her first opera, Miss Haven Romiley has won the hearts of people young and old, not only in London but in all of England. People are traveling from various distances to attend the Theater Royal just to hear Miss Romiley. They have named her the Angel. Her innocent and clear voice is like none other. Her performance is flawless, as is her fair beauty. Miss Romiley is indeed heavenly. The queen herself has been to the theater to hear the Angel herself. England's adoration grew to new heights at last night's extraordinary performance. You will not want to miss the upcoming performances.'" Trenton sighed with satisfaction when he finished and laid the newspaper on the table.

"This is simply wonderful!" Haven stated.

"Are you pleased? Your name is known in all of England!" Trenton quietly asked and smiled proudly.

"I couldn't be happier."

CHAPTER NINETEEN

May 2, 1836

aven and the others on stage all took hands and bowed together at the end of the curtain call. The crowd clapped so loudly it echoed in the great auditorium. It sounded almost like roaring.

The actors and actresses followed Haven's lead as she motioned to acknowledge the orchestra before them, below the stage in the pit. They all waited for the curtain to swing closed. However it never did. Haven looked around in confusion. Just then, the orchestra played a short little ditty, like some sort of introduction. It caused everyone's cheers in the audience to quiet down.

Haven glanced to the left of the auditorium where Trenton always sat, but he wasn't there. By the time she moved her gaze to the others on the stage, she found Trenton walking towards her. He was strangely gazing at her. He quickly covered the distance between them and took her hand in front of everyone.

"What are you doing?" Haven quietly asked. Trenton didn't answer. Instead, he lowered onto one knee. The crowd erupted in gasps and loud whispers.

"Haven Romiley, would you do me the honor of accepting my hand in marriage?" he asked loudly for all to hear. Everyone grew silent all at once in suspense as they awaited her answer.

Haven felt everyone's eyes on her. It finally hit her as her breath caught in her throat. She raised her gloved hand to her mouth in astonishment. For one brief moment, Haven recalled the last time someone had asked the same question. Her relationship with Derek was far different in comparison to this one. Haven figured she would never have the same love for anyone else ever again. She knew Trenton loved her, and so did she, yet not in the same way.

Her heart beat loudly as she forced herself to push away thoughts of Derek and her past. Derek was gone, and she had to move on.

"I will!" Haven blurted happily. She almost flinched when

cheers exploded in the theater. Trenton smiled from ear to ear as did Haven.

"I can hardly believe it!" Haven squealed with delight as she and Trenton bounded off the stage. The passing cast and crew offered their congratulations then made their way downstairs to the dressing rooms. Haven and Trenton were left alone backstage amongst the countless props.

"You've made me the happiest man in the world," Trenton exclaimed over the sound of the crowd leaving the theater. He took both of her hands in his. "Are you pleased?" he asked in all earnest. "This is a dream come true. It's everything we've ever hoped for," she replied breathlessly.

"Of course it is. I always get what I want." That being said, Trenton leaned closer and kissed Haven. "Forgive me for being too forward." Haven smiled her approval. "I had better go and greet the important guests."

"Oh wait," she reached out and gently wiped some of her red rouge off of Trenton's lip. Haven watched him leave, almost in a daze. Part of her wondered at what he meant about always getting what he wants. She didn't have much time to think, for when she turned to leave, she caught sight of someone sitting on a wooden chair in the corner of the dim stage. She was a little startled until she took in the man's black hair and warm eyes and realized whom it was. Derek, dressed in his usual blue waistcoat and white shirt sat back against the chair.

"Derek! Where have you been? I've missed you," Haven asked, pained as she recalled the day she needed him so badly. He didn't answer but grinned at her.

"Remember our first kiss?" he asked. Haven remembered the day like yesterday. "You promised always to love only me, no matter what," Derek said as if betrayed. Haven felt a pang of guilt but it was soon washed away with anger.

"Yes…yet the next morning, you died," she spoke up and stood aloof from him. "You left me!" she teared up with emotion. "I have to let you go. I can't keep going on like this…I have to," she said the last few words when Derek vanished. Haven blinked back tears and made her way to the dressing room.

CHAPTER TWENTY

Everyone cheered and gave Haven a standing ovation. Some shouted for an encore but since they'd already given them one, Trenton gave them the signal to end from where he sat in the nearest box to the left of the stage.

Haven, along with the other actors and actresses bowed one last time before the heavy curtain closed between them and the cheering audience.

"Well done, Haven. Yet another grand performance," Wren congratulated her as they made their way backstage and to the stairs leading to the women's dressing room. It was separate from the men's, which was located downstairs.

Lindsay cut right in front of them, causing Haven to nearly trip over her extravagant full skirt. It was decorated with beaded rushing and appeared to sparkle in the gaslights on stage.

Lindsay didn't have a single leading role ever since Haven arrived. Everyone in the entire cast could sense her bold animosity towards Haven. She watched Lindsay ascend the rest of the stairs and only sighed. Her rude behavior didn't really bother her anymore. Haven had won Trenton's affection, along with the people of England.

Once the women arrived in the dressing room, they began to change out of their heavy costumes. A ladies maid, part of the Theater Royal staff, came up to Haven. She helped her slip off the scarlet gown. The other actresses did likewise. Haven donned her pastel dressing gown then went to work removing her thick rouge and blush. The women sat in a row in front of long candlelit mirrors, talking and laughing, all but Lindsay, who sulked in the corner alone.

"Wonderful performance tonight," Christine stated.

"Yes! You mesmerized the crowd once again," Bernice chimed in.

"Thank you. You all did a splendid job as well," Haven replied. She reached for her bag that lay on the counter beside her and pulled out a few of the bigger items inside to find a small hairpin at the very bottom. It was a gift from Trenton and Haven wanted to put it on before they saw each other later for a late dinner.

"Where did you get that?" Bernice gasped as Haven secured the ivory pin in her hair.

"Where did I get what?" Haven turned from the mirror. Bernice pointed to the Romani journal as if she was afraid to touch it. The look on her face was that of great concern. Haven glanced at the journal as well.

"Do you know what that is?" Bernice asked. She acted as if it was some sort of poison. None of the other ladies paid any attention to them and one by one slowly made their way out of the dressing room as soon as they finished.

"Well, it's a journal," Haven replied incredulously. "I haven't written in it since coming here. I don't have the time." Haven went back to the counter to pick up her things, putting them back in her bag.

"It's a journal, yes. But do you know what kind of a journal it is?" Bernice asked with urgency in her voice. As far as Haven was concerned, she was done and needed to leave to meet up with Trenton.

"What difference does it make?"

"Do you know what the inscription says on the cover? This is no ordinary journal."

"What are you talking about?" Haven was about to reach out to pick it up when Bernice pointed to the symbols on the brown leather cover.

"My grandmother was Romani and I know their language. According to this inscription, this journal has a curse on it," Bernice explained with all seriousness. Haven couldn't help but chuckle. When Bernice saw she didn't believe her, she finished reading it. "Anyone who writes in it is also under its curse." She looked up and met Haven's gaze. "Do you still have the pen that belongs to it?"

"What does the pen have to do with it?" Haven's smile slowly faded. Could Bernice be speaking the truth?

"Once the pen is broken, the curse begins its purpose."

"Purpose?"

"Its purpose to fulfill what has been written in it." Haven took in what Bernice was saying a little more to heart than before. The truth was, she didn't have the pen any longer. It had been missing ever since she left the gypsy camp.

"I don't want to frighten you, but you need to know what this truly is. It's nothing to take lightly. Romani curses are powerful." That being said, Bernice picked up her own things and left.

Haven glanced down at the journal. She recalled Sabina and when she had given it to her. Haven didn't doubt that the older woman would something like this.

But she did tell me to write my dreams in it. Did she give it to me to cause good to come my way? But then again, why is it called a curse? Haven slowly came back to the present. She didn't want to be late in meeting Trenton.

She stood up, put the journal back in her bag, and shook off the notion.

CHAPTER TWENTY-ONE

May 9, 1836

 y the time Haven and Trenton sat down to have dinner together, she had all but forgotten about what Bernice said. Following dinner, they talked while before parting ways. They both had busy mornings with rehearsals at the theater. Trenton had his carriage bring Haven from the fancy restaurant and back to her townhouse. Since becoming famous, Trenton

surprised Haven with her very own townhouse. It was located near the theater and came with a household staff.

Haven walked through the front door and immediately went to bed. This was the time when the conversation about the journal chose to come back to her. Haven tossed and turned but could not fall asleep. She couldn't get rid of the thought that what Bernice said was true. There was no reason why she would lie about it.

Haven finally huffed and threw aside her blankets. She got up and went to her writing desk to light the candle on top of it. She then fetched the journal. She sat down, opened the book, and carefully flipped through the pages, reading intently. This time, however, she read it in a new light. Questions burned in her. What Bernice had said repeatedly played in her mind. Was it true? Did the words in her journal have the power to come to pass?

Haven had to somehow find out for herself, to see if what she'd written had come to pass as of yet. The fact that the pen was missing made her feel a bit alarmed. It had been so long since she'd written in the journal. Haven wanted to refresh her memory of just what exactly was in it.

She paged through until she came upon one of the first entries.

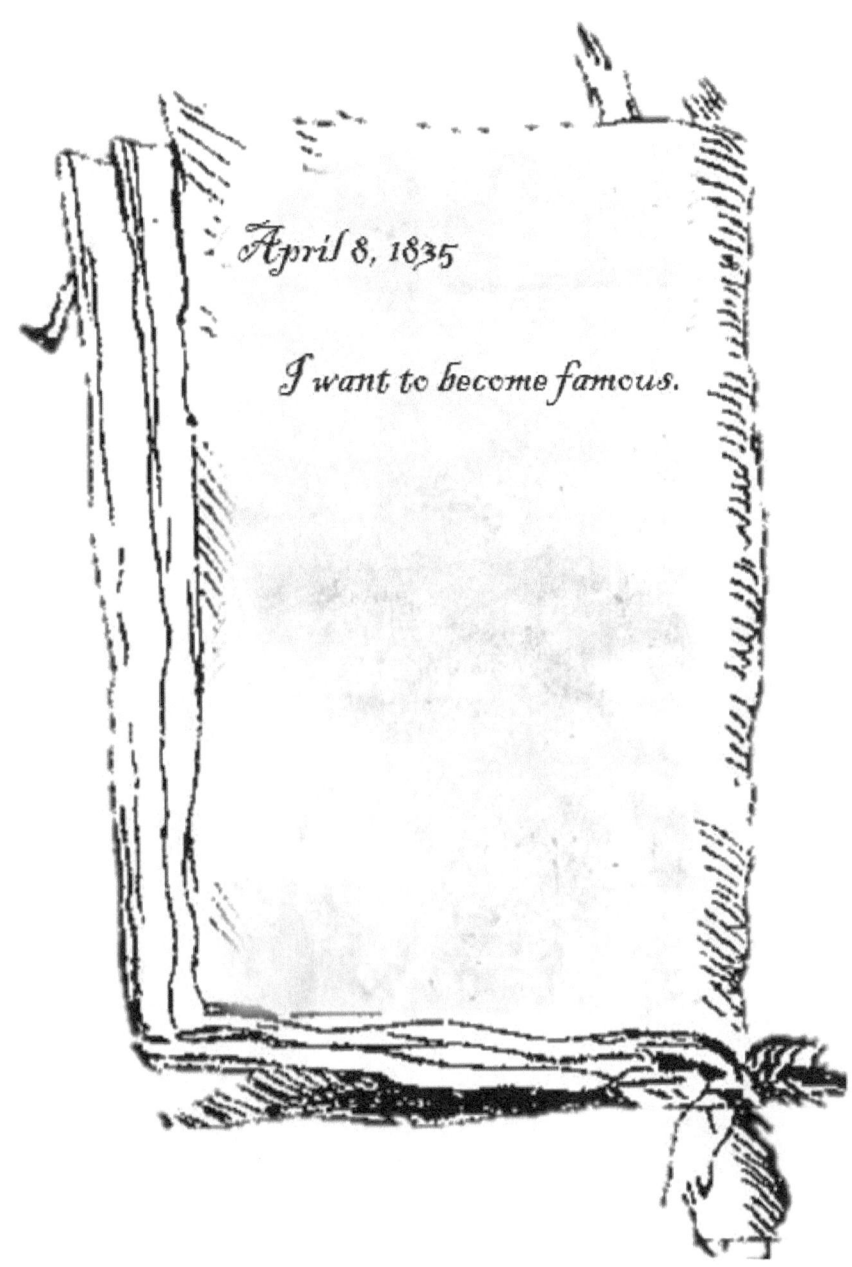

April 8, 1835

I want to become famous.

The simple desire seemed harmless enough, so Haven went on.

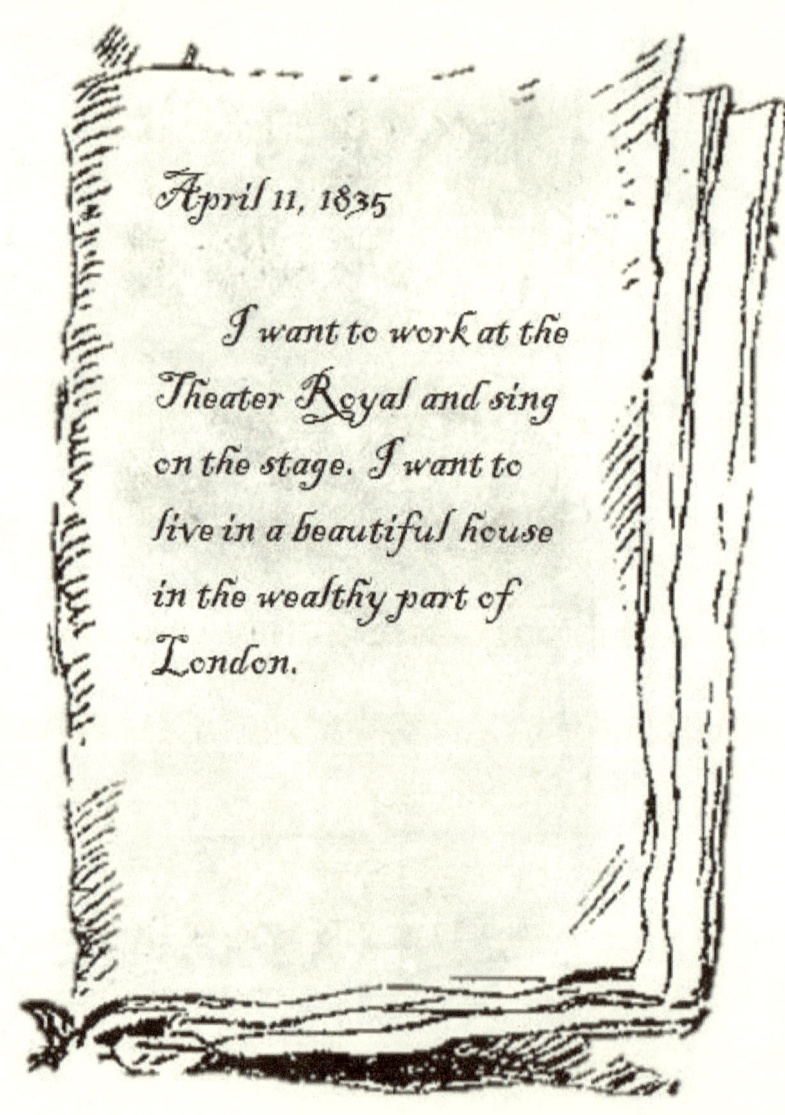

April 11, 1835

I want to work at the Theater Royal and sing on the stage. I want to live in a beautiful house in the wealthy part of London.

Haven stopped reading for a moment. This undoubtedly came true.

But it's not enough to prove anything. And besides, this isn't a curse. This is a blessing! There was nothing more to do but go on reading.

I want to meet a handsome and wealthy man, who is kind to me and treats me well.

She stopped once more. She was again taken back by the exactness of what she had written compared to what had taken place.

I want to have all of my needs met and not have to worry about money.

Haven thought for a moment. She truly did not have any wants that she could think of. Everything from food, clothing, to a roof over her head, had all been provided. With all the money she was making from the theater, it was certainly more than enough.

May 2, 1835

I want a man of great
means and power to propose
to me in an elaborate way.

If she was starting to wonder before, this entry startled her for this just happened. The present date was May ninth.

Why, it was a week ago that Trenton proposed. He proposed on May second! Exactly one year ago. Haven placed her hand over her mouth. How could she keep telling herself it was only a coincidence? The dates written in the journal did not lie.

How can this be? Now she was more alert and read all the more carefully.

Instead of paging through, Haven now turned the page and moved her finger down along the words, taking in each line intently. There was a large gap where she didn't write anything. She soon reached the last entry. In very sloppy writing, she read the few words.

Haven stared at the words and blinked several times. She had all but forgotten about her sorrowful entry in the midst of her grieving state after she had learned about the death of her family.

September 9, 1835

She reread the date countless times. All the confusion and wondering was gone and all that was left was fear, a fear so great it was almost tangible. Everything she had written up until now were good things, such as dreams and goals. But not like this.

"The journal is cursed." Bernice's words came back to Haven in full force. She had no choice but to realize what she had said was very real.

How can this be? It's impossible! Haven tried to reason with her unsettling thoughts.

"Romani curses are very powerful. Don't take this lightly." Bernice's words were relentless, invading her mind to no end.

Haven finally shut the journal as if the act would stop its power.

Perhaps Bernice is merely mistaken and read the inscription wrong, Haven stood and went back to her bed. She needed to clear her mind and find some relief. Surely, there was a reasonable explanation.

She lay down and gazed up at the white lace of the canopy bed. She knew it was foolish to hope to escape her troubled thoughts for they came over her straight away. The more she tried to reason the matter away, the stronger the reality of it arose. Haven was forced to accept what was told her to be real, just for a moment at least.

Bernice said something about a pen…the pen that came with the journal. How could I lose that pen? Haven spent the rest of the night going over it within herself.

May 10, 1836

The next morning, Haven walked into the auditorium of the theater.

"Good morning, dearest," Trenton immediately greeted and approached.

"Morning," she replied halfheartedly.

"How are you?" he asked when he took in the dark circles under Haven's eyes.

"I'm alright…I just had a sleepless night."

"Oh…well, are you up to rehearsing?" he put his hand on her back so she would look up at him. She seemed very preoccupied about something.

"Yes," Haven only met his gaze for a swift moment before looking away, walking past him to the stage.

In the next half an hour, she tried her best to rehearse the songs she was to sing that very night for the performance, yet she was failing miserably. She missed her cue, along with the words during almost every try. The orchestra, fellow actors, and even Trenton noticed something amiss right away for Haven would usually practice without error.

Trenton didn't know what to do other than knowing this couldn't go on. The orchestra was growing weary of playing the same three songs over and over. Not only were they getting tired, but he could also easily see Haven was just as frustrated. While he had to do something, Trenton didn't want to embarrass her in any way. He finally stood up.

"Please stop a moment," he announced and quickly marched his way onto the stage.

"Haven, are you sure you're feeling alright?" he tried to put all the kindness he could in his voice.

"I'm fine! Why does everyone keep asking me that?" Haven snapped.

"It's just that you don't seem yourself today." Trenton didn't want to keep thinking about all that was at stake concerning this rehearsal, albeit, this was getting them nowhere. "I think perhaps we should all take a break," he suggested. Haven was about to object. However she truly was exhausted and still burdened with her thoughts.

"Well, alright." Suddenly an idea came to her that could possibly help her problem.

"How long do you need?" Trenton asked.

"Perhaps an hour or two."

"Very well."

Before Trenton was able to announce the break to everyone else, Haven went for the stairs. She had renewed purpose. It would have to be carried out quickly if she was to make it back in time. Haven hurried down the aisle and towards the gallery. Her carriage was parked a ways away on the street beside the theater.

Wren was just coming in at the same time Haven was leaving. They were both in a hurry, so they ran right into one another.

"Oh! Is practice over already?" Wren asked and glanced at the stage nervously. "I was told not to come until now because my scene is—"

"We're taking a break," Haven swiftly informed.

"Is everything alright?" Wren asked when Haven started to continue on her way. It wasn't like her to be so curt.

"Yes, yes," Haven stopped again and said exasperatingly. "I have to go somewhere quickly before we resume rehearsal."

"Oh…I'm sorry," Wren's dejected tone made Haven come to a halt. Wren was always kind to her.

"No, everything is fine. I didn't mean to sound brash. I just…." Haven raised her hand to her forehead, trying to keep from crying. She had managed to hold it in all morning but it was becoming too difficult.

"Haven, are you in some kind of trouble?" Wren immediately rushed up to her. Haven gulped back the tears and met her concerned stare.

Should I tell her? The temptation to let it all out was hard to fight. The matter was so absurd and Haven didn't know all the answers, nor did she even comprehend it completely.

She will only think I'm foolish for even thinking it might be true. Best to keep it to myself for now.

"You can tell me."

"I…well…not really anything troubling. It's just something I have to do. I must go," she forced herself to keep the matter secret and moved to the entrance.

"Do you want someone to accompany you?" Wren offered. Again, Haven slowed. No one had ever genuinely cared for her like this, other than Derek and Trenton.

It would be nice for her to come with me but would this only make matters worse? Would she know too much?

Wren must have noticed her indecision for she went on.

"You don't have to tell me anything. I could just be there

for you."

"Thank you," Haven nodded and fought her emotions. Both ladies then went to Haven's carriage.

"Please take us to the Port of London. There's a gypsy camp on the way. Please stop at it."

"Yes, Miss Romiley," the driver helped both women into the carriage and closed the door. After hearing what Haven had said, Wren became more than a little curious.

Gypsies? What does Haven have to do with them? Though she remained faithful to her word and didn't ask a single question on the way, Haven never did provide any information and kept silent.

"You are certain this is it, miss?" the driver asked again. Haven ignored his question and stood just outside of the carriage with her gaze fixed on the open area. She was surer than anything that this was the grassy spot was where the Romani camp was. It was completely abandoned now. The only evidence left was the dark ashes in several small circles that dotted the place where they had built fires.

They're gone...where could they have gone? Haven helplessly gazed at the place where Sabina's wagon once stood.

"Haven?" Wren quietly spoke up from inside the carriage.

"Let me just have a quick look around, alone," she replied. Wren nodded, respecting Haven's privacy.

Well, they were gypsies after all. They move from place to place. Haven scanned the ground as she strolled through the grass. She didn't know what to do now. She had hoped she would somehow come upon the pen she was seeking. *This is next to impossible! The pen is long gone.* Haven would never know the fate of it or if it was broken or not. *If Sabina knew the journal was cursed, there's no telling what she did once she found out I fled. Perhaps it isn't broken after all. Maybe it fell out of my bag upon my escape?* Haven sighed. Not knowing her fate was worst of all.

There was nothing more to be done, so Haven slowly turned back to the carriage.

My entire fate lies with a pen...perfect! I certainly can't tell Wren such a preposterous story. Maybe that's all it is...a story. There are so many unanswered questions. Perhaps all the things I read in the journal are merely a coincidence. Haven was so tired she couldn't think anymore.

"Are you alright?" Wren asked once Haven returned and got inside.

"It was foolish to come out here. Thank you for coming with me even though it proved to be a waste of time.

Haven and Wren returned to the theater and finished rehearsal. Haven forced her mind to calm down since there was nothing more she could do. Not knowing what had become of the pen, proved to be difficult enough to process, there were still many variables that the pen was perfectly fine and was only lost somewhere. This fact only brought her a small amount of peace.

The performance that evening went smoothly, and for that, Trenton was thankful. He was used to working with moody actresses and even some actors. Though Haven had always been easy to work with, the pressure was always there and would usually get to even the most experienced singer, sooner or later.

CHAPTER TWENTY-TWO

 oodnight! Well done tonight," Haven called to the other ladies as she parted from them in the lobby of the theater after the performance. She and Wren were the only ones left as they made their way to the entrance.

They walked out onto the well-lit porch when Wren suddenly spoke up.

"Oh, I almost forgot." Wren held up her reticule. "The necklace I borrowed from you. Let me find it now, otherwise I will forget." They both slowed to a stop and Wren dug through her purse as Haven waited. "It probably fell to the very bottom. I have too many things in here," Wren pulled out a few larger items to see inside better.

Haven had to cover a yawn for she was beyond tired after the long day. That's when she saw it. Wren pulled out what appeared to be a pen, then continued to search for the necklace.

"Wait!" Haven quickly took ahold of Wren's wrist. "What is that?"

"What?" Wren looked at all the items she held in her full hands. Haven reached for the pen. It was only half of a pen for it was broken.

"Where did you find this?" Haven, no longer tired, was now very alarmed.

"When we went to the…." Wren didn't even know what to call where they had gone earlier, "When you took a look around, I got out of the carriage and stood just outside of it. This was on the ground and it caught my eye. I don't know what made me pick it up. It's very ornate. What a pity it's broken." Wren glanced up from the pen to find Haven's gaze fixed on it. She looked as if she was ill. "What's wrong?"

"I uh…have to go…goodnight," Haven retreated and rushed through the colonnade and down the steps, leaving Wren more confused than ever.

Haven hurried to her carriage. The driver no more than shut the door when she began to tremble and gasp for air. She leaned against the seat and tried to breathe but found it quite hard.

This is the very pen…the pen that belongs to the journal…and it is broken! The curse has begun! What can I do? Haven felt like she was in some kind of a daze as she held the pen tightly in her hand inside the dark carriage.

Once she arrived at her townhouse, she said nothing to anyone as she marched through the foyer, to the staircase, and to her bedroom, slamming the door shut behind her. She walked across the room aimlessly, still holding the broken pen. The only light came from the fireplace. It flickered on the violet damask walls.

She reached her writing desk and groped around until her hand came upon the engravings on the cover of the journal. The crackling of the fire was drowned out by her sniffs. Haven wiped her eyes as a thought came to her. She slowly picked up the book and turned around to face the fire.

I know how to get rid of this curse once and for all. New determination rose up in her as she stepped closer to the flickering flames.

"Sabina, your plan will not succeed!" Haven gazed at the journal and spoke aloud before thrusting the book into the inferno. She stared at it for some time, watching it begin to burn. As it disintegrated, so did her fears. Now she was free to go to bed and sleep without the dread hanging over her. She was free!

May 11, 1836

The late morning sun shined through the window into Haven's bedroom as she slowly woke up. She had slept very well, after getting rid of the troublesome journal and was thankful to have a day off from rehearsals. She did, however, have a lunch appointment.

Haven got out of bed and headed to the door that led to the dressing room. Along the way, she glanced at the mahogany fireplace. By now, it was completely out. Something dark sat on the very top of the grey ashes. She instantly stopped to take a second look. A shiver ran down her back at the sight.

What? No, it can't be! She rushed over to the fireplace and gasped in horror, for it was the journal. It was in perfect condition and wasn't burnt or even smoking.

But I watched it burn last night! I saw the fire engulf it. Haven reached out to the mantle to steady herself for she felt lightheaded all of a sudden. All she could do was stare at the book until she recovered her shock. She then bent down and picked up the journal, immediately opening it. As she took in each untouched page, soot covered her nightgown and hands. Everything written inside was just as it was before. It was as if it had never met the flames.

A quick knock at the door made her jump.

"A...yes?"

"Miss Romiley?"

"Come in." The ladies maid opened the door but froze when she saw Haven kneeling on the large rug in front of the fireplace, in her filthy nightgown.

"What is it?" Haven asked as if she didn't know. Her ladies maid came every morning to help her dress. It was always the same.

"I'm here to help you get ready for your luncheon."

"Oh...right," Haven hesitated. *I can't possibly go! I'm much too overwrought to meet Trenton and pretend everything is alright. I just need time to figure this out...I need time to think!* Her thoughts flew.

"Please send word to Mr. Martel and tell him I'm not feeling well I will have to meet him another day."

"Yes, miss," the maid nodded then left. Haven returned her gaze to the book when another idea came to her. She got to her feet but didn't care to wipe the soot off of her. She held the journal open in one hand. With the other, she grabbed one of the pages and ripped it out. One, then another, and another. Haven ripped every page from the binding in an almost crazed manner. Once each page was out and lying on the floor, she picked up each one and began tearing them into smaller pieces. It took her quite a while for the book contained at least two hundred pages.

There! Haven sighed as she dropped the last few pieces of paper into a wastebasket. Unfortunately, she didn't feel the least bit of satisfaction, but only more apprehension. After seeing the journal, following the burning flames the previous night, Haven didn't know anything other than fear. This attempt of ripping it up was her last.

Haven picked up the wastebasket and went to the door. She opened it just as the scullery maid walked by.

"Could you please dispose of this for me?"

"Yes, miss." Haven handed her the basket and watched her walk down the hall and out of sight.

"Mr. Martel, how may I help you?" the butler opened the front door and greeted.

"I'm here to call on Miss Romiley."

"I'm sorry, sir. She's not accepting visitors at this—"

"I know. She'll see me," Trenton stated assuredly. He was well aware that he had the upper hand since the entire staff was under his employment. "Please tell Miss Romiley to ready for my visit. I'll wait for her in the parlor."

"Uh...yes, sir," the butler moved aside and held the door for Trenton.

Haven awoke to a soft knock at the door. Shortly after she had donned a paisley dressing gown, she got a book to read in attempts to get her mind off the dreaded journal and eventually fell asleep. Whoever was at the door slowly opened it.

"I'm sorry to disturb you, miss. Mr. Martel is here to see you. He awaits in the parlor."

"What?" Haven immediately became alert and sat up. "He's here? But I sent word to him, canceling our luncheon! Why is he here?" she gazed at the maid, nervously. "He can't see me like this! Tell him I can't see him for I'm ill and indisposed." Haven didn't want to seem like she was avoiding him but she truly didn't feel up to it. Her pounding headache was one thing, but her appearance was another. Her hair was still down, and the dressing gown was meant only to be seen by close relatives and not during courting by any means.

"Yes, miss," the maid replied.

Trenton heard someone approach him, so he got to his feet, thinking it was Haven. Instead, it was a maid.

"I'm sorry Mr. Martel. Miss Romiley is not feeling well enough to see you." The maid started to leave for there was nothing more to be said. However, Trenton was not about to be swayed.

"Is she dressed and decent?" he boldly asked. The maid turned back to face him; eyes widened at such a question.

"What? Well...yes, but...." Trenton didn't wait for her to finish and curtly walked passed her.

"Mr. Martel!" the maid gasped, "But you can't!" she called out after Trenton when she watched him march to the stairs. "You simply can't go to her room! It wouldn't be proper," she cried but he completely ignored her and quickly ascended to the second floor.

When he reached her bedroom, he found the door open a little. He quietly peered inside and saw Haven lying on the settee in her private sitting room with her arm draped over her forehead. Trenton knocked.

"What is it now, Florence?" Haven moaned. When no one answered, Haven removed her arm from her head and glanced at the door. She was horrified to see Trenton instead of the maid. All she could do was gasp.

"Don't get up," Trenton approached her.

"What are you doing here?" There was no missing the anger in her voice.

"I'm sorry to intrude like this, but I had to make sure you were alright," he pulled up a chair beside the settee.

"I really wish you wouldn't," Haven squirmed in embarrassment. They were alone, without a chaperone or anyone for that matter. This only added to her discomfort.

"I have a terrible headache and I must look affright," she nonchalantly felt her hair to make sure it was somewhat in place. As she did, Trenton reached over and took her hand in his.

"Dear, you haven't been yourself lately. I took the liberty of bringing my personal physician with me in case you would like to see him. He's in the carriage."

"No thank you. I'll be fine...after I get some rest," she hinted to make him leave her alone. Haven knew nothing was wrong with her except what was brought on by constant worry and wracking her brain to try and figure out a way out of this strange predicament, not to mention lack of sleep.

Trenton must not have noticed her suggestion for he still sat before her. He released her hand, only to reach up and caress the side of her face as if checking for a fever.

"Is there anything I can do to help you feel better?" He persisted.

"Nothing, other than leaving me alone to rest," she replied coldly.

"Are you sure you won't see the doctor?" He wasn't used to being refused.

"Yes," she sighed.

"I only want to ensure you don't fall behind from all your hard work...and fall short of the expectations upon you," Trenton hoped Haven understood well what he meant. She was a little confused at first but eventually caught on to his meaning. He might care for her and be engaged to her but he was still a businessman. There was a lot at stake concerning her performance. The theater would no doubt suffer a significant loss if she missed even one night.

"I said I'll be fine...with rest," she repeated herself. Thankfully there were two full days without performances. Trenton didn't leave or say anything at first as he stood to his feet and gazed over her, hoping she would change her mind and see reason. She didn't and returned her arm over her eyes.

"If you change your mind, please let me know." Haven nodded but didn't look at him. "Rest well, my dear," Trenton's loving remark reminded her how much he did care.

CHAPTER TWENTY-THREE

May 12, 1836

irdie, Birdie!" Haven ran down the hall, shouting as she went. "Have you seen Birdie?" she asked when she met the butler. "She is downstairs, miss," he meekly replied. He didn't know what to think of her absurd behavior of late.

Haven quickly retraced her steps toward the staircase just as she spotted Birdie.

"There you are!" she blurted loudly and met the ladies maid on the landing.

"Is everything alright?" Birdie asked in concern and shifted the basket she held on her hip.

"Nancy…I gave Nancy the wastebasket yesterday…to dispose of…do you know what became of it?" Haven asked, breathlessly, referring to the scullery maid. Birdie didn't know what to think of the strange question, nor how upset Haven was over it.

"I uh…she did as you asked. I saw her bring it downstairs and disposed of it with the other garbage."

"Oh, alright. Good…thank you," Haven didn't look relieved or angry at the reply. Perhaps a bit embarrassed.

Haven turned and slowly walked back up the stairs. Birdie watched her and tried her best to try to understand what had just happened.

What should I do now? Haven slowly trudged back to her room and glanced down at the journal in her hands. She discovered it when she awakened that morning. It was sitting on the floor right inside the door, in perfect condition. Sadly, she wasn't really shocked this time but this attempt to destroy the book was her last hope. Haven had no choice but to face the fact that she couldn't escape it. She couldn't avoid the curse.

I'm going to die… Tears filled her eyes as she made her way down the hall and back to her bedroom.

"Miss Romiley has arrived, sir," the butler entered the drawing room of Trenton's grand apartment. It was actually a part of the Theater Royal. It was located behind the stage near the woman's dressing room. It was as spacious as any wealthy townhouse.

"Splendid. Show her in and let me know when dinner is served please." Trenton set down the newspaper he'd been reading on the plush footrest in front of the warm fire.

"Yes, sir."

She must be feeling better, he happily thought. He had hoped she wouldn't cancel their dinner plans as she did the luncheon the day before.

He got up as Haven was shown in.

"My dear, I'm glad to see you." They both neared one another when Trenton saw the same worried expression on Haven's face. This time, however, it was accompanied with very red eyes as if she had been crying.

"How are you feeling?" he carefully asked. Haven had indeed been weeping all day, up until she began to get ready. She was doing all she could not to start again at his question.

How much longer can I keep up this poor façade? "A little better. I'm sorry I'm a bit late."

"Not to worry. I was just reading the paper," Trenton began when the butler reappeared.

"Dinner is served," he announced. Trenton offered Haven his arm and they leisurely made their way to the dining room.

"As I was saying, I was reading the paper and saw there is a benefit this weekend for…oh, I can't recall the name…but it's for some wealthy noble. I think you and I should attend for there will be many people there that would be very advantageous for you to meet," Trenton explained.

"I'll have to see." The last thing on Haven's mind was a social event. Everything was different now.

"People who would be influential to your career," he continued as if he didn't even hear what she said.

Haven didn't say anything more, yet she was wondering if her visit was a mistake. She would have canceled the evening, albeit there were two things she wanted to accomplish in seeing Trenton. One of which was to consider if she should reveal to Trenton what was truly going on with her or not. By his continual focus on business, Haven was beginning to realize what the answer was.

Trenton pulled the chair out for her then took his own seat across the table.

"Will you be alright to rehearse tomorrow morning?" he asked as the meal was served.

"Yes…" she sighed and decided to go on with it. "I need to talk to you about something," Haven put down her fork, though she had yet to touch her food. Her nerves were too out of control to eat and it worsened at the thought of telling Trenton.

"What is it?"

"I…well," she opened her mouth to speak as she remembered his words to her the first day when he'd given her the job at the theater.

"There's just one thing. It takes dedication and commitment to sing here and certain said favors that are expected."

How could she tell him? It would change everything.

How can I let him down after all he's done for me? Haven couldn't do it. Instead, she resorted to the second reason why she was there.

"I was...wondering if I might see your doctor after all." All day Haven had been contemplating her fate and how it would happen. She couldn't escape it. One of the possibilities was her health. She figured seeing a doctor couldn't hurt and he might find something. She was starting to get desperate.

"Why certainly. I'll have him stop by tomorrow before rehearsals begin," Trenton replied. He was both glad and relieved she finally agreed to it.

May 13, 1836

The following morning, Trenton's doctor did indeed pay Haven a visit. He quickly examined her and was on his way within twenty minutes.

Trenton waited until the doctor climbed inside the carriage, parked outside Haven's townhouse, and sat down across from him.

"How is she? Did you find anything?" he quickly asked.

"Physically, there's nothing wrong with her, other than perhaps a few sleepless nights," the doctor informed.

"Good...good," Trenton mumbled, deep in thought.

The doctor's positive analysis gave Haven no relief from her haunting thoughts whatsoever. At first, she thought seeing him would help somehow. It did nothing of the like. It merely eliminated one of the many possibilities of how her death would come about. All she had left was time to wait and think.

I can't do this! I can't wait to die! She miserably thought as she laid across the settee in her sitting room yet again. The clock struck nine o'clock in the morning. *Oh, I must get ready for rehearsal...but what is the point?* Tears came to her eyes. *I can't sit here and waste another day crying!* Being alone with her thoughts was growing darker with each passing hour. If she only had four more months left on the earth, Haven didn't want to waste it.

I only have a limited time left, she helplessly let her sad lot wash over her in finality. More than anything, she wished this dreaded curse wasn't upon her, yet now that it was certain she couldn't get free of it, Haven had an important decision to make.

What do I want to spend it doing? What would bring me the most happiness? Haven got up and walked to the window. She peered out of it and saw people busily going about their business on the sidewalks that stretched out before her townhouse. She took in the skyline, etched with tall buildings and smoke billowing from the factories. She thought over the few precious things she had left in her life. Her greatest dream was to sing on the stage of Theater Royal, yet now her fame seemed to matter less and less. She had no family. All that was left was Trenton, who couldn't understand what she was going through. There was Wren and Bernice.

That's it! I want to be around people. That will help keep my mind off things. I'll go to rehearsal, after all...maybe then I can escape a little of this dreariness and stay busy. There's nowhere else to turn to. Even though there wasn't an ounce of hope to be found, it was better than staying cooped up in her townhouse.

CHAPTER TWENTY-FOUR

May 20, 1836

Haven starred at her reflection in the brightly candlelit mirror in the theater's dressing room. Though it was impossible to escape the curse, she had managed to keep the sorrowful matter at bay to a certain extent. She still had to constantly fight her thoughts and couldn't find sleep at night.

The only peace she could find was when she was singing on stage in front of thousands of people.

Haven finished applying some rouge as the other women talked excitedly while they each put on their costumes behind her. She stood up and smoothed the long pointed waist and pale blue skirts, made of delicate watered silk. She hardly noticed what they were saying. It all seemed like nonsense to her now. On the outside, Haven did her best to hide all she was going through. As long as she kept herself busy, it was all right. The moment she stopped and let her mind have a chance to wander however, everything piled over her all over again.

There was a loud knock at the door.

"Ten minutes until showtime!" Trenton announced after he opened it and poked his head inside. "You are all looking splendid as always," he commented as he walked inside and approached Haven. Even though Haven was fully ready, her gaze remained fixed on the mirror, deep in thought.

"Feeling alright, my dear?" Trenton leaned against the wall, beside Haven and asked quietly. She eventually glanced at him.

"Is it a full house out there?" Bernice unintentionally interrupted and asked as she walked by.

"It is completely full!" Trenton exclaimed in excitement. Everyone in the cast knew they were setting records in attendance. It was all the more true, for it wasn't even the busy London season yet. Trenton couldn't be more pleased. "And guess what, ladies? The queen herself is present!" Everyone gasped. Her Majesty had been to one other of Haven's performances but not the present opera.

Trenton glanced back at Haven, still awaiting her answer. She said nothing, nor did she seem even the least bit excited over the news.

"Dearest…you're feeling alright?" he asked again. What

could she say? She couldn't let him down, not after everything. This performance meant a lot to him. Haven nodded and forced herself to smile. "Good. You'll do wonderfully…as you always do," Trenton turned to go and spoke to the other women, "Five more minutes to show time! Five more minutes!"

Everyone got to their places on stage behind the curtain. Haven was to sing the first song, so she stood front and center, along with Wren, who stood to her left. They heard the orchestra begin playing the overture. All they had to do now was to wait for the song to end before the curtain opened and the first scene to take place.

Haven was occupied with going over the lyrics in her mind as she waited.

"How does it feel?" Wren suddenly asked. Haven turned to look at her. The music was fairly loud, so it was difficult to hear her.

"What did you say?"

"How does it feel?" This time Haven heard, but she was still confused. Perhaps she wasn't hiding her troubles after all and Wren was catching onto something. Wren must have seen her confused expression for she went on.

"How does it feel to be the most famous woman in all of England? You are adored by everyone." Her words were so thought provoking, Haven forgot all about the lyrics and even the performance. She had nearly forgotten the fame she earned in the past year.

There was no time to think of a reply for just then, the overture ended and the heavy curtain opened. Trenton hadn't exaggerated when he'd told them the auditorium was packed. Haven had never seen a full house such as this. Her gaze began with the several enormous crystal chandeliers high above everyone under the covered ceiling, then slowly moved downward. All three tiers of boxes, the upper and lower galleries in the horseshoe shape, were filled with people. They were looking at her, excitedly waiting for her to begin.

Though she felt a bit strange after Wren's question, she was forced to go on and begin her first ballad. Her voice was as clear and effortless as ever, however, she was finding it hard to focus.

"How does it feel to be the most famous woman in all of England?" Wren's innocent question, merely intended to encourage haunted Haven's mind. The heat coming from the bright gas lanterns, surrounding the stage, seemed warmer than usual. Sweat formed on her brow as she sang the second verse in Italian.
"You are loved by everyone…"
How does it feel? Haven now asked herself. *It's meaningless! What is the point of any of this?* she fought her thoughts, trying to keep up with the orchestra and in time with the song.

Besides the heat, her corset felt tighter than ever. A wave of nausea swept over her.
I'm going to die!
"You are loved by everyone!" Wren's words echoed in her. *I might be loved, but I feel utterly alone. I'll die alone.* Haven envisioned her breathless body, dressed in her very best, laying in an elaborate coffin. Her funeral taking place in a graveyard with not one person present except the priest.

The director caught her eye from his place in the orchestra pit. He glared at her and waved his baton violently, trying to hurry her along to keep up. Haven knew what he was telling her yet all she could feel was herself growing warmer all the time under her heavy gown. Her tight corset felt as if it was becoming tighter all the time. It was affecting her breathing.

She was just finishing the second verse when she missed a word. The mistake befuddled her so she couldn't find her place again.

Get it together! I can't let everyone down...I can't let Trenton down. The orchestra didn't know what to do; other than continue playing the song without her. The next words to come to mind were that of Trenton's.

"It takes determination...certain said favors...." Haven raised her hand to her pounding head to think. Time seemed to stand still.

When she found the words to continue with the song, she opened her mouth but no breath was there. She tried again but couldn't speak. She couldn't breathe. Panic washed over her and with it, more nausea in waves. Haven glanced back at the director of the orchestra and tried to cry for help but could only choke for air. When it was apparent that something was wrong, the music fell silent.

"Haven! Are you alright? What's wrong?" Wren shouted from the other side of the stage yet it sounded distant to Haven. It was as if she was under water. Haven knew she would collapse any second. The person she glanced at next was Trenton. He was in the bottom tier and was standing by now. He glared at her furiously. Through her dazed and alarmed state, fear arose in her at seeing how angry he was. She had never seen such fire in his eyes.

For the first time since Wren's question, Haven was able to focus on one thing. Run! She stumbled off stage. Everyone in the crowd whispered to each other in confusion. Haven gasped for air and rushed out of the back door of the dressing room, onto the dark streets. She hurried down one street, and then another, and another. Along the way, she shed some of her heavy costume to keep from hindering her. Her shoes were the first thing to go. She came to a quick halt to bend over and untie the silk ribbon on her ankle to remove the uncomfortable brocade satin slippers. She then took off a long oversized necklace and bulky decoration in her hair and threw them to the ground. Her light hair fell from its once neat state. Haven didn't bother to try and secure it for she had to move on for fear of Trenton finding or following her.

Over an hour later, she came upon a bridge. She looked over the side and realized it was very high. It was too dark to see very well, but the moonlight that cast over it, made it look like the river had a strong current. She walked out to the middle of the bridge to the highest point then slowed to a stop. She stared at the black water.

Why did I think I could just go on like everything was fine? What is the point of going on when I'll be dead in a few short months? I'm going to die... Tears streamed down her face as she glanced up at the clear black sky. *Why is this happening to me? I haven't done anything wrong.* More than the hopelessness and despair that hung over her, what she hated most was it was out of her control. She couldn't stop it.

"Derek...," she said the name but grew quiet. When she was only given silence in return, she became more desperate. "I'm sorry for pushing you away. I need you...I need you more than ever before. You're my only hope," Haven reached for the rock atop the thick stone wall of the bridge and threw it into the water spitefully. After which, she began to weep harder, leaning against the wall for support. Just then, a thought slowly came to her.

There's one thing I still have control over, Haven wiped her eyes. *I could beat this dreadful curse after all...by taking matters into my own hands. This is my only choice...my only way out of all this.*

She stood up straight and assessed the height of the wall. It wouldn't be easy with her bell-shaped skirt but she was determined to climb over. With some maneuvering, she swung her legs over and slid to the other side of it. There was a small ledge, the space of one foot, to stand on. Haven's heart raced as she held onto the wide railing behind her to balance herself. Up until now, she had completely forgotten what was in her pocket. It was the very thing that was causing her all the pain and making her do the unspeakable. Haven carefully pulled the journal from the deep pocket of her skirt.

"You have ruined my life! My dreams of singing...and marriage to Trenton," she mumbled between sobs. "All I ever wanted was peace." At present, Haven couldn't remember the last time she had peace. It vanished when Derek died. *Now he's abandoned me too. I'm to die alone.*

Looking over the water, Haven drew back her arm to throw the book into the river when suddenly someone caught her wrist from behind. Haven gasped for she lost her footing.

"Watch it there!" the man tightened his grasp on her arm to keep her from falling. Once she regained her balance, she glared at him. She couldn't really tell his age because his face was covered in a straggly beard and unkempt hair that was nearly shoulder length. He was dressed like a filthy street urchin.

"Let go of me!" she demanded. Being interrupted at such a time as this was one thing, but by this blighter made her even more aggravated.

"Climb back onto the bridge," the man stated. When he spoke, she smelt spirits on his breath.

"Just leave me alone!" she cried and tried to pull away but she was unsuccessful. She refused to be swayed from going through with her grave intent.

"Not until you come here. Come on," he urged. At first, it appeared that she would comply, for she slightly turned toward him. Instead, she did it to free both of her arms to escape his hold.

"No, don't do this!" Haven desperately endeavored to loosen her arm just as she lost her footing again. She was fully prepared to hit the icy cold water only to realize the man still held onto her.

"Let me go! Just let me die," she screamed but was ignored as the man pulled her back up and over the rail to safety. Haven was now outraged.

"Are you alright?" the minute her feet hit the ground, close to the stranger, he released her.

"Why couldn't you leave me alone?" Haven slapped the man across the face.

"I was only trying to—" she then kicked his leg, though without any shoes on, it did little.

With that, Haven spun around and ran down the dark street.

"Well, that's the thanks I get," he watched her until she was out of sight. Her fancy gown baffled him. It was the very last thing he thought he would see, especially in the east side of the city. The few high society people he knew, never dressed so lavishly.

Why would someone, who looked like she has everything, want to forsake it all and kill herself? What problems could she possibly have?

There was nothing more to be done so he went on his way when something caught his eye. A book lay open, face down on the cobblestone street. He quickly realized it was the book the young woman held before he stopped her. He went to it and picked it up.

"Oh, uh…miss?" he called out but knew it was too late. The woman was long gone by now, nor did he think she would ever come near him.

Once he turned the book to look at it, he realized it wasn't a book at all, but a journal. He glanced back down the street before continuing on his way.

CHAPTER TWENTY-FIVE

"Stupid man! Why did he have to stop me?" Haven stomped down a secluded street. She purposely stayed out of the busier areas in fear of Trenton finding her. However, she was growing weary of walking. What was she to do? Where was she to go? It was the middle of the night. There was only one thing Haven wanted, one thing she desired, to finish it once and for all.

"But how?" Haven wiped away her angry tears to see more clearly. It was only then she saw the moon reflecting off of the water. The same fast moving river, under the high bridge, must have curved around and was now before her. The very street she walked on was parallel with it. She immediately drew closer to it. Unfortunately, there was no bridge.

"Blast, it's not very high," she mumbled to herself when she reached the bank. Her plan was ruined.

Haven's head ached. She was much too distraught and exhausted to try to figure something out any longer. Instead of taking another step, she sat down on the edge of the riverbank and contemplated her sorrow. She didn't know how much time had passed before she heard movement behind her. It sounded like someone approaching. Haven didn't move for she didn't care anymore. There was no fear for her own life because her only desire was to end it all.

"Miss?"

Oh, now what? Haven sighed at the interruption, *Can't I be left in peace?* She still didn't move to see who it was.

"Miss, are you alright?" the voice was that of a woman. When the young lady remained still, the woman stepped up to Haven's side to see her face. The young lady's gaze remained straight ahead and her face wet with her tears.

"Miss?" Haven felt the stranger put her hand on her shoulder. *What is she doing?* Haven slowly looked up at her and sniffed, hoping the woman would go away. Unfortunately, she did no such thing and sat down on the bank next to her with a huff.

Haven eventually wondered if the woman merely sought after money because she was dressed so finely. They sat in silence with only the sound of the trickling from the river. When it was apparent the older woman wasn't going to leave anytime soon, Haven glanced over at her. She was a bit surprised to find it was a woman in her seventies. Her greying brown hair was neatly pulled up in a simple bun under a simple hat. She wore a plaid cloak and held a closed umbrella. The woman gazed at her with compassion and a very kind smile.

What was a lady such as this doing on the streets at such a late hour? Haven wondered.

"What do you want? I have no money," Haven finally asked curtly.

"I don't want anythin', golden dove," the woman calmly picked a handful of grass beside her and fingered it in her hand as if it was a leisurely chat. Now Haven was more confused than ever. Before she could ask further, the woman spoke.

"My name is Hephzibah Weston." Her caring gaze searched Haven's. It caused her distrust to lessen. Haven didn't know why, but she felt compelled to open up a bit to this perfect stranger.

"Haven Romiley," Haven blurted. Hephzibah instantly recognized the name, yet held her tongue for she was quite shocked to find the famous opera singer, here of all places.

"Can I 'elp thee in some way, Haven?" The sincerity in her question caused Haven to tear up anew. She looked back to the river and sighed heavily.

"No one can help me," she broke down.

"There's always 'ope," Hephzibah patted her hand.

"No," Haven shook her head in despair, "There's nothing that can stop it."

"Stop what?" Hephzibah carefully inquired.

"You wouldn't understand," Haven pulled away from her touch.

"Well since, as ya say, there's no 'ope of you gettin' out of whatever hangs over ya, there's nuffin' to lose...you might as well tell me about it," she stated cheerfully and shifted on the grass to get more comfortable. She fully intended to remain there as long as it took.

Haven saw her determination and quietly huffed.

"You wouldn't believe me if I told you."

"Try me," Hephzibah met her gaze.

"You'll only think I'm mad."

"I've heard quite enough of your excuses." Although she didn't want to push too hard, Hephzibah felt she had to urge a bit more than before if she was ever to reach the poor girl and do some good.

Haven didn't speak as she tried to think of a reason not to tell the persistent woman. Sorrow hung over her every thought. She had to find an escape.

"I'm...I'm going to die," she finally confessed and met Hephzibah's gaze to find her not surprised in the least. At first, she thought perhaps the older woman didn't hear what she'd said. "I'm going to die...very soon," she stated again, this time more slowly.

"We're all goin' ter die, love."

"No, you don't understand. I'm under a curse. It pursues me at every turn. It will not relent until I perish. I can't get free from it. I've tried...I'm going to die and I know the very day. I can't bear to sit here and wait. I must take matters into my own hands and—" Haven abruptly stopped, tears brimming in her eyes. "There's no hope for me. I told you it sounded absurd.

Hephzibah was indeed astonished upon hearing her story. It wasn't at all what she presumed.

"A curse, ya say?" She prayed for guidance under her breath when all of a sudden, it came.

"Yes, a powerful, terrible, haunting curse...more powerful than anything!" Haven exclaimed. Hephzibah suddenly perked up at what she said. The answer poured over her all at once.

"There is a way," Hephzibah spoke up quickly. It surprised even her. She felt force on her words, not her own.

"I already told you, I've tried everything! It keeps coming back," Haven sniffed. "How could you know anyway?"

"Sounds to me loike ya 'ave nuffin' to lose by trustin' me," Hephzibah stood up with a grunt and wiped off the dew on her dress. "What does thee say?" she reached her hand out to the young woman. Haven gazed at it. She spoke the truth. She didn't have anything to lose. Anything was better than sitting on the damp river bank all night, contemplating her end.

Haven finally took Hephzibah's hand, though reluctantly and followed her. They walked for about four blocks until they reached a small home. It was on the corner of the cramped housing, deep in the city, near the harbor. It wasn't shabby like others Haven had seen during her long walks.

"You can bo-peep sleep 'ere for now. Me brovwer is a captain and onny ports 'ere for a week at a time. I figure we can make otha arrangements then," Hephzibah showed Haven around the house then ended with the quaint but cozy bedroom. It was fairly small but kept extremely clean. It had a very homey feel.

Other arrangements? Haven thought, *How long does she think I'm staying here?* She wasn't expecting to stay at all. *She's merely going to show me how I'm to escape the curse, isn't she?* Haven didn't have much time to think for Hephzibah spoke again. She was swiftly finding out that the woman enjoyed talking very much.

"It's much too late to start discussin' why thou came wif me. I'll fetch you somethin' ta eat then I'll say goodnight. We can talk tomorra." In a way, Hephzibah was testing her to see if she truly wanted to know how to gain her freedom from the curse. She knew if she was to get through to her, the young lady had to long for it on her own. It couldn't be pushed on her by someone else.

She stepped out of the room and was about to close the door when Haven put her arm out to block it.

"Wait, I need to know what it is you think can save me. I can't possibly eat or sleep until I know."

"Oh...well, I guess we can do that," Hephzibah tried to hide her satisfaction at Haven's ardent response. "Aye, cum to the chuffin' sittin' room and sit by the bloomin' fire. I'll put on a spot of tea then join thou," Hephzibah bustled to the kitchen. Haven marveled at the strange way she spoke.

Minutes later, they both were seated and sipping their tea.

"So what is it?" Haven asked hastily, though deep down she knew this was a waste of time for she was confident there was nothing to be done. She was more than ready to abate anything Hephzibah presented.

"Well, before I can give thee the details, thou need to tell me a bit more abaht this curse business." Her question seemed fair enough.

"The simplest way I can explain it is, a gypsy gave me a journal and instructed me to write my dreams in it. I did as she said and filled up half of it. Soon after, I found out my entire family...perished on a ship."

"Oh, my dear girl," Hephzibah put in but Haven swiftly kept going to keep from choking up.

"I was in such terrible distress; I wrote in the journal that I wanted to die. Months went by when someone told me the engravings on the journal proved it wasn't just any journal but a curse was on it. I didn't believe it at first, however, when I looked back at my past entries, I realized every single thing I had written came true exactly one year later. It's only a matter of months before I will die. I've tried burning the book and tearing it to shreds, yet the next morning, it's sitting in my room in perfect condition. There's nothing I can do! I'm going to die. So you see, there is nothing that can save me from the dreadful curse."

Haven was still speaking when Hephzibah got up and went to the other side of the room to a table. She came back holding a large book.

"I know wot can save thee from this."

"What?" Haven eyed her skeptically and asked.

"The answa is in this book," she held it up. The front of it was titled The Holy Bible.

"A book? How can the answer be in there?" Haven snorted. *I knew this was a waste of time.*

"Why not? The bloomin' curse over thee began with a book. Why can't the answa be in one? This isn't just any book." Hephzibah sat down again and began paging through it. Haven set down her teacup, preparing to leave at any moment.

"Ah yes…here it is," she stopped and put her finger on the page, "It says here, 'Christ hath redeemed us from the curse.'"

Haven's interest was instantly aroused at the mention of a curse.

"Wait, what?"

"Let me explain," she briefly lowered the book and met Haven's intense gaze. "Afta the first man and woman ever created, sinned, a curse came upon all mankind. The enemy became the rula over us and we were separated from God. There was seemingly no 'ope but then somethin' glorious happened. God sent His Son ta earth. Jesus gave His life for us. Because He 'ad never sinned, and died in our place, He won the keys of hell and death, hammer and tack back from the enemy. He became a curse for us, so we could be free from the terrible curse on the entire world. Anyone who puts their trust in Jesus, repents of their sins, and confesses Him as their

Savior, shall be saved. They shall be saved from the curse."
Hephzibah came to a stop and waited for Haven's reaction to
all of this. The young woman leaned forward and rested her
head on her hands, trying to process her words.

"Can this be true? I don't know this…Jesus, you speak
of." Hephzibah could see a glimmer of hope in her eyes, ready
to grow.

"He knows you."

"Why would he do all of what you say, for me?" Haven
asked.

"Ya said the bloomin' curse is pursuin' thee to no end.
Well, there is a greater One who is pursuing ya. He has been
ever since ya took your first breath. You might not 'ave ever
felt it, but He is always wif ya. Thee are never alone,"
Hephzibah explained.

Haven sat back, stunned at her words. She wanted so badly
for this to be true.

"Just think of the length He has gone ta reach thee. Of all
the places, in all of England, we meet in wee diddle of the
night on a riverbank. He did it all for you." Compassion poured
over Hephzibah. How much God loved this dear, frightened
girl, arose, and flowed out of her. She leaned forward in her
chair and took Haven's hands. "God wants ya to know the
peace you've desired so deeply. It is Him. He is thy peace."
Haven was overcome and deeply touched. It was the one desire
she wanted more than anything else. Tears filled her eyes. No
one could have possibly known this. It was real! This was true.
The walls around her heart came down.

"Let me tell you what God's desire is…for thee to know
Him as He knows you. He wants to come and live within
ya…to have a relationship with you, His daughter. All you
must do is ta ask. Do you wanna?" Hephzibah gently asked.

"Yes…how?" Haven wiped her eyes. Hephzibah led her in
a simple, tearful prayer.

When they finished, Haven opened her eyes and met the older woman's loving, motherly gaze.

"My dear lass, thou are now His bairn child. And because of it, this verse belongs to ya," Hephzibah lifted the book from her lap and handed it to Haven. She took ahold of it as Hephzibah pointed to a verse.

"Christ hath redeemed us from the curse of the law, being made a curse for us: for it is written, Cursed is every one that hangeth on a tree: that the blessing of Abraham might come on the Gentiles through Jesus Christ; that we might receive the promise of the Spirit through faith."

Haven read the precious, yet still very mysterious words to herself.

"It means Jesus rescued and purchased thy freedom from the curse. It wasn't a small price by enny means."

"What was the price?" Haven asked in wonder.

"He bought our freedom by his right own blood," Hephzibah replied. Haven's eyes widened at the wondrous thought. "He took your drum place and took the curse on Himself so you can be free. Thou art free!" Hephzibah's last few words rang in her ears.

"How do I know more?"

"There is so much more, dear. Start by readin' 'ere," Hephzibah gently reached toward the Bible and turned the pages. "Start at the Gospel of John. But, it's much too late ta begin naw," she secured a bookmarker in the pages and shut it. She then glanced at the tiny watch, pinning to her brown shawl around her shoulders. "My my! It's nearly dawn. Why don't we bof get some shut eye and we'll talk rabbit and pork more tomorra." Haven hadn't realized just how exhausted she was until the mentioning of sleep.

Haven was more than tired, that is, until a little while later as she lay in bed. She began thinking over everything Hephzibah told her. She thought about how deeply God knew her and how much she didn't know in return.

Haven glanced up at the wooden beams of the ceiling. "God," she spoke quietly. She had never spoken to God all by herself before. Even saying His name felt quite austere and foreign. "God, I've been told You pursue me...I've been told You are my peace. I've been told You want to have a relationship with me," her voice was filled with emotion. "I want to know You...show me how to begin." Her tears flowed anew at the disparate, almost childlike plea. She closed her eyes. Then, at that moment, something glorious happened. The very presence of God seemed to fill the small room. It was as if He, the creator of the universe, stepped into her room. It was more real than anything. In addition to His presence, a love so great washed over her, almost like warm honey. It washed away all her feelings of dread and sorrow. The power was so great, Haven couldn't have stood if she wanted to. She wept as she let it soak into her heart. She had never felt such piercing, unconditional love. Now, more than ever before, Haven longed to know Him more.

She eventually opened her eyes, fully expecting to see something or someone. The room remained the same but it didn't move her in the least. She was more convinced of anything that she wasn't alone. God was very near. She forgot all about sleep and quickly lit a candle. In an almost crazed manner, Haven reached for the large Bible, Hephzibah lent her, and swiftly opened it to the Gospel of John. It was as if Haven was starving and had to learn of this Savior, who loved her so.

She began at verse one.

'In the beginning was the Word, and the Word was with God, and the Word was God. The same was in the beginning with God. All things were made by Him; and without Him was not any thing made that was made. In Him was life; and the life was the light of men. And the light shineth in darkness; and the darkness comprehended it not.'

Great excitement and expectancy rose up in her as she intently went on. It felt as if she was on the verge of all adventure.

Haven lost all track of time and remained there until she heard the clinking of pots and pans in the kitchen. She removed her gaze for the first time and realized the sun was shining.

How long has it been? Haven wondered. She put the bookmarker on the pages to save her place and nearly jumped out of bed like a giddy child.

"Hephzibah!" She hurried to the kitchen where, sure enough, she was scurrying about, making breakfast. She stopped and when she glanced up at her, gasped.

"My my!" Hephzibah clicked her tongue. "You look loike an entirely new person!" Haven looked down at the white nightgown borrowed to her the night before. It was much too big for Haven's slender frame. Without any rouge and other cosmetics, she knew she must look very different.

Hephzibah instantly saw the young woman mistake what she said literally.

"I'm not referrin' ter thy appearance. I mean your heart. There's a lightness abaht ya and...." Hephzibah hesitated and took one more step closer to see Haven's smiling face. "You are flowin' over with 'ope!'"

"And peace," Haven happily finished. "It's all so true. I feel as if a terrible weight is lifted and I can breathe free for the first time."

"Oh my dear girl," Joyous tears filled Hephzibah's eyes, "I'm sa glad. T' gran' Lord is so good. He nivva ivva disappoints." Haven couldn't hold back any longer. She lunged forward and fell into Hephzibah's embrace.

"All thanks to you. Thank you for showing me the way. I didn't sleep a wink last night. All I could do is read and read," Haven backed up. "And I'm not tired in the least. I feel quite the contrary. After breakfast, I want to continue on!" she ranted on so, Hephzibah had to chuckle.

"Aye, thou can never get too much of it. In fact, it onny makes ya want more!"

CHAPTER TWENTY-SIX

May 21, 1836

"Did you find her?" Trenton asked through clenched teeth. He stood with his back facing the door, peering out the bay window, as if there was a chance he might spot her on the busy streets. He leaned over the desk in his office in frustration when he heard the knock at the door.

"No sir," one of the several men on Trenton's staff stepped

forward and stated. "We searched all the streets surrounding the theater but there's no sign of her except this...." Trenton finally turned to face him to see that he held one of Haven's slipper. He slowly walked toward him and took the shoe from him.

"I want her found, do you hear me?" Trenton nearly growled his order. He swiftly continued when the man opened his mouth to speak. "No one rests until she is found...I don't care if you have to search all of England."

"Yes, sir." With that, the handful of men left.

Trenton gazed down at the shoe.

"Where can you be hiding?" he sauntered back to the window. He had never been so angry. For one, several members of London's high society had demanded a refund from the previous night's performance. They didn't hold back in expressing their anger and displeasure over it. There was only bound be to more. He dreaded the newspaper articles that would no doubt surface in the next day or two. Haven had completely ruined him!

Trenton miserably leaned against the windowsill.

Why would she do something like this? I've given her everything! She didn't have a care in the world. Why would she want to depart from the money, fame, and adoration? Trenton asked himself over and over. *And then there's me...why would she leave me...her fiancé. She adores me.* At least, he thought she adored him. *Unless...she's in love with someone else. It can be the only conclusion.* Trenton painfully reasoned. It made him all the angrier.

His grip tightened on the dainty slipper.

She'll be sorry...she doesn't know what I'm capable of. Without warning, Trenton threw the shoe across the room where it banged against the wall.

CHAPTER TWENTY-SEVEN

May 24, 1836

arrett's eyes slowly opened. He groaned as he sat up, for his head pounded from spending the night at the pub, partaking of ale. He remained seated on the side of his bed and rubbed his face. In truth, he was trying to come up with a

reason to get up. Any purpose he once had was gone.

"Oh, my head," he mumbled. There was only one thing he could think to do to gain some kind of relief.

Garrett forced himself to get dressed. He then trudged down the stairs. As he descended, the front door opened and Leiston walked in.

"Good morning...well, there's not much left of the morning it seems," he greeted. Garrett merely nodded at his roommate and went to his coat that lay on the floor in the middle of the small sitting room. He was in no condition or mood for a chat.

I have to leave before the lecture, he told himself.

"Where are you off to in such a hurry?" Leiston asked.

Oh, here we go, Garrett rolled his eyes, for his back was hidden from Leiston's prying eyes.

"Out," he hurried to the door.

"Out where? Why are you trying to hide it?" Leiston approached and caught Garrett's arm.

"What do you care? I know what you're doing...and you can stop. I don't recall asking you to be my mother," he spitefully said. Leiston wasn't prepared for his ill temper. He realized this was a bad time to push him, so he backed down and helplessly stepped aside.

Garrett grasped the door handle then hesitated.

"Don't get me wrong, I'm grateful for all you've done for me, allowing me to stay here," he referred to the quaint townhouse that Leiston's father owned. Leiston was Garrett's friend from college. His father actually owned a series of row houses. The one they resided in was a bit larger and nicer than most. They were superior to the majority of homes east of them because it was located toward the wealthier part of London. Leiston was living in the house while attending law school, for it was only a short distance from it. "And for letting me lay low here," Garrett went on. "For understanding my plight…however, I don't need to be lectured day after day."

"I'm only worried—"

"Don't be," Garrett cut him off. "I'm fine," he opened the door.

"Oh you are, are you? Going to the pub day after day and staying late into the night… drinking yourself into the grave."

"I don't go every day!"

"Well, if you don't go to the pub, you just bring the ale here and sleep the entire day," Leiston argued. "Something needs to change. I'm your friend. I care that you're throwing your life away."

"I am not. You're exaggerating," Garrett quickly defended himself.

"It was an accident, Garrett. Stop blaming yourself," Leiston finally blurted what he'd wanted to say for some time now.

"I told you never to bring it up!" Garrett angrily stomped outside and slammed the door.

He doesn't understand. He clenched his fists as he walked down the street. While he'd told Leiston about the horrendous accident, Garrett never revealed the truth about his false family. It was too painful. All he wanted to do was forget.

"Ah, Mr. Stirling, nice to see you this fine day," the barkeep greeted when Garret entered the pub.

"Mr. Stirling?" He had all but forgotten the fake name he'd given the barkeep. The man behind the counter looked steadily at him.

"Oh, uh…" Garrett suddenly recalled. "I'm well," he lamely replied and took a seat at the counter. The place was empty at this early hour.

"What'll you have?" the man asked. Garrett reached into the pocket of his jacket for a coin when he felt something hard. He slowly pulled out the journal he'd put there. It was the last time he'd worn it. It was only then that he remembered.

The book from that night! It belongs to the girl I stopped from jumping off the bridge.

The barkeep cleared his throat loudly as he waited for payment, yet Garrett's interest in ale vanished in his curiosity.

"Uh, never mind…I have to go."

"Alright, Mr. Stirling. I'll see you later I'm sure," the barkeep chuckled as Garrett left. He couldn't go home when Leiston was there, so he walked down the street. He had to find somewhere to be alone.

The first secluded spot he found was a sunny alley. Garrett lifted a half broken crate and placed it upside down to sit on. He then pulled out the journal and opened it. The more he thought about the young woman he'd found, the more curious he was about who she was. The fancy gown she wore baffled him.

Why was she in the east side of London and barefoot no less? He remembered that particular detail well, for after she slapped him, she kicked him in the leg before running off.

Garrett hoped he would find a name in the book or something to reveal whom it belonged to. The symbols on the journal looked very old, yet it was in fairly good condition, other than some ware from much use.

He opened it and read the date on the first page.

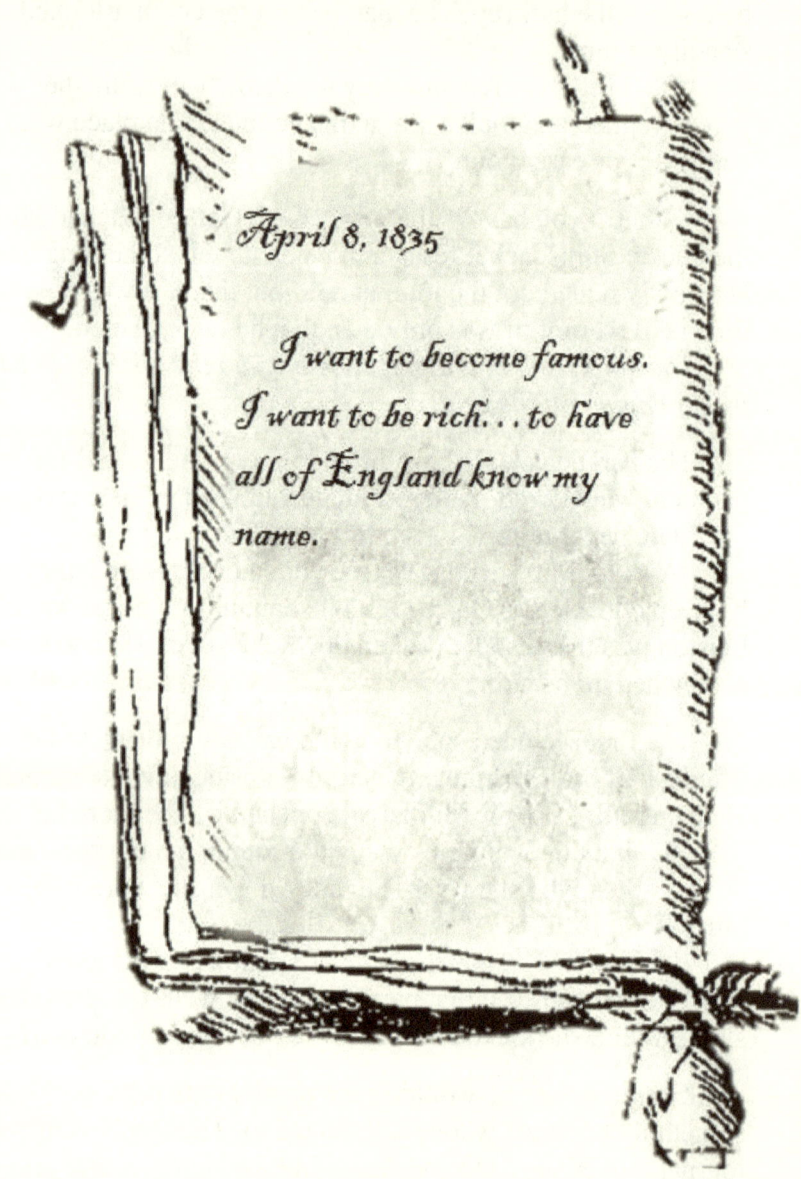

April 8, 1835

I want to become famous. I want to be rich. . . to have all of England know my name.

He read a few more lines then slammed the book shut.

I knew it...the aspirations of an ignorant girl. I'm not reading this. I shouldn't anyway. Garrett leaned back against the brick wall behind him. His thoughts were consumed with the mysterious young woman.

Someone dressed like she was, must surely be wealthy. Yet, why was she at the bridge in the east side of the city...and so upset?

Just then, he remembered when he came upon her, she was about to throw the very book he now held. He looked down at the journal again for some time before he couldn't take it anymore and opened it again. He mostly skimmed the pages until he came upon something that could possibly reveal who the woman might be.

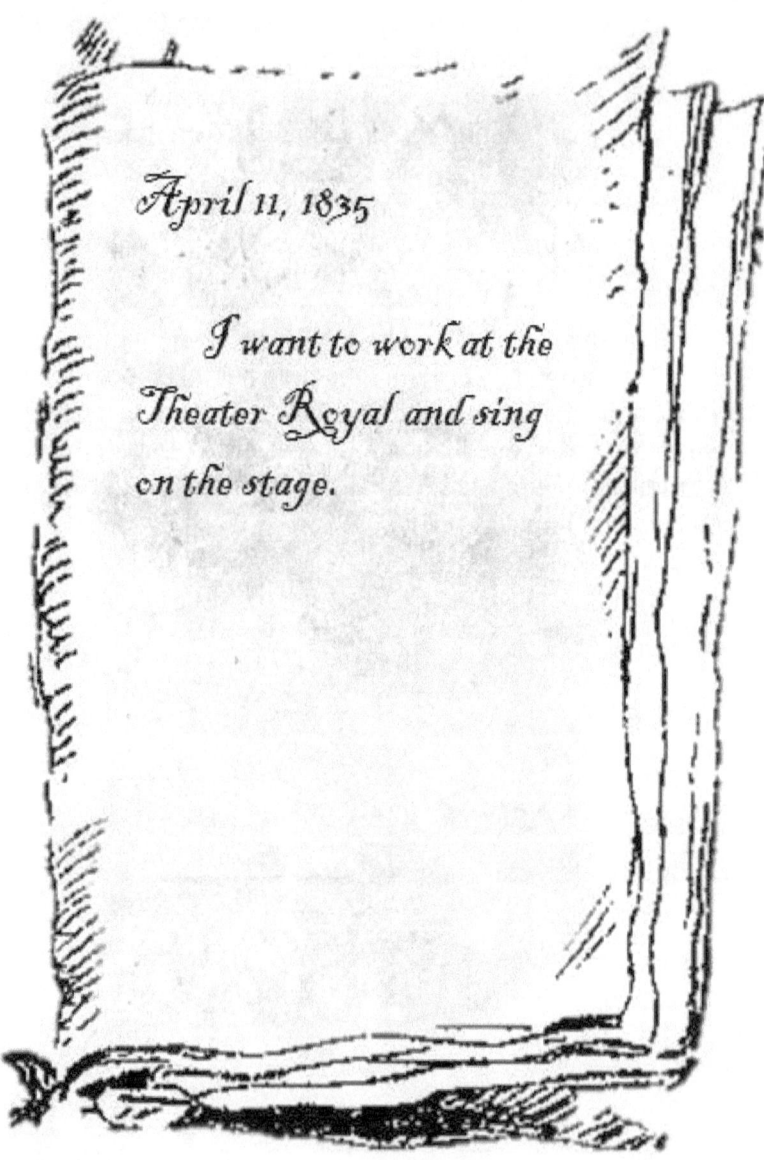

April 11, 1835

I want to work at the
Theater Royal and sing
on the stage.

Garrett felt as if he was coming on to something valuable, so he slowly turned a few more pages.

May 2, 1835

I want a man of great
means and power to
propose to me in an
elaborate way.

There still wasn't a name mentioned. He was quickly beginning to lose hope and interest. It wasn't the worst thing if he couldn't return it to whomever it belonged.

Instead of slamming the book shut like before, he fanned the pages one last time in case something caught his eye. About three fourths through, an almost blank page made him stop. He opened it fully and saw the date written at the top.

Garrett's brow furrowed at the strange and sudden change. Up until now, everything written in the journal was about dreams and goals.

And now this? Garrett suddenly jumped in surprise when three children chased one another through the alley. They swiftly ran passed him and into the street. Once they were gone, he looked back down at the open journal.

This is absurd...what am I doing? Wasting my time. There's nothing here to lead me to the owner. Garrett stood up and dropped the journal on the crate before walking out of the alley. He continued for nearly half a block before abruptly coming to a halt.

Yet, what else is there to do?

As much as he hated to admit it, Leiston was right. He was wasting his life away. There was something about the strange journal that kept him pinned there. It beckoned to him as if there was something much more in it than just scribblings.

Without so much as another thought, Garrett spun around to retrieve the book.

Leiston wasn't there when he walked in to the small townhouse. Garrett wandered upstairs to his room and looked around. Needless to say, the room was a mess. Clothes, empty bottles, and old newspapers were strewn on every surface and across the floor.

He still held the book in his hands as he walked to the bed and sat down. One of the queer entries written in the journal came back to mind.

"I want all of England to know my name." It sounded almost familiar somehow.

But how could that be? Garrett lay on the bed to think when his head landed on something. It crinkled under him. Garrett reached up and found a newspaper under the unkempt blankets. The date on it was April 8, 1836.

Before throwing it onto the floor, one of the bold headlines caught his attention. In big, bold letters, was written,

"ALL OF ENGLAND KNOWS HER NAME."

He pulled the paper closer to him to get a better look.

"Miss Haven Romiley is the newest addition to The Theater Royal. She has instantly become well beloved by everyone who has heard her beautiful talent."

Garrett lowered it to his lap.

That's it! Her grand appearance made much more sense now. *Wait,* he thought. The headline was somehow strangely very familiar to him.

Garrett quickly sat up and took ahold of the journal he'd set aside. He hurriedly flipped through the book and searched for the place he'd read before.

Here it is, he stopped and read it.

I want all of England to know my name.

He then moved his gaze to the top of the page.

April 8, 1835

He had to blink a few times to make sure he was reading correctly. The date was exactly a year earlier.

How can this be? Impossible! He turned to another entry.

May 2, 1835

    I want a man of great means and power to propose to me in an elaborate way.

Garrett stood with a sense of renewed purpose. He went around the room and picked up each newspaper, searching for the date. If it wasn't the one he sought after, he tossed it behind him.

"It has to be here somewhere!" he grumbled when he was nearing the other side of the room. There were only two wrinkled papers left. He bent down and picked them both up but hesitated, wanting so badly to find one dated May second and to prove whether or not this strange notion held any merit.

The first paper said May 20, 1836. He nearly cringed and took a look at the very last paper. May 2, 1836. He sighed with relief and almost ripped the page as he opened it. Sure enough, the very first and largest headline read,

"THE ANGEL OF THEATER ROYAL SAYS YES!"

His gaze immediately moved to the article below it.

"After last night's performance, everyone was aghast when Mr. Trenton Martell, the manager of the theater, appeared on the stage. He lowered himself on bended knee and asked the talented Miss Haven Romiley for her hand in marriage. To everyone's pleasure, she said yes. What an elaborate and extravagant ending to the glorious evening."

In an elaborate way, Garrett put down the paper in astonishment. *The exact same words she wrote in the journal, precisely one year before it came to pass.*

As the truth of the matter slowly dawned on him, so did concern. He couldn't begin to understand what was going on here. One thing was certain, there was no way it was a mere coincidence. Another thought struck him unexpectedly. It was what he had read in the journal, earlier in the alley. Garrett dropped the newspaper and immediately returned to his bed. He picked up the book and hastily paged through it. The entry he sought was easy to find for it was very near the end and had a single sentence written.

Garrett's gaze lowered to the lonely words on the page.

If the previous entries came true...this could only mean....
Garrett solemnly shut the journal. He pictured the beautiful woman, standing on the edge of the bridge, ready to end her life that forlorn night.

"I've got to warn her!" he spoke aloud. "I've got to warn her before it's too late." Garrett quickly put on his well-worn coat and slid the book in the inside pocket, before leaving the house once again.

CHAPTER TWENTY-EIGHT

ome in," Trenton said as a knock sounded on the door. Malcolm Barstow, Trenton's assistant, opened it and peeked inside the office.

"Sir, there is someone here to see you."

I'm much too busy to be bothered. I told you—"

"Yes, but it's about Miss Romiley," Malcolm informed.

Trenton immediately stopped to listen.

"Who is it?"

"Some man. He wouldn't offer his name. He actually asked if Miss Romiley is here."

"Is that so?" Trenton set his pen down on his desk. What did this man have to do with Haven? In the process of getting to know Haven, she had told him about her family and their sudden deaths. She had no one in the world left, other than her adoring fans.

Perhaps he's found her...or, Trenton's mind reeled. *What if he knows why she left...or whom she left with? Why, he could be the very man himself...who stole her away from me!* Trenton angrily stood.

"I showed him to the east entrance hall to wait," Malcolm finished.

Garrett tapped his toe on the floor as he nervously waited for Haven on a bench in the elegantly decorated hall. What would he say once she got there? Would she recognize him from the bridge? Would she be happy to see him? Garrett recalled when she slapped him before running away.

If she's truly the person the journal belongs to, he thought. His doubts were beginning to creep in. Only an hour ago, he was more sure than anything about what he had discovered.

He couldn't sit anymore and got to his feet just as he heard someone walk in.

"May I help you?" Garrett turned to a man wearing a frock

coat, vest, and stiff notched collar.

"Uh, yes. I was hoping to have a word with—"

"She isn't here at the moment. Who might you be?" Trenton asked curtly. He eyed the man intently. He was very homely looking and possibly even homeless by his old, somewhat tattered clothing, much less the long hair and beard. Trenton tried to cover his astonishment at how his beloved Haven could have anything to do with the likes of him.

Garrett's uneasiness doubled. If Haven Romiley wasn't at the theater, Garrett wanted nothing more than to get out of there as fast as he could. The businessman and the entire theater made him more than a little uncomfortable.

"Oh, it doesn't matter really. I'll just come back another day." Garrett placed his hat on his head and headed for the entrance. Trenton followed close behind.

"Do you want to leave her a note? I could give it to her when she returns," Trenton lied. For a moment, Garrett thought about taking him up on his offer.

"No thank you," he swiftly declined. There was something about the man he instantly disliked, yet he couldn't put his finger on it.

"Might I at least tell her who called?" Trenton tried one last attempt to find out who the foul looking stranger was. Garrett didn't reply as Trenton saw him through to the east door.

"Thank you anyway," he mumbled then left.

The door no more shut when Malcolm appeared.

"Who was he?" For some unknown reason, even to him, Garrett hesitated on the regal porch. He overheard them talking inside. In his curiosity, he carefully moved closer to hear better.

"He didn't say...but he knows something."

What's going on here? Garrett listened all the more intently at this.

"How could you tell?" the other man asked.

"He's hiding something. I want him followed," Trenton ordered. Garrett was startled. Why did he want him followed? Where was Miss Romiley, anyway?

"Yes, sir."

"I'm certain he will lead us to Haven," Trenton stated in a desperate and dark tone. Garrett had heard enough. The last thing he wanted was to be followed and possibly discovered for his past.

What have I done? He thought. He scrambled off the porch while trying his best to remain quiet. *He doesn't know where Haven is either? What's going on? Why didn't he just tell me that in the first place?* His heart raced as he hurried to get as far away from the theater as possible. He was now more confused than ever, although, Garrett knew there was much more going on with the mysterious young woman than his findings from the journal.

May 27, 1836

"Knowing this, that our old man is crucified with Him, that the body of sin might be destroyed, that henceforth we should not serve sin.

For he that is dead is freed from sin.

Now if we be dead with Christ, we believe that we shall also live with Him:

Knowing that Christ being raised from the dead dieth no

more; death hath no more dominion over Him.
For in that He died, He died unto sin once: but in that He liveth, he liveth unto God.
Likewise reckon ye also yourselves to be dead indeed unto sin, but alive unto God through Jesus Christ our Lord."

Haven was sitting up in her bed at Hephzibah's house. She had grown accustomed to reading late into the night ever since first opening the Bible. She was dozing off, her head slowly leaning against the headboard behind her, when she heard a soft voice.

"I love you," a voice she knew all too well, whispered in her ear. Normally, Derek's caring tone brought her comfort. Yet this time, it sent chills down her spine. Haven's eyes shot open. She glanced around the room. In the flickering shadows from a single candle, Derek was sitting on the only chair in the room. He wore what he always did. It was the last thing Haven had ever seen him wear before he died. The only difference was, he wasn't smiling and his gaze downcast. Haven had never seen such a forlorn expression from him.

"Derek, where have you been?" She recalled when she needed him most on the bridge, but he never appeared.

"Remember…all the wonderful memories we made together…all the plans for the future," he stated as if betrayed and hurt. "You promised only to love me, no matter what." Derek had said this so many times. However, it was never in an accusing way, as he did now. Instead of feeling any guilt like she usually did, something deep inside Haven rose up in her.

"I have found someone who is always there for me," she said and clutched the Bible close to her.

"You promised," Derek met her gaze for the first time.

"Well, you promised never to leave me. I have found someone else to give me hope," Haven briefly motioned upward. "And He will never leave me, nor forsake me."

"But you gave me your word," Derek urged.

"I don't need you anymore." Part of her couldn't believe the words that came from her lips. For so long, Derek was everything to her. All of her hope and everything she lived for.

"What?" Derek nearly gasped. "But I love you, Haven." A small pang of sorrow hit her. Would she relent and succumb to the old, familiar grief? Instead of feeling all alone in her attempts to overcome, there was a power in her this time. It was as if someone stood with her, supporting and strengthening her.

"You aren't real. I don't need you anymore. I have fulfillment now. I've found peace."

Derek stared at her, stunned. When it was apparent she wouldn't be moved, he stood up and turned toward the wall with a closed window.

"Goodbye forever," he sighed then walked to the wall. He didn't stop and kept walking until he stepped through the closed window and disappeared.

Haven didn't feel at all lonely but empowered. She had released the final burden and was free. The sorrow would haunt her no longer.

CHAPTER TWENTY-NINE

May 31, 1836

"See you later!"

"Goodbye," Garrett replied as he exited the pub and started to walk home. The sun was about to set behind the houses. Just as he turned to go down the next block, Garrett caught sight of something in his peripheral vision. It was a man and he was following him but staying at a close distance behind him. It didn't surprise him in the least. It had been going on ever since Garrett went to the theater. Though he might have gotten somewhat used to it, he didn't like it one bit. He tried several different attempts to lose them. Everything from going to crowded areas, to running to get away, even slowing his pace and turning around to face the men. Nothing worked.

He guessed there were now two or more men in pursuit, for one morning, he finally got a good look at the bothersome men. He'd glanced out his bedroom window to find two suspicious characters talking to each other and glancing at the townhouse once in a while. Garrett was at a loss as to what to do anymore. He hoped they would tire in their efforts and realize Haven wasn't anywhere near him.

He tried one last time to turn and face them, yet they always remained far enough behind him to easily stay hidden. Garrett quickened his pace as much as he could while still keeping them in his sights. If he were going to try anything, it would have to be quick. They apparently already knew where he lived so if he did somehow get away from them, he wouldn't be able to return to Leiston's.

The sun went down and it was swiftly growing dark with every passing minute.

I know these streets well, Garrett reasoned. *I could easily navigate it blindfolded.* Just then, an idea came to him to escape for the last time. He dearly hoped his pursuers didn't know that particular part of town as well as he.

Garrett glanced to his side one last time before breaking into a run. Sure enough, one man was still behind him. Garrett sped down one block, then another. He didn't want to completely lose them, not just yet, but wanted to get far enough ahead of them to follow through with his plan. He knowingly led the way to a street that was filled with old discarded crates and broken furniture.

He turned one more corner when he'd arrived. It was only a matter of seconds before the men would show up. Garrett didn't have much time. He hurriedly scanned the dark street for something fairly heavy to grab. He finally went for a broken chair and backed up against the cold brick building, closest to the corner. He tried his best to quiet his fast breathing so he would better hear them approach.

"Where'd he go?" Garrett heard a man ask. It sounded like they were only about a block away from him.

"That way!" another man gasped.

So there is more than one, Garrett concluded.

"You go that way...I'll check over here." Garrett listened and silently waited. By now the sky was entirely dark so he hoped he would be able to see the man right away. He strained to hear the nearing footsteps on the cobblestone street. It seemed to take forever. Garrett pulled back the wooden chair, his gaze fixed on the corner, waiting to strike. The man then appeared into view. This was it! Garrett swung the chair through the air and right into the unsuspecting man's head. The chair crumbled over him and he loudly fell to the ground. The man lay, unmoving. Garrett carefully leaned over him and found he was out cold. It worked! The crash was quite noisy so Garrett knew if he wished to get away for good, this was his chance. The other man would inevitably come upon his comrade shortly.

Garrett rushed down the rest of the block and was gone. Sure enough, the other man found the other, lying on his back with a nasty cut on his forehead and a bloody nose.

"Harvey! Wake up!" he knelt beside him and shook his shoulder. Harvey slowly came to and winced when he felt a handkerchief press against his head to stop the bleeding.

"Where did he go?"

"He knocked me over the head...got away, I spect," he

moaned as the other man helped him up.

"Mr. Martel won't be happy about this."

CHAPTER THIRTY

June 1, 1836

"Sir, we've had a minor setback," the man employed by Trenton entered his office and declared solemnly.

"What kind of setback?" Trenton firmly set down some papers firmly on his desk in anger. The man turned to open the door when Harvey walked in. His face was black and blue and a bandage wrapped around his head.

"What has happened now?" Trenton sighed in frustration.

"The person you instructed us to follow clobbered him and got away. We've searched everywhere. He hasn't returned to his house either."

"You two are worthless. One homely man easily outsmarted you."

"Sir, it was dark and he knew the area better."

"Just go," Trenton mumbled and held his head in his hand.

"But sir,"

"I don't want to hear any more of your excuses. Just go! Get out!" he shouted as he stood to his feet and angrily pointed to the door. Both men instantly heeded him and scurried out of his office.

"Is everything alright?" Malcolm must have heard the shouting, for he came right after the others left. He took one of the two seats in front of Trenton's desk. Trenton plopped back into his chair.

"I thought we would have found her by now. I don't understand how she could have vanished...without the help of someone, that is," he stated, implying the nameless man who'd come seeking Haven.

"I've wanted to keep things quiet and not gain unwanted attention from the public...to keep attendance up," he referred to their present arrangements in Haven's absence. The show had to continue on with Lindsay taking the leading role in Haven's place. Trenton was growing tired of the complaints and questions from the public and newspapers, demanding to know where the beloved angel was. Trenton could only lie and say she was ill for so long. Everyone would find out sooner or later. In all honesty, Trenton nearly cringed to find out what had actually become of Haven, fearing she had truly run off with another man.

"What else can be done?" Malcolm broke into Trenton's hopeless musings.

"I dread if we are going to discover her whereabouts, I'm going to have to tell the newspapers the truth of her disappearance. All of England knows who she is and what she looks like. It shouldn't take long."

"Perhaps you could offer a reward for any information to speed up the process," Malcolm suggested.

"What if I didn't mention that she fled from here? What if she was kidnapped?" Malcolm quickly caught on to Trenton's idea.

"It would surely make some very interesting news."

"Yes it would. And, it would keep the theater in good standing with the public. It would most likely boost our profits. Everyone would be consumed with bringing her back to me."

"Shall I send word to the reporters?" Malcolm stood and asked.

"Yes...and the authorities."

"The authorities?"

"To report Haven is missing," Trenton smiled, "And can you guess who the main suspect will be, whom we will report?" Malcolm shook his head no.

"The mysterious man who came here looking for Haven," Trenton finished.

"Brilliant!" Malcolm replied before going to do Trenton's bidding.

"It won't be long now," Trenton sighed and happily leaned back in his chair and folded his hands.

CHAPTER THIRTY-ONE

June 5, 1836

"Oh, daffy dahn dilly silly me!" Hephzibah gasped when she walked into the kitchen.

"What is it?" Haven was just coming downstairs when she heard the commotion. Hephzibah met her at the bottom, holding a medium sized bag.

"Weston left without this. It's filled wif scones. I make up a bunch for 'im every time he sets sail. He keeps askin' me ta accompany him on his happeny dip ship to cook. Can you imagine me…on a ship full o' men…for months on end, mind you?" she chuckled at the very thought. "So I make him treaties so it's like I'm there after all.

"It would be rather amusing," Haven smiled. It was a far cry to their first meeting when Hephzibah found her utterly hopeless. "I could bring it to him," Haven offered.

"That is sweet of ya, but he's prolly launched by naw."

"Maybe not. He didn't leave very long ago."

"Are ya sure? I mean, he could fair without them."

"It's a nice day for a walk anyway. It would do me good," Haven grinned and put her hand on Hephzibah's.

"Alreight. Does thee still know the bloomin' way since we welcomed me dear brother home a fortnight agoa?" she asked. Haven nodded in assurance and happily took the bag. She donned Hephzibah's plaid cloak then left.

Haven cheerfully strolled to the harbor, enjoying the beautiful, late afternoon weather. There was a market located right before reaching the port. Before she neared it, Haven raised the hood of her cloak as she did every time a crowd of people was close by. Thankfully, at the present time of day, it wasn't overly busy. The various merchants were beginning to pack up for the evening.

At the busiest corner, a boy was stacking up what was left of the newspapers he hadn't sold. Haven walked passed him and smiled as she glanced down at the paper on top of the stack. A large headline instantly caught her eye.

The London Ledger

England's Angel Kidnapped!

"Haven Romiley, known as the Angel of the Theater Royal, is missing. She was found missing, May 21th. There is one suspect so far, known as a bearded man, around thirty years of age, about six feet tall, and dressed in homely attire. There is a reward for any helpful information. If you know anything about this, please go to the Theater Royal or the London City Police."

"ENGLAND'S ANGEL KIDNAPPED!"

Haven came to an abrupt halt and stared at the newspaper, horrified.

"Do ya want one, miss?" the young newsy asked.

"I…I," she stuttered in shock. "I don't have any money."

"That's alright. I'm leavin' anyway. You can just take one." He picked up the one her gaze was still fixed on and handed it to her.

Haven took in the article under the headline in concern when the boy went back to work, organizing his papers.

"Haven Romiley, known as the Angel of the Theater Royal, is missing. She was found missing, May 21th. There is one suspect so far, known as a bearded man, around thirty years of age, about six feet tall, and dressed in homely attire. There is a reward for any helpful information. If you know anything about this, please go to the Theater Royal or the London City Police."

Haven jumped when two villagers walked by and startled her. They looked at her strangely and continued on.

"Are you alright, miss?" the boy asked.

"I won't need this after all," Haven immediately stepped back to try and hide her appearance as the paper slipped from her grasp. "I have to go," she continued backing up until she rammed right into a tall, gruff blacksmith.

"Pardon me," she gasped and tried to hide her face with her hood. She had to get out of there! She had to get back to Hephzibah's house.

Haven forced herself not to run, for it would only attract more attention. She hurried down some quiet streets, slowly peering around each corner to make sure the coast was clear.

CHAPTER THIRTY-TWO

*G*arrett awoke when he heard tin cans clinking together. "Sorry bloke…didn't mean to wake ya."

Garrett yawned and stretched out on his sad looking bed he'd made out of newspaper. Ever since he'd rid himself of the two men following him, he'd been sleeping on the streets. He couldn't go back to Leiston's townhouse for he knew what was most likely awaiting him.

It wasn't long before he met Harris, another homeless man, much older than he. He had been kind enough to show Garrett a few pointers and allowed him to stay in the same cold, damp street as he.

"The city is in an uproar, my boy," Harris sat down on a crate adjacent from Garrett.

"What do you mean?" Garrett yawned again.

"There moeight be some 'ope for we street urchins yet…a way ta make some money." Garrett didn't say anything and just listened to Harris go on. He was an eccentric man who enjoyed long chats and coming up with odd ideas to get ahead. He was also very hyper and seemed to be unable to sit still, moving constantly.

"It's all right here in this newspapa." Garrett knew by now it was pointless to question the man but to let him finish. "It says reet here, *'reward for any helpful information.'* So the way I see it, all we have ta do is keep a close eye for anything to do with Miss Haven Romiley," Harris explained importantly. Garrett's head shot up at him upon hearing her name.

"Wait, what?"

"Aye…here's what we should do…tomorrow we should go—"

"Wait, what did it say about Miss Haven Romiley?" Garrett got to his feet in urgency yet Harris kept talking.

"We need to go to the busiest part of town and—" Garrett finally marched up the to the ranting man and ripped the paper from his hands.

"Let me see that!" he snapped more harshly than he intended but silenced Harris. Garrett hurriedly read the large headline and article underneath with the details.

He froze when he neared the end.

"There is one suspect so far, known as a bearded man, around thirty years of age, about six feet tall, and dressed in homely attire."

They think I'm the one responsible? Just because I went to the theater asking for her? What have I gotten myself into? Not only could he not return to his parent's home, but Leiston's townhouse as well.

Now I can't even be left alone on the streets. Garrett glanced at Harris. He was digging in his jacket pocket, searching for something. The man obviously hadn't read all the details of the article for he surely would have voiced it by now.

Garrett recalled what he overheard from the owner of the theater when he had gone there looking for Haven.

"He didn't say...but he knows something."

"How could you tell?" the other man asked.

"He's hiding something. I want him followed," Trenton ordered.

"Yes, sir."

"I'm certain he will lead us to Haven."

There was much more going on. The nosey man at the theater was covering something up, albeit Garrett didn't have time to try and figure it out. He had to hide somewhere before he was spotted and reported to the authorities.

Garrett put the paper under his arm and went to work shoving his very few belongings in an old potato sack.

"What are you doin'? Where ya goin'?" Harris immediately asked.

"I'm leaving," he simply replied.

"But why? We've work to do. Tomorrow we must nip on to the west side."

"I'm sorry. I have to go now. Thank you for everything." Garrett took off down the street without another word. Harris watched him until he was out of sight when he remembered something.

"Hey, come back! I need that newspaper!"

CHAPTER THIRTY-THREE

hen she got far enough away from the market, Haven started to run. She had to get back to Hephzibah's before someone recognized her. *Lord, help me! Help me hurry!* She was so focused on hurrying, she didn't see the protruding rainspout. Her foot caught on it, causing her to fly forward. Thankfully, she regained balance quick enough not to hit the ground. The rainspout was very old and fragile so the impact made it crumble. It echoed loudly as it fell to the ground.

Haven glanced in front of her to the street and gasped for she was no longer alone. Two men were present. One was on a horse and the other was holding his horses leg up, inspecting its shoe. They were both staring right at her from the loud noise. Haven instantly recognized the man on the horse as the same man who she had seen work for Trenton. What was she to do? Where could she run? Both men glanced at each other. They didn't say anything, but they undoubtedly knew who she was.

Haven didn't wait around to find out what they were going to do next. She darted down the street to her left, away from them.

"Come on! She's gettin' away," the man atop the steed, shouted to his partner.

Haven ran for her life. Fear rose up in her until it was so great, she struggled to breathe. She willed her legs to move faster but deep down, she knew she was no match for whoever was after her on horse. They would surely be upon her at any moment.

Don't look back! It will only slow you down. Keep going! You have to find a place to hide. Haven's panic urged her onward, through the dark and dingy streets. There was no doubt other unsavory characters in that part of London to fear besides the ones after her.

"Oi! What's your hurry, pretty lass!" Sure enough, a spindly old man spewed as Haven rushed by. The frightful act distracted her for only a second. That was all it took for her to stumble over her filthy skirt. She tripped and fell to the damp ground. Her hands and knees burned from her attempts to catch herself on the cobblestone. She swiftly glanced behind her. Over her wild heartbeat, she could hear possibly more than one horse beating the street with their hooves at a fierce rate. Was she caught? Was her brief fall the end of her? Haven didn't care to wait around to find out. She lifted herself to her feet. Her lungs ached from already running so far. Where could she go? Where could she hide?

Why...why did I have to leave when I knew it wasn't safe? Regrets flashed through her mind. *But there's no time for that!* Her pursuers would round the corner any minute! Haven picked up her skirts and hurried down the narrow street. *Where can I go?* The alarming question followed her every gasp. She tried her best to watch where she was going and at the same time desperately searching for a place to hide. There, out of the corner of her eye, a dark side street came into view. Though she doubted it would provide a quick hideaway that would cause her to disappear completely, it was her only choice. She slid to a halt, almost falling in the process for the street was fairly wet, and dashed into the other street. She didn't have time to think of the possible dangers that dwelt in the shadows. Her only focus was the people after her.

The horses sounded closer and closer. When they raced down the very street she had just stood in, Haven drew back against the cold, brick building and tried to calm her gasping breaths.

Please don't let them see me! She hoped against hope as she glanced up at the dreary clouds that covered the moon. It was then that the horses past by the street where she stood. She pressed in further against the building and into the shadows. She felt as if she might faint as she froze. Haven didn't look but heard the horses bound down the street and to the next block. She breathed a sigh of relief, however, deep down she knew she wasn't safe quite yet. There was still a substantial distance between her and her safe abode.

"Miss?" The low voice behind her made her jump. She peered down the alley where the mysterious voice came from, but it was completely dark. "Miss Romiley?" A man stepped out of the shadows as he said her name. He moved slowly, trying not to frighten her in fear that she might bolt.

"Who—" Haven began to ask when she realized what he held. It belonged to her. He slowly held the book out to her, freely offering her to take it. Haven gazed at it. When she glanced back up at the man's face, she finally recognized who he was. He had seemed nice enough upon first observation but she didn't know for sure if he could be trusted. She remained guarded just as the sound of horses echoed again.

Oh no! It can't be them! Instead of taking the book, she spun around. She had to get out of there and find another—

"This is yours," the man spoke, swiftly drawing her attention back to him.

"Did you read it?" she hurriedly asked. The man lowered his gaze to the book in his hand. He struggled with a reply. This only caused Haven's panic, which had returned when she heard the horses growing closer. She didn't have time to wait any longer! *Doesn't he know there's someone after me?* "I must hurry. Did you read it?" she urged sharply. She again turned to glance behind her swiftly. The faint sounds were growing louder.

"I uh…that is…." the man stammered. It now appeared that it was painful for him to let it out.

"Well?" Haven took one step back, getting ready to make her escape!

"You're going to die," he blurted at last. He almost winced as he said it. Haven looked at him intently, trying to take in what he'd just stated. The man seemed relieved now that he'd gotten the heavy truth off of him.

"I know," Haven suddenly replied in assurance. The man's mouth dropped open. It was the very last thing he thought she would say in response to such devastating words. The calmness and almost determined tone in her voice baffled him above all else.

"What? Wha—" he was cut off by the sound of a loud neigh from the street.

"Hurry!" Haven breathed, "We must hurry! They will never stop looking for me…I have to get back to Hephzibah's." By now, she was horribly turned around.

"Where is it located?"

"It's near the row houses on Posey Lane. Do you know of it?"

"Follow me," the man gently grasped her arm before they carefully moved on. They didn't breathe a word to one another as she followed the mysterious man down several streets. They no longer heard any horses pursuing them and for that, Haven was relieved. Now that her panic was beginning to subside a bit, questions arose about the man before her. Could he indeed be trusted? Why was he helping her? Haven recalled their first meeting when she slapped him and fled.

They rounded the corner when Haven finally recognized her surroundings. There was Hephzibah's welcoming house! Haven breathed a heavy sigh of relief, her gaze filled with tears. She had been so frightened she'd been caught.

Haven rushed to the house. Hephzibah must have been worried, watching for her to return because before Haven reached the door, it opened.

"Haven, me dear girl…there ya are!" Hephzibah embraced the upset young woman in her motherly way.

"I'm so glad I made it back."

"Wot happened? I was prayin' so hard for thee to return safely," Hephzibah said then took in the straggly character, nervously standing behind Haven.

"He helped me find my way," Haven pulled away and glanced at him.

"Come, let's get inside quickly."

"Got 'em!" the man breathed as he gazed at the threesome making their way inside the small house. Not only was Miss Romiley found, but the so-called suspect as well.

"Do we go?" the other man asked.

"No...we know where to find them now. You keep watch. I'll inform Mr. Martel."

CHAPTER THIRTY-FOUR

ephzibah immediately saw to Haven's bleeding knees and helped her get cleaned up before going downstairs. She then bustled into the kitchen, always the perfect hostess, and set some tea to boil. While she did so, Haven told her about the headline in the newspaper. She felt a little awkward with the perfect stranger sitting across from her at the small table.

"I ran as fast as I could to get back here then ran right into the two men…I know they work for Trenton. How could he do such a thing?" Haven asked, clearly still upset. "I don't understand why he would presume I was kidnapped."

"Maybe he doesn't," Garrett spoke up for the first time but never looked up from his lap. Haven gazed at him intently. What did he mean?

"Here we are," Hephzibah approached them and placed the tea set on the table then took a chair. "This will 'elp thou get rid of the cool night air in ya. And dear, I just thank God you are all roeight," she patted Haven's arm.

"I became very lost in my panic. I don't know if I could have found my way if it weren't for…." Haven meekly met Garrett's gaze for the first time since they came inside the house.

"Wot was your name young man?" Hephzibah asked just as he was sipping his tea. He swallowed and was about to tell them his name but stopped. He swiftly recalled all the trouble this strange matter had already caused him ever since setting foot in the theater. He decided to keep some things to himself.

"Stirling…Patrick Stirling." Both women eyed him curiously by his peculiar response.

"And you were sayin' ya two 'ave met before?" Hephzibah asked. Haven blushed when she recalled the night of their first meeting. Garrett glanced at her to see if she would answer but she remained quiet, looking down at her cup.

"Not exactly. We more or less came upon a chance meeting." Haven was taken back by his well-mannered speech. It was not at all what one would think by the look of him. His long, matted beard and terribly dirty clothes, not to mention the smell, left much to be desired.

Before Hephzibah asked more questions, Haven spoke up before things could grow more uncomfortable.

"We met the night I almost…well, a few hours before I met you, Hephzibah."

"Oh, I see."

"I better be on my way," Garrett abruptly stood at this.

"So soon? Surely ya need ter rest a bit longa," Hephzibah offered.

"Thank you for your kindness," he hurried to the door. Haven longingly watched him go. There were still so many things she wanted to ask him. Why did he know the journal said she would die? What did he mean by what he said about the headline? Was he the very bearded suspect mentioned in the newspaper? How did Trenton suppose it was him that kidnapped her? She was helpless to do anything other than listen to him bound out of the door.

CHAPTER THIRTY-FIVE

June 10, 1836

aven was sleeping soundly. She didn't hear the window of her bedroom, being slowly pried open. It was only when a large, strong hand covered her mouth; Haven startled awake. What made her alarm intensify was when she tried to scream, she found out she was unable to breathe. She flailed around, gasping for air as the man dragged her from the bed and toward the window. In her panicked attempt to break free from his hold, the lamp beside the bed fell to the floor with a loud crash.

They were nearly to the window. Haven felt like she might pass out at any moment. The intruder lifted her up when, from out of nowhere, the side table flung through the air and hit the man on the back of the head. Haven didn't know what had happened; only that she was released at long last. She violently gasped for air on the floor, then looked up to see Weston, Hephzibah's brother, standing in the doorway. He must have heard the crash and thrown the table.

Haven moved her gaze to her attacker. His face was hidden by a black mask of some sort. She couldn't speak, but could only shake with fright.

"Heavens! Wot is this?" Hephzibah ran into the room an nearly choked as she pointed at the man. He had come to and quickly escaped out of the window and into the darkness before Weston could catch him.

"Are ya jannock all right?" Hephzibah instantly moved to Haven's side and helped her up. Haven didn't answer but glanced at Weston, who stood before the window.

"Thank the Lord, Weston was home with us," Haven eventually stated with quivering breath.

"Thank God indeed!" Hephzibah agreed. It was a miracle he was present just at the right time. The last shipment he'd taken was a rarity for the destination was very close. He only ended up being gone for five days. Typically he was gone for months at a time.

"What if he comes back?" Haven shuddered at the very thought.

"He won't…that is, if he's wise," Weston said, still gazing out the window. "I'll board this up." He left to get his tools.

"I'm so glad you're safe," Hephzibah spoke up.

"I'm just so sorry to put you through all of this."

"Don't ya worry none abaht this. This is where God wants thee," Hephzibah hugged Haven reassuringly. "Come, let's get some tea. It will 'elp calm us." Haven followed her lead but before leaving the room, she stopped. She caught sight of the Bible, sitting on the floor. It had been knocked over during the struggle. Ever since she'd met Hephzibah and was told of the Man who'd given His life to free her from the curse, Haven only wanted to know more. The dear older woman continued to allow her to read it whenever she wanted. The moment she began, Haven was enraptured by every word. The words itself seemed to breathe life into her. It didn't matter if she didn't quite understand it, nor did she care. It brought her peace, something she hadn't possessed since she could remember. Before Derek died, Haven thought her life was perfect. Yet even then, she didn't have the inward peace she held within her now. She couldn't understand it. She had no money, no home, nothing to call her own, yet after almost being abducted, her heart still abounded with hope.

CHAPTER THIRTY-SIX

June 16, 1836

hree days after the concerning ordeal, Haven and Hephzibah tearfully said goodbye to Weston. He had another shipment, this time it was a longer trip. He left them a pistol for safe keeping. Haven was thankful they prayed together before he departed. They ultimately resolved that the masked man was desperate for money and wanted to turn Haven in for the reward.

The next few days, the ladies were a little on edge. The day finally came when Hephzibah had to go to the market. She hated to leave the young woman but they had no other choice for their food was running low.

Hephzibah departed early in the morning and left Haven with strict instructions not to open the door unless she heard her voice.

Hours later, Haven was reading on the couch in the cozy sitting room. The drapes were drawn over the windows for her safety. All of a sudden, there was a knock on the door. Haven stiffened in sheer terror. It surely wasn't Hephzibah back already, nor would she knock on her own door. Haven froze, hoping whoever it was, would go away. There was another knock. She held her breath and slowly reached for the gun that sat on the coffee table in front of her. There it was again, this time louder.

"Haven?" a young woman's voice meekly called through the door. "Haven, it's me, Wren." Haven stood to her feet at this. It did sound very much like her friend from the theater.

Haven crept to the front door, gun still in hand. There was a small window on both sides of the door. She carefully peeked out one of them and did indeed see Wren. She appeared to be alone and wore a worried expression. Part of her felt foolish for holding the pistol as if she'd ever be able to go through with using it. She merely put it behind her back and drew near to the door.

"I know you must be frightened. I must speak to you…for your own safety," Wren went on. Haven was hard-pressed as to what to do.

How did she find me? Even if it was safe, if I answer, it will only prove that I reside here. Haven reached out and gingerly touched the lock on the door but hesitated when Wren spoke again.

"Please Haven…trust me." Tears sprung to Haven's eyes at her sincerity. How she missed Wren. She couldn't deny her any longer.

"Are….are you alone?" Haven asked through the door, her voice was filled with emotion.

"Well, not entirely. Haven, Trenton is here." Fear washed over her at the mention of his name. His face flashed before her, nearly a month earlier, when she fled from the stage. It was filled with nothing but rage and disappointment.

"I promise you he's not angry. He merely misses you and is very worried. He cares for you deeply and only wants to speak to you," Wren urged gently.

"I…."

"He says after he speaks with you, he'll leave and you can stay here if you wish." Haven's anxiety lessened upon hearing this.

Perhaps it's time to settle this, once and for all and be done with it. She set the gun down on the stairs behind her. She unlocked the door then opened it, only a little at first. She glanced at Wren then looked passed her to Trenton. He stood outside of the enclosed carriage in the distance. His face held no anger or resentment. Only that of concern.

"Haven, we have been so worried about you," Wren said, blinking back tears.

"How did you find me?" Wren didn't answer Haven's question as she embraced her.

"Wll you not speak to him?"

"I will," Haven eventually relented. She found herself very nervous to face him after the way she left.

Wren turned to Trenton and gave a quick nod. Haven couldn't be certain, but it looked as if he was choked up when he neared her.

"Dear, I've missed you terribly," he touched her shoulder as he drew near and kissed her on the side of her face. It made her heart flutter, much like when she first met him and he'd shown interest in her.

"I apologize for leaving the way I did. I can't really...." She struggled to find the right words.

"You don't need to explain. There's something I need to discuss with you. It's very imperative."

"A...alright."

"Along with telling you, I must show you something," Trenton stepped back to prepare to walk back to the carriage.

"Wait, please," Haven said. "Before I go anywhere with you, I must know something."

"Yes, anything," he replied eagerly.

"How did you know I was here?"

"Haven," Trenton began to interject but she held her ground.

"And why does the newspaper say I was kidnapped...and the mentioning of a suspect, no less?" Haven gazed at him intently as he sighed and shifted side to side, almost nervously.

"Dearest, I promise you, your every question will be answered once I show you. I beg of you to just accompany me to the theater. I'll bring you right back here once we are finished if you so desire," he stated in all earnest. Haven glanced back at Hephzibah's home in indecision.

"Let me leave a quick note before we go," she darted back into the house. She wrote a short note and walked over to the coffee table. She set it partly under the open Bible she'd been reading. For a brief moment, she longed to take along the beloved book but was distracted when she heard the horses outside. She took one last look at the house, that had become somewhat of a refuge for her, then made her way back to the door.

CHAPTER THIRTY-SEVEN

hen the carriage arrived at the theater, Malcolm Barstow was waiting to meet them. He walked up and opened the door before the driver jumped down to do so. Trenton emerged first and met Malcolm's gaze. He gave him a quick nod. Malcolm glanced behind him and saw Haven in the carriage. He now knew what the nod meant and quickly left the group.

Trenton turned to help Haven out, followed by Wren.

"Would you care for a cup of tea?" he suggested, trying to stall.

"Didn't you say you have something to show me of great importance?" Haven asked yet tried to keep the tone of her voice light.

"Yes, yes of course. Right this way," Trenton led the way inside then through the circular gallery. His slow pace confused Haven since he seemed so urgent at first. As they passed by the countless statues, she saw a large banner, advertising the present opera. It had Lindsay Adair starring in the very show Haven had, only weeks ago. A small pang of something struck her.

What did I expect to happen once I left?

She continued to silently follow him through the lobby and to a side door. There were a few sheds on the property used for storage. Haven had never been near them. When they headed in their direction, she thought it very strange.

"Where are we going?" she couldn't hold back her curiosity any longer, especially when the door to the largest shed opened and two men emerged.

"You will see," Trenton solemnly answered.

Malcolm was the third person who came out of the shed. Trenton slowed until Malcolm nodded at him quickly. Trenton then turned to face Haven.

"Now you must trust me and ready yourself."

"Why? What's inside?" Haven anxiously asked. Instead of saying more, Trenton opened the door further. Haven slowly stepped inside the dimly lit room. There was yet another man inside. She swiftly glanced at Trenton and saw him motion to her to go deeper in. He appeared to be standing guard over something further inside. She apprehensively walked toward the man standing guard as her eyes slowly adjusted. A shudder went through her when she finally saw what lied before her. It was the masked man, from the dreaded night. He lay on his back, unconscious at the feet of the guard. Haven gasped loudly. He wore the exact same disguise when he'd attempted to drag her from her room.

She felt Trenton gently put his arm around her. It was only then she noticed tears were streaming down her face.

"It's all right. He can't hurt you," he comforted and drew her closer.

"I don't understand...how did you catch him? This was the man who broke into my room only days ago."

"I know. My men found him late last night. When we questioned him, he confessed of his actions against you and told us where you were. Now that you've confirmed this, I'll notify the police. They can come and claim this criminal."

"Who is he?" Haven trembled and asked.

"See for yourself," Trenton said. Haven gazed up at him to see he was serious. "Don't worry. He's quite harmless now. We had to restrain him for he was quite violent." Haven wiped her face then meekly stepped up to the man. She knew well how violent and strong he truly was. She bent down near his head and glanced back up at Trenton one last time.

"Go ahead," he reassured. Haven carefully reached out, took ahold of the black mask, and pulled it off his head. Her heart plummeted into her stomach when she recognized his face! It was Patrick Sterling, the man who had stopped her from jumping off the bridge and helped her get back to Hephzibah's house.

Why would he try to abduct me? She shivered anew when she recalled the feeling of being dragged from her bed and the tight hand over her mouth that horrible night.

"I know this man!" she cried. Trenton approached and crouched down beside her.

"Now you know why I suspected this man of kidnapping you. He is a notorious street urchin who preys on innocent young women. He'd been caught doing this many times before," he informed in all seriousness. "I'm glad we found him. He'll finally be handed over to the authorities so he can never hurt anyone ever again." Trenton took Haven's hand and they both stood up.

"Haven," his voice lowered as he looked into her eyes. "I don't know what made you leave the theater or what your feelings are towards me. All I've ever wanted is your affection. I care for you deeply. You can trust me. I can see the doubt in your eyes, and it brings me great pain. I beg of you to let me fix whatever has come between us. Please let me regain your trust somehow," he besieged and blinked back his own tears. Haven was cut to the heart at his vulnerable entreat. Perhaps her assumptions about him were foolishness.

"The police will be here soon to take him. We had better leave now." Trenton escorted Haven out of the shed and back to the theater. She thought hard over what he'd said as they walked along. Really, the only reason she left the theater was because of the cursed journal. Now that she was free from its power, could she move on? Could she return?

How long could I impose on Hephzibah and her brother anyway? She quickly searched her heart. Haven's life had been restored to her. Perhaps it was time.

"I'll have my driver take you back to—" he began.

"Trenton, wait," Haven spoke up. "About what you said."

"Yes?" Trenton piped up with excitement.

"I do believe you…and, while I'm not ready to explain why I left, I think I'm ready to stay. That is, if you will allow me to return to the theater."

"Of course, my dear! Nothing else would make me

happier." He was visibly overjoyed and Haven found herself relieved to put all of this behind them.

"Well, instead of taking you back, I'll have him take you to your townhouse. I'll let you get settled after this trying affair. Perhaps we can have dinner together tomorrow?"

"That would be lovely. Oh, one more thing, could you send word to Hephzibah…the lady I was staying with…I need to let her know I'm fine. I don't want her to worry."

"I'll have someone take care of it straight away."

"Thank you," Haven stated, causing Trenton to smile.

He walked her to the carriage then she was on her way to her townhouse. Trenton was very pleased to have her back, not to mention the star of the theater.

The door to the shed opened and light poured into the dark building.

"Did she go for it?" Malcolm asked Trenton in hushed tones.

"Yes. She has agreed to return and is off to her townhouse as we speak," Trenton replied, very pleased with himself. "She thinks the police are on their way to take him," he gazed down at the man lying on the straw-covered, dirt floor. "Is he awake?"

"He'll come to shorty, I'd say."

Garrett's eyes sluggishly opened as he overheard what was being said. He gazed up at the dust and cobwebs of the shed ceiling. The same men who had followed him from the very start had attacked him late the previous night, where he slept on the streets. After he was brought to the shed, Trenton came and had him beaten while questioning him thoroughly about his relationship with Haven. Garrett repeatedly told them they hardly knew each other but Trenton wouldn't believe him. Strangely enough, Trenton instructed his men to leave his face alone, while being pummeled. He didn't know it was all part of Trenton's scheme. His head pounded from being hit over the head and knocked out. After witnessing Trenton's cruelty first hand, he now knew above all else that Haven was in grave danger in having anything to do with the likes of Mr. Martel.

"What do we do with him?" Malcolm asked. Garrett tried to focus all the more when he heard him, yet the pain made it difficult. He quickly shut his eyes not to let on he was coherent.

"Just get rid of him," Trenton instructed as if he was merely taking care of a mundane daily task. He took his leave of the shed and shut the door. Fear washed over Garrett, knowing what was intended for him. He had to get out of there! He desperately tried to get up when a moan escaped his lips from the pain caused by the beating. Malcolm ignored him and looked at the two nearby men, waiting for their orders.

"Well, you heard him. Get rid of him. I've got work to do before tonight," he referred to the performance that was to take place in only a matter of hours.

Once Malcolm left, the two men stepped up to Garrett.
"Let's get this over with, shall we?"
"Wait," the other man shoved the other out of the way.
"Wait for what? You heard him."
"I know what he said. But he didn't tell us how we had to do it. You forget he's the one who smashed a chair over my head and broke my nose."
"Oh yeah!" the other chuckled.

"I wanna show him a thing or two before we finish him off," he swung his leg back and kicked Garrett in the stomach.

CHAPTER THIRTY-EIGHT

"Haven, it's me, Hephzibah," Hephzibah spoke through the door. When no one came, she knocked on the door. Again nothing. Concern rose up in her.

"I pray she's all right," she whispered. Although she had locked the door before leaving hours earlier, she grasped the door handle.

Oh no, she gasped when it opened. Hephzibah carefully looked around the tiny entryway before crossing over the threshold. All was quiet. The minute she stepped in further, she instantly spotted the pistol. It was sitting on the stairs, located directly across from the front door.

"Haven dear?" she called out and went further in. There was no sign of any struggle or foul play.

After searched the entire house, Hephzibah ended up in the small sitting room.

"Lord, where is she?" she prayed aloud, nearly in tears. "It's all my fault. I knew I shouldn't 'ave left her alone." Hephzibah picked up the Bible that sat on the coffee table. She'd lent it to Haven to read. She picked it up when she found Haven's note under it and quickly read it.

Dear Hephzibah,

Please don't worry. I'm alright and am accompanying a friend on a quick errand. I shall return as soon as I'm able.

Haven

While she was relieved that the young woman wasn't abducted, she dearly hoped Haven made the right decision in leaving so soon. She loved her much like her own daughter.

"Dear Lord, protect 'er," she sat down on the couch and held the Bible and note on her lap. Even though the note made it sound as if Haven would return at any moment, Hephzibah had an overwhelming notion she wouldn't see the dear girl again. "I kna there is a great reason You brought her into my life…to find freedom from the curse and to serve Thee. I pray

she'll continue to remain close ter You. Thank You for bringin'
her into my life. Please show her the right way to go, and wot
to do. Be wif her now, watch over her kettle and hob in Jesus'
Name."

CHAPTER THIRTY-NINE

eiston startled awake. He swiftly looked about his room. He was sure he heard someone knocking on the door over and over.

I must have been only dreaming... he resolved and reached for the pocket watch, which sat on the nightstand. He held it up to the small amount of moonlight coming from the window. *A little after three in the morning,* Leiston laid back against the pillow. He closed his eyes when there was a loud knock on the door downstairs. Leiston's eyes shot open and his heart jumped. It was a strange, almost eerie banging as if very urgent. It made him wonder all the more of whom it might be.

He quickly sat up and lit a candle then rushed downstairs. When he opened the door, there was a queer figure, hunched over with its back to him.

Who in the world could it be? Is it merely a drunk street urchin or a poor bloke who is lost and thinks this is his home? Leiston asked himself. His concern momentarily subsided a bit and was replaced by anger. He after all, had an early morning coming all too soon.

"What do you want?" Nothing could have prepared Leiston for what he saw once the figure turned to face him. The man held his midsection and winced in pain at every little movement. Leiston saw blood on his hands and the rags he wore. His gaze moved upward and ultimately took in the person's face. His beard was caked with mud and blood, while his face was badly swollen and bruised. Leiston squinted to try and make out who it was. He was at a loss, that is, until the man spoke.

"I....t's me,"

"Garrett!" Leiston gasped and immediately went out to help him walk inside. Garrett moaned with each step.

"What happened? Where have you been? I need to get a doctor!"

"No," Garrett managed to speak, through clenched teeth. He put his bloodied hand out and placed it on Leiston's shoulder. He seemed to have trouble concentrating enough to say more.

"I...I'm sorry," all of a sudden, his legs gave out and he started to fall. Leiston tried his best to catch him.

"Garrett, stay with me! Garrett!" Leiston clutched his jacket but Garrett passed out. Everything in him told him to go against Garrett's wishes and fetch a doctor, yet he knew what Garrett had done and it surely wouldn't bode well.

Yet, who did this to him? He's obviously in danger. The doctor would no doubt question what happened. Leiston frantically tried to think of what to do as a hundred other questions rose up in him. He quickly decided to agree with Garrett for now. He would try to nurse him to health and hopefully get some answers when he came to.

CHAPTER FORTY

June 30, 1836

T he next two weeks felt like a whirlwind to Haven. The minute word got out that she had returned, letters came pouring in, along with requests for her to attend luncheons and social engagements with members or nobility. Trenton wasted no time in creating an opera for her to star in and began practicing straight away.

Haven barely had time to think, much less settle into her townhouse and daily routine.

Lindsay Adair was quite miffed by her return as was expected. The rest of the cast welcomed her warmly. Trenton surprised her a few days after she came back to the theater with a private dressing room. It was right behind the grand stage and lavishly decorated.

One night, after the last dress rehearsal before opening night, Haven sat at the large white vanity, removing her makeup when there was a knock at the door.

"Come in," Haven presumed it was Trenton, to ask if she wanted to have dinner with him.

"Haven?" Instead of hearing him, however, Wren meekly entered.

"Oh, Wren, please come in. How are you?" Wren slowly came closer and sat down on the seat nearest Haven.

"I'm fine. How are you settling in?" she asked in a melancholy tone. She wasn't her usual cheerful self. Haven noticed a change in her ever since returning. She had yet to really get a chance to speak with her.

"I'm well…perhaps a bit tired. I'm not used to practicing night after night."

"I suppose," Wren replied halfheartedly.

"Is everything alright?" Haven asked.

"Well, I've been meaning to ask you something," Wren seemed relieved to finally get the opportunity to bring it up.

"Yes, what is it?"

"Ever since you've come back, something is different."

"What do you mean?"

"There's a change in you. I mean, you appear happier and brighter…free," Wren had a difficult time finding the right words. "I don't know, just different. Might I ask what it is?"

"I suppose there has been a change. It's been a long time and so much has happened since last we spoke. I very nearly take it for granted now."

"What is it?" Wren asked, and sat on the edge of her seat.

"I met someone who showed me this," Haven pulled open the top drawer of the vanity and took out a book. It was a Bible. Haven had purchased it as soon as she could after leaving Hephzibah's.

"A book?" Haven couldn't help but smile when she recalled those very same words had come out of her mouth at Hephzibah's home.

"It's not just any book. It holds the words that can make one free...words of truth," she explained. "And the peace I've found is...," Haven sighed. How could she possibly explain the precious experience she had her first night at Hephzibah's. How God's presence visited her with overwhelming love and the peace she'd longed for all of her life. "It's all so wonderful and it starts right here," she ran her hand across the Bible that contained her life. Wren was more than a little interested, so Haven continued and showed her the same verses Hephzibah had shown her.

Haven was grateful that Trenton never did visit her dressing room. She and Wren remained there until well past midnight. By the time Haven got home, she felt as if she was floating. She couldn't be happier, for Wren chose to make Jesus the Lord of her life.

CHAPTER FORTY-ONE

July 6, 1836

 tell you, you won't believe me!" Garrett said once again from his place on the couch in front of the fireplace. He was slowly recovering and was out of bed, though very slowly, and very sore.

"Garrett, it's been almost three weeks since you came in, looking the very picture of death and you haven't said a word about who did this to you. Now, I'm not leaving this chair until you tell me," Leiston folded his arms against his chest in determination.

"You are a stubborn one, you know that?" Garrett sighed.

"I'm waiting," Leiston wasn't swayed in the least. Garrett finally decided just to tell him the facts and leave the unbelievable details alone. At least then, he would get off his back about it. Regardless of his persistent questions, Garrett was very grateful for Leiston's help in recovering. He had abided by his wishes and didn't call for a doctor. The least Garret could do in return was to reveal what happened.

"It's a long story but somehow I got involved with Miss Haven Romiley. She's in some kind of trouble and they think I'm involved. That's why I haven't come back here. I was being followed constantly until they eventually caught me."

"Who?" Leiston asked.

"He's the owner of the Theater Royal. He's behind all of this. They caught me and brought me to a shed…somewhere. Anyway, they questioned me and beat me."

"What did they question you about?"

"My relationship with Miss Romiley," Garrett finished.

"I see. How did you escape?"

"When I came to, the owner fellow told his men to get rid of me. They pummeled me again…I was barely conscious when I was carried into a carriage and driven to an abandoned street. They threw me out in an alley, filled with rubbish. It was dark…," Garrett did his best to recount that night. "Before they left, I heard one man say to the other, 'He told us to get rid of him. I doubt he'll live much longer but we better make sure.' Then they shot at me two times. It was so dark and so many things in the alley; I can see how they missed. One bullet grazed my leg. The two men left me there. I managed to get here, though it took several hours. There you have it," Garrett stated with a sighed. Silence filled the room as Leiston took in what he'd said.

"So, Miss Romiley...the famous opera singer...has something to do with you?" Garrett could see Leiston try to hide his amused skepticism.

"I told you that you wouldn't believe me," he carefully got to his feet and winced. "This is no laughing matter. The very moment I'm able, I must warn her. She is in danger."

"You're serious," Leiston grew more solemn at Garrett's earnestness.

"The man they're blaming for her disappearance in the newspaper is me! I'm going to bed."

"Garrett, I'm sorry. I just find it a little hard to grasp," Leiston called out after him but he continued to trudge up the stairs, one by one.

CHAPTER FORTY-TWO

August 16, 1836

renton hurried behind the stage, down the stairs, and into the noisy green room. The actors and actresses congregated together for some refreshments. Everyone was talking excitedly amongst themselves.

"Could I have everyone's attention please?" Trenton had to nearly shout over them before they began to quiet down.

When Haven met his gaze, he offered his arm to her so she would move to his side.

"Another grand performance! I dare say, each one is better than the last. I just came from a private meeting with the queen. She wanted to see me to tell me herself that she hasn't seen a better opera in all of Europe. Well done, well done indeed!" Everyone in the room gasped and cheered with delight.

Trenton turned to face Haven and happily kissed her cheek.

"All thanks to you," he whispered to her. Haven smiled and slightly blushed at his praise. As she did, something caught her eye behind Trenton. Wren was watching the couple very intently. She looked exceedingly concerned and troubled over something. Haven was noticing whenever Wren was present while Haven and Trenton were together, the same look would come upon her face.

"Dear, the other reason I came down here was to tell you the queen wishes to meet you before she departs."

"She wants to see me?" Haven gasped.

"Yes, we mustn't keep her waiting."

"Well I'd say not!" Haven picked up her heavy skirt to go back up the stairs after briefly glancing over at Wren again. Sure enough, she was still staring; however, when she realized that Haven was looking at her, she lowered her gaze in embarrassment.

I'll have to speak to her when I can. Haven didn't have much time to speak or think on it for long. Trenton took her hand and led her to the stage.

By the time Haven returned to the green room, Wren had already left. There was nothing else to do but to go home as well. Haven planned to retire early for she was to attend a high society brunch the next morning.

She got into bed and read some of the Bible. She then blew out the candle and tried to fall asleep, but it wouldn't come. She was still very excited about meeting the queen. Yet, it wasn't the only thing on her mind. Wren still troubled her thoughts. She tossed and turned, trying to quiet her mind but she couldn't shake the concern over Wren.

"Lord, what is it? Something isn't right," her prayer stopped short when there was a quiet knock on the door.

"Yes?" *Who could it possibly be at this hour?* Haven wondered and gazed at the door.

"Sorry to disturb you, miss," the maid slowly opened it and poked her head in. "A woman is here, Miss Wren I believe. She wishes to speak to you…says it's urgent," she informed.

"Uh, please tell her I'll meet her in the private sitting room." Haven sat up.

"Yes, miss." The maid seemed quite surprised that Haven agreed to see Wren at such an absurd time. Haven very nearly jumped out of bed and put on a shawl. She was anxious to speak with Wren and find out what was going on.

Once she entered the sitting room, Wren stood up nervously, wringing her hands together.

"I'm sorry for coming so late."

"Don't worry at all. I was hoping you'd come," Haven

approached and put her hand on her arm as Wren met her gaze. The strained look on her face changed to astonishment.

"You were?"

"Yes, of course. I wanted to find out what's weighing on you so," Haven said. Wren turned away at this before Haven could see her eyes fill with tears.

"Wren, you can tell me." Haven presumed to see a considerable change in Wren after she drew near to God, yet a dark cloud seemed to remain over her.

"I don't know how to say it," Wren went to the window, her back toward Haven. Though she tried to keep her voice calm, she was failing miserably. Haven finally walked over to her and came up beside her.

"Ever since I became a believer last we spoke...I can't stop thinking about this...I can't keep it a secret any longer," Wren took hold of the nearest chair and sat down in it. That's when Haven saw the tears brimming in her eyes and how she trembled.

What terrible thing is she hiding? Haven almost dreaded to hear what it was.

"Trenton...he uh...." Wren forced each word. "He isn't all he seems to be. I've worked at the theater for nearly ten years...in that time, I've witnessed him do things...terrible things, to ensure he always gets what he wants. And...I'm afraid to say, you are no exception."

"I'm no exception? What kind of things are you referring to?"

"When he found out where you were, he knew you wouldn't come if he came seeking you alone. So I," she grew more upset with every word she spoke. "I helped him...in the lies. Everyone is frightened of what he would do if they don't assist him in his terrible deeds, but I can't do it anymore! I can't," Wren broke down in sobs. Haven put her arm around her until she settled down enough to speak. She didn't know what to think of the discomforting words.

"Haven, you're in danger if you stay here any longer," Wren's voice quivered.

"What kind of danger?" Haven dared to ask.

"I know it's hard to believe but Trenton cares more about profit than any person. He says and does things in his charming way, only to further his gain. It's as I said, I've seen it many times before. Your very life is in peril. You need to leave and get as far away from here as possible."

"When? What will I do?" Haven's mind reeled. She once again remembered the look on Trenton's face right before she stumbled off stage, ruining the show. There was such a fury kindling in his eyes. It was so unlike his charm and caring ways toward her that it was frightening.

"I don't know but it must be tonight."

"I know…I can go to Hephzibah's. She'll know what to do. I'll pack my things straight away," Haven glanced at Wren. She was still trembling and hugged her arms around herself in evident fear. Compassion washed over Haven at the pitiful sight. She then knew what she must do.

"You must come with me."

"What? No, I can't."

"But what are you going to do? With how dangerous you just described Trenton to be, you surely can't stay here," Haven reached out and took Wren's hand only to have her pull away.

"No, you don't understand. He has people who watch from everywhere. If I don't return to the ladies townhouse, Trenton will find out."

"I won't leave without you."

"I'm too afraid of what might happen. It's safer for me to stay and just pretend I don't know where you went." When it was clear she wouldn't be swayed; Haven was forced to pack a few things. She quickly finished gathering her things and put them in a bag. It was the same carpet bag that held her mother's jewelry when she ran away from the ship. Haven quickly got dressed in a plain, dark colored dress to stay hidden more easily.

"I'm forever indebted to you…my dear friend," Wren said as she smiled at her, yet it was sad.

"I beg of you to come with me." Wren was about to protest but she continued, "If not tonight, that's alright. I'll go to Hephzibah because she'll know how to get away quickly without being seen. Once I talk it over with her, we could meet you on the corner of the townhouse…the servant's entrance."

"I," Wren's hesitancy gave Haven some hope. She apprehensively nodded slightly.

"Good. We will meet at first light," Haven sighed with relief.

"A…alright."

CHAPTER FORTY-THREE

*H*aven tightened her hold on the bag she carried then stepped into the dark of night. She exited out the back door to be more secretive. Her heart pounded as the truth hit her like the damp night air. Trenton was yet another person in her life she thought she could trust but turned out to be her enemy. She was beginning to wonder whom she could lean on.

"I know You will never leave me, Lord," she said breathlessly and started walking, quickly.

For the first time since returning to the theater, Haven realized how she ached to see Hephzibah again. She'd dearly missed their long talks about the Bible and the things of God. Just then, a noise made her jump. All she could think of was what Wren said about Trenton's men who watched everything. She remembered well the night she was chased. She quickened her pace without looking behind her.

"Help me get to Hephzibah's unseen," she prayed. There was the strange noise again. Haven grasped her skirt and began to run. It was still a considerable distance to cover to reach Hephzibah's house.

She ran down several small streets in hopes of losing anyone who might be following her. She couldn't run forever and finally had to stop for just a moment to catch her breath.

Only a little further! Haven got another wind for she knew she was getting closer. She took a step forward when all of a sudden, someone placed their hand over her mouth from behind and pulled her back into the shadows. She tried to scream but couldn't.

"Don't scream, it's me…Garrett," he spoke softly to try and calm Haven and to remain quiet. He slowly released her. Haven spun around to look at him, fear evident on her face.

"You!" she gasped loudly and turned pale as if she'd seen a ghost. "Stay away from me!"

"I need to explain," Garrett began but Haven backed away from him. "Wait, I have to tell you that you're in danger!" he reached toward her and took ahold of her wrist to stop her.

"Don't you dare touch me!" in her panic, she kicked his leg so hard it hurt her foot. He winced, giving her a chance to escape. Garrett immediately limped after her. He couldn't understand why she was so terrified of him. Their last meeting was entirely different.

I have to make her listen to me. This might be my only chance.

Haven ran as fast as she could, her foot pounded in pain. She had to force herself to keep from shouting for help to quietly get away.

How did he escape the authorities? How did he find me? Haven didn't know what to think. She recalled the last time he helped her get to Hephzibah's. He seemed to know the area well. *He knows where Hephzibah lives! Where can I go to hide?* She ran down many streets and thought she might have lost him. Haven briefly looked behind her and was glad he wasn't there. She turned back to see where she was going and ran right into the very man.

"Let me go!" she cried and tried to pull away but Garrett held her arms.

"Just listen to me. I'm trying to explain." But she didn't listen. She wouldn't be reasoned with so Garrett knew he had to do something, anything to contain her long enough for him to tell her. He took in his surroundings for an idea as Haven began to cry out.

"Help, someone help!"

"Keep quiet…please!" Instead of staying put any longer so all of England could hear her, Garrett took action. He contained the young lady and pulled her down the block, wrapping his arms around her tightly.

"Let me go…where are you taking me?" Haven shouted and thrashed. Garrett did his best to cover her mouth while dragging her, yet it proved to be somewhat difficult. Thankfully he didn't have to go far.

The man then did the unthinkable and opened the front door to one of the row houses, and hauled Haven inside. He swung her in so quickly when he released her, she went flying to the floor. This gave him enough time to shut the door and lock it.

"What do you want with me? Where are we?" Haven very well thought he had broken into a random house.

"You gave me no choice. I have to make you listen," Garrett stated, out of breath as he leaned against the door. His ribs ached every time he inhaled. He was still somewhat recovering from being beaten almost to death and was pretty winded from the struggle.

"What could you possibly have to tell me? I don't want to so much as look at you. I hate you! I demand you let me go."

"Not until you listen to what I have to say," Garrett took a step forward once he caught his breath enough and felt a little better. "Now sit down," he stated sternly. Haven had no choice but to slowly take a seat, all the while scanning the room, searching for a way to escape. The house was small and very plain looking. There were no decorations. However, the furniture was ornate. It was surprising to see grand possession in the tiny row house in the east part of town.

"What is all the racket down here?" Leiston came downstairs while putting his robe on and tying it. He suddenly stopped when he spotted the woman. Haven stood up at once.

"Please, you've got to help me. He's forced me into this house and won't let me go," she rushed up to Leiston and begged him for help.

"What's going on here?" he met Garrett's gaze, completely baffled.

"I'm only trying to explain to Miss Romiley here…"

"This is Miss Romiley?" Leiston ignored Haven's persistent inquiring. This made her angry. Out of desperation to be heard, she clasped the collar of Leiston's robe.

"I beg of you to help me." Leiston's eyes widened and looked to Garrett again.

"Now, let's just settle down and talk a bit," he calmly put his hands on hers and pulled her grip off of him. "Let's all have a seat."

Oh, no...he is in on this...whatever this is, Haven thought in defeat.

Leiston led her to the sitting area and motioned for her to sit in the chair beside the one Garrett took. Instead of going anywhere near the awful man, Haven defiantly went to the far end of the room and remained standing.

"Please have a seat," Garrett beckoned.

"No."

"Fine. Then just listen," he sighed as Leiston sat down. "I don't know why you are so afraid of me this time since I've only ever tried to help you...as I do now." Haven snorted at this.

"So you are trying to help me? Keeping me here against my will."

"Only to make you listen."

"No, you listen!" Haven shouted. "How did you escape the authorities? Why did you attempt to abduct me from my bedroom at Hephzibah's? I will never trust you."

"What are you talking about? I never—" Garrett began when Haven suddenly rushed to the unguarded door. In her hysteria, she had forgotten that Garrett locked it. She tried the door handle and, sure enough, it wouldn't budge.

"Let me go!" she screamed. As soon as she felt a hand on her shoulder, Haven turned to face her capture and hit him on the chest over and over with her fists. "Don't come near me! Just let me go to Hephzibah's!" Angry tears poured down her face. Both men felt for the frightened young woman.

"I never did what you suggest," Garrett calmly said repeatedly until Haven stopped.

"You have to believe me," he held onto her forearms to stop her from hitting him. "Did the man who's in charge tell you I did such a thing?" Haven glanced up at him. She searched for the truth in his blue eyes as she recalled all the things Wren told her, only hours ago.

"I don't understand," she wiped her eyes and realized just then how exhausted she was.

"His men brought me to him…they beat me and tried to kill me. That's all I really know about it. I wanted to warn you for I overheard something he said. I didn't understand most of it, but I know you are in great danger around him," Garrett explained and stepped away from her.

"What he says is true," Leiston chimed in. "When Garrett returned here, he was beaten so badly I wasn't sure he would live. I assure you Miss Romiley, he is only concerned about your safety…and I vouch for his character."

"If what you say is true, why is he calling you Garrett? Why did you lie about your true name?" Haven asked and eyed Garrett suspiciously.

"My true name?" Garrett's brow furrowed in confusion. Leiston glanced at him in question as well. Garrett then remembered the fake name he would use to keep his true identity hidden. It seemed like an eternity since he'd given Haven and Hephzibah his false name. He'd completely forgotten about it.

"What is she talking about?" Leiston asked.

"Oh yes, well…while it is true I did lie about it; I had good reason why I had to do it then. I'm sorry," Garrett explained as best as he could.

"Who are you then…really?" Haven asked and put her hands on her hips.

"I'm Garrett Blakeslee, I promise you."

"He speaks the truth," Leiston put in.

Haven remained silent for a moment as she compared everything Wren told her to what Garrett said.

"If this is all true, what can I do? What should I do?" she finally looked back up at Garrett and asked.

"Don't go to Hephzibah's."

"Where else?"

"The owner of the theater…"

"Trenton Martel?"

"Yes. He has spies everywhere it seems and the authorities are possibly on his side as well," he stated. In truth, he was unsure of what to do as well.

"My sister and her husband have an estate in the country. The town it's nearest to is Dolbury. They would have more than enough room if we fled there until other arrangements could be made," Leiston offered.

"That would surely work," Garrett readily agreed then met Haven's gaze. "You're free to go to Hephzibah's, or we can go to Dolbury. The choice is yours."

"Why should I trust you?" Haven asked. Garrett had to think of how to reply.

"Because we only want to help. I have no ulterior motive, nor do I seek your money. I've merely experienced Trenon's cruelty and I don't want you to have to suffer it as well." Haven was taken back by his heartfelt explanation. Why did he care so? Perhaps what he said was true. What other choice did she have?

Haven's mind reeled. She wasn't absolutely certain these two men could be trusted, albeit, the last thing she wanted was to bring Hephzibah into this present danger.

Lord, what should I do? She searched her heart.

"Alright…I'll go to Dolbury."

"That's it then. We can walk to the edge of the city easily enough while it's still dark then hire a carriage," Garrett quickly came up with a plan.

"Wait, there's one thing I must do before we leave," Haven suddenly remembered.

"What?" both men asked.

"My friend…from the theater. I gave her my word that I wouldn't leave her. I told her I would meet her at the corner of the townhouse where she lives at first light." Garrett glanced at Leiston.

"If we do it, it might put us at risk of getting out of

London unseen."

"I gave her my word," Haven stated in all seriousness.

"Alright, we will chance it."

"I will not leave without her."

CHAPTER FORTY-FOUR

 he threesome went through with the first part of their plan and traveled by foot to a busy part of the city and hired a hackney carriage. They rode in strained silence to the townhouse, which was located near Theater Royal.

"Just park over there," Garrett instructed the driver. Haven's gaze was fixed on the servant's entrance into the townhouse. Meanwhile, Leiston and Garrett kept close watch of their surroundings.

Come on Wren. Come out...please! They surely couldn't wait much longer. *Lord, help her to overcome her fear of leaving!* Haven silently prayed.

"Over there, look," Leiston pointed out the man on the street to Garrett. "He's paying much more attention to us than a mere bystander."

"We need to leave now."

"But what about Wren?" Haven turned from the window and glanced at them.

"I'm sorry but we've waited as long as we can. We can't risk being caught any longer," Garrett replied. As much as Haven knew he spoke the truth, she was distraught over Wren and the danger she was putting herself in by not escaping while she could.

"Driver, move on...quickly please," Leiston hurriedly declared.

"I am sorry," Garrett spoke softly. Haven didn't reply but only turned to look out the window, a single tear rolled down her cheek.

The carriage made its way out of the winding streets of London. Haven was preoccupied with praying and thinking about Wren. In a way, she was grateful for it kept her mind off of her nervousness. Traveling with two complete strangers into the unknown, left her a bit unsettled.

Four hours dragged by before the estate came into view. Caragin was a friendly looking cottage like estate, surrounded by woods and hedges. As they got closer, the carriage rode over a small bridge with a brook flowing beneath. There had been no time to write and let the family know of their arrival but Leiston assured it would be alright for them to seek refuge with his sister and her family.

They came to a halt in front of the brick home. Leiston opened the door and stepped out, as did Garrett. He turned to take Haven's hand to assist her, while Leiston went to the front door.

"May I help you?" a maid answered it.

"We are here to see Mr. and Mrs. Kinsey. I am Mrs. Kinsey's brother."

"Please come in," she opened the door for them and formally led them to the drawing room. It was a very cheerful and homey place.

Haven was just going to sit down on the couch when she heard a woman's voice coming from the foyer. Garrett and Leiston still stood when she quickly entered the room.

"Leiston! I thought it was your voice I heard," she approached and hugged him.

"Hello sister."

"What a surprise! What are you doing all the way out here? Aren't you in the middle of classes?"

"Yes well, something else has taken precedence at the moment. I apologize for not sending word of our visit. It was imperative that we left London straight away," Leiston motioned to Garrett and Haven. "Mary, you remember Garrett Blakeslee?" Leiston's sister's expression swiftly changed from one of curiosity to great concern. Haven watched their interaction closely to see if she could gain any insight of who Garrett truly was. She was still very guarded and apprehensive about the whole situation. Even though she knew this was the safest plan, it was nothing like what she had anticipated. Haven would much rather be with Hephzibah.

"Why Garrett, you look…." Mary hesitated to find the right words. "You look quite different since last seeing you."

"Yes ma'am," Garrett shook her hand.

"And this is Miss Haven Romiley," Leiston presented Haven. "Miss Romiley, this is my sister Mary." Haven got up and took her hand, forcing herself to smile.

"Pleased to meet you. Pardon our intrusion."

"No need to apologize," Mary warmly welcomed her. "Wait, are you Miss Romiley from the Theater Royal?"

"Yes."

"Oh, my! That's why I recognized your name. I've read so much about you in the newspapers. I regret to say, I haven't been to the theater for several years. I'm very honored to make your acquaintance," her brown eyes seemed to shine with delight. Her kindness instantly made Haven rest at ease and melted away some of the nerves that weighed heavily on her. Mary looked much like her brother, with dark brown hair, and the same bright smile.

"Please have a seat. I'll have the maid bring us some tea," Mary motioned to the sitting area and they all sat down. "What brings all of you to Dolbury?"

"Well, it seems we've found ourselves in a bit of trouble," Leiston stated calmly.

"Trouble? What kind of trouble?"

"Is Stephen here? He should probably be in on this conversation."

"What conversation?" Stephen walked into the room as if on cue.

After the introductions were made and they were all seated again and sipping their tea, Leiston got to the point.

"Our real reason for coming was, we are helping Miss Romiley escape from someone in London. We're trying to hide, that is if you are favorable with our plan, until…well, until," Leiston glanced at Garrett, and then to Haven.

"Until other arrangements can be made," Garrett finished reassuringly. Haven remained silent and let them explain. In truth, she didn't exactly know what the next step was. She just dearly hoped Garrett wouldn't bring up the cursed journal. Haven's uneasiness that had lessened only moments ago returned in full force as she sat there, listening to people she didn't know discuss her absurd predicament. It felt as if she was listening to a horrible story about someone else, yet this was her very own life. Hearing someone else speak about it made the realization of it hit her in a way she couldn't have anticipated. In a way, Haven thought after she'd given her life to the Lord and finally obtaining freedom from the dreaded journal, everything would be easy and wonderful. At that moment, a verse came to mind she had read the previous morning.

"In the world ye shall have tribulation: but be of good cheer, I have overcome the world."

Lord, only with You was I able to get free from the journal's curse, and only with You will I also overcome all of this. I trust You, she prayed within herself.

"Miss Romiley?" At the mention of her name, Haven was quickly drawn from her musings and found everyone in the room staring at her.

"Oh, pardon me. What did you say?"

"We were just saying we will be more than willing to help by having all of you stay with us as long as you need," Stephen informed.

"Thank you," Haven was surprised by their exceptional

kindness towards her, a perfect stranger. And if that wasn't enough, Mary did something that altogether astonished her.

"I'm so sorry to hear all the things you've gone through. I read some of the reports in the paper, which I now know aren't entirely true," she gently took Haven's hand and patted it. "Anyway, I can't imagined how terrible it must be…and then to be forced to trust Garrett and my brother, whom they tell me, you barely know. I hope we can be of some comfort to you while you're here."

"Thank you very much," Haven nearly chocked as she fought back her tears. The love that poured from Mrs. Kinsey was like none other she had ever met, besides Hephzibah. She so badly wanted to see Hephzibah. She imagined so many times running into her arms and weeping together, releasing all the fear and emotion bottled up in her. All of the emotions washed over her all at once at Mary's compassion.

"Mother!" A young girl abruptly ran into the room. When she saw the visitors in the room, she stopped and blushed in embarrassment. "Oh, I'm sorry. I didn't know we had company."

"That's quite alright dear. Come in," Mary stood. Haven was grateful for the interruption so it would give her time to compose herself.

"This is our eldest, Scarlette," Mary rested her hands on her daughter's shoulders and introduced her to Haven.

"Pleased to meet you," Haven stood and shook her hand. Scarlette was adorable and the very image of her mother.

"This is Miss Romiley and she is a very famous opera singer from London," Mary informed as Scarlette's eyes widened in wonder. As soon as the girl saw Garrett and Leiston, she began to giggle.

"Uncle!"

"Why hello my favorite niece," Leiston stood as she ran to him.

"Oh and here comes the rest of the crew," Stephen announced when three other young children came happily gallivanting in. The two youngest held the hand of their nursemaid. Haven couldn't help but smile when they rushed to their mother, grinning and as happy as could be.

"Scarlette is ten years of age and this is Stephen Jr. He is seven. Then there are the twins, Andrew and Phillip. They are only three."

"How precious," Haven replied.

"Well, I'm sure you're all exhausted from the journey. I'll have the maid show you to your rooms and will have your luggage brought in. We'll allow you some time to rest before dinner is served," Mary took charge of the group, showing she was the perfect hostess.

CHAPTER FORTY-FIVE

et us pray over the meal, shall we?" Stephen asked. He sat at the head of the table in the dining room. Haven was delighted that they said a prayer. She very swiftly glanced across the table at Garrett. He didn't close his eyes during the prayer but merely gazed down at the table. When he finished praying, dinner was served.

"Miss Romiley, how did you become an opera singer?" Scarlette asked.

"Well, I've always wanted to sing at the Theater Royal and...I finally got there."

Some dream that turned out to be, Haven thought.

"Do you have family in London?" Mary then inquired.

"No, I don't." Haven gave a quick answer then took a bite of food.

"Where are you from, might I ask?" Leiston now took a turn.

"A small town in northern England. Arbor Side is the name. Have you heard of it?"

"Oh...I think I know it. Do your parents reside there?" Stephen spoke up.

"Uh, no. They are...gone," Haven hesitantly answered just as she met Garrett's gaze. It was as if he was trying to tell her he felt for her and knew how awkward this stream of questioning was.

"Will you go back to sing at the theater soon?" Scarlette asked in her adorable innocent way.

"Scarlette dear, that's enough questions. Eat your dinner now, please," Mary must have sensed the growing tension and put a stop to it.

"Please excuse me, I'm a little tired," Haven pushed her chair back from the table, placed her napkin on the plate, and quickly left the room before the men were able to stand. She rushed up the stairs and to her room before her tears had a chance to fall. Haven leaned back against the closed door.

"My one and only dream of singing at the theater is over forever," she cried, "I can never go back now. Lord, please help me. Help me to let go."

Garrett also made his way to him and Leiston's room following dinner. He felt badly about Haven yet there was nothing he could do. He picked up a book that sat on the shelf inside the spacious guestroom and lay down atop his bed. Try as he might to get his mind off her, the novel did little to distract him.

Two hours had passed before he slowly began to doze off. That is until Leiston entered.

"You alright? Have you been up here since dinner?" he walked to the opposite side of the room and sat down on his bed, going to work loosening his tie.

"I'm fine. Just concerned about Haven—Miss Romiley, I mean," Garrett caught himself.

"What? Oh, she's fine."

"You really think so? She seemed upset when she excused herself early. I can't blame her for reacting that way with all the questioning." Leiston looked at him, incredulous. He pulled off his necktie and set it next to him.

"It kind of reminds me of someone else I know who dislikes questions."

"What is that supposed to mean?" Garrett asked defensively.

Haven finally emerged from her room and slowly walked down the hall to the stairs. It was only then she heard raised voices in one of the nearby rooms. She stopped and couldn't help but tiptoe closer before carefully leaning forward toward the door. She glanced down the hall and saw it was empty then carefully leaned forward.

"You don't like questions any more than Miss Romiley

did down there. It's only normal for my sister's family to be curious. They are gracious enough to take her in and help. Why does it bother you so much?"

"Why attack me? This isn't about me," Garrett replied rather curtly.

"Isn't it?" Leiston would not relent. "I think she reminds you of yourself."

"What? That is preposterous."

"Why? You're hiding just as much as Miss Romiley is."

Haven tried to listen all the more intently at the mentioning of her name.

"Well, you're correct to say I'm hiding. Indeed I am. You saw how badly beaten I was," Garrett huffed.

"That's not what I'm referring to," Leiston stood to his feet and spoke in all seriousness. "What I mean is, you are running from your family and hiding under that hideous beard and rags…like a criminal."

"Why shouldn't I? If they ever found me…after all I've done, they would very well take me as one."

A criminal? The hairs on the back of Haven's neck stood on end. Trenton's words came back to her all at once.

"He is a notorious street urchin who preys on innocent young women. He's been caught doing this many time before."

"You'll never change," Leiston rolled his eyes and turned away from him. The act angered Garrett.

"You think I'm a coward, don't you?" He swung his legs over the side of the bed and sat up. Leiston turned back to face him.

"Yes."

"What do you expect me to do?"

"I don't think this has as much to do with that man dying as you let on. Ever since then, all you've been doing is sulking and feeling sorry for yourself. When are you going to stop hiding and start acting like a man?" Leiston let into him like never before.

"You know nothing about it!" Garrett immediately stood up and marched to the door. When Haven heard the floor creak, she swiftly backed away from the bedroom door and hid against the wall in the shadows. The second she did, Garrett angrily swung open the door and rushed downstairs.

Upon hearing what she did, it did little to lessen her apprehension.

CHAPTER FORTY-SIX

August 18, 1836

A s much as Haven wished she could remain cooped up in her room, she knew it would be impossible. Besides, no one knew just how long she would be hiding at Caragin. She also didn't want to appear rude, especially to Mary and how kind she had been towards her. This was another matter that weighed heavily on her mind.

From what she overheard the previous night, it made it sound as if Garrett was indeed some kind of felon.

Why would such kind and gracious people be acquainted with such a man? She asked herself nearly all night long. She only hoped she could somehow find out more about him as time wore on.

Haven finished fixing her hair then went for her Bible. She planned to go for a walk and read after breakfast. She took a deep breath and exited her room. She made her way down the hall when a small piece of paper fell out of her Bible. Haven bent down to pick it up. When she stood back up and started once again, she was shocked to find a man standing right before her.

"Oh! Pardon—" the minute Haven saw his face, she froze.

"Good morning," Garrett, that is, it sounded like him, greeted. He was clean-shaven and his hair neatly cut. He looked like an entirely different man. Haven was mostly surprised by how handsome he was, hiding under a scraggly beard. His blue eyes seemed to pierce hers when he smiled.

"Good morning," she eventually replied, her face warm with embarrassment.

"Are you going down to breakfast?"

"Yes."

"As am I."

They both started down the hall.

"I hope they didn't scare you with all the questions last night, as innocent as it might have been."

"I'm fine. Thank you," Haven quietly replied, willing herself to stop blushing and get ahold of herself.

Everyone shortly arrived at the dining room and sat down. Haven had to fight the urge to glance at Garrett during the meal. The change in his appearance baffled her. The once old, repulsive man she'd run into in the dark streets of London, now looked entirely different. He looked sophisticated, kind, and his smile caused a fluttering in her stomach.

"Could someone please pass the jam?" Stephen asked. Haven reached in front of her, as did Garrett, to pick up the jam when their hands brushed up against the other. Haven froze yet again and their eyes met. Without saying a word, Garrett continued to pick up the dish and passed it. Haven couldn't understand what was happening in her. She managed to get through the rest of the meal before she could get away for a walk and to be alone with her thoughts.

CHAPTER FORTY-SEVEN

August 21, 1836

here she goes once again. Garrett stood at the window of his room. He watched Haven stroll through the gardens behind Caragin and down the grass covered path that led toward the creek. For days now, Garrett watched her do the same thing day after day. She always held a book as well. He was growing more curious about what she was up to. Today, he decided to find out for himself.

Garrett made his way through the house and to the back door. He walked past the gardens and onto the same path. Once there, he slowed his pace and tried to be very quiet. It wasn't long before he heard something. It started out soft then slowly grew louder. Garrett soon realized it was singing. He snuck to almost the end of the path and came upon the creek. There was a wooden bench there and sure enough, Haven sat on it. Garrett carefully gazed through the trees at her. The sun shined on her and made her already whitish blonde hair, nearly glow. Almost like an angel. He now knew why the newspapers and all of London called Haven Romiley the Angel. Her cherublike appearance, as well as her singing, proved the very nickname.

He'd never heard the song she sang. It wasn't a opera type of song for she sang in falsetto and softly. He intently tried to listen to the words and found her to be singing to God. Right at that moment, she stopped and gazed at the book sitting open on her lap. She read for some time.

Garrett turned and started to leave when Haven abruptly spoke.
"Why?" Garrett froze in mid-step, fearing he'd been caught spying on her. "Why am I here? I don't understand my purpose here."
Who is she talking to? His brow furrowed in confusion as he turned to look. Haven was still gazing at the creek.
"Lord, what am I supposed to do while I'm here? I mean…I can't stay here forever. What then?" she went on with her casual prayer. All Garrett could do was watch in wonder. All at once, he began to feel ashamed to be eavesdropping while Haven poured her heart out to God. He very quietly, backed away unnoticed to let her be alone. He had never seen

anyone pray the way she did. She spoke to God as if He stood before her. It was much like talking to a close family member.

He made his way back to the house, more than a little bewildered.

CHAPTER FORTY-EIGHT

August 24, 1836

O h, hello…" Haven nearly jumped at the sudden interruption. She quickly glanced up from the Bible she held and saw Garrett in the doorway of the drawing room. Haven was sitting in front of the fire, enjoying the time alone. Everyone was readying for bed a few hours after dinner, leaving her alone.

"Pardon the intrusion. Have you seen Leiston?"

"No, I haven't," Haven answered simply.

"Alright, I'll let you return to your reading," Garrett said as Haven lowered her gaze to continue. He started to leave when he caught sight of the journal. It was on top of the ottoman near Haven. He hadn't seen the cursed book since he'd given it back to her in the alley. If truth be told, Garrett wasn't searching for Leiston at all. He was hoping to get a chance to speak with Haven. He'd all but forgotten the strange thing she'd said to him in the dark streets of London, until now. Perhaps they could discuss it.

"I uh...might I have a word with you?" Garrett asked awkwardly. Haven met his gaze again.

"Alright," she closed her Bible as Garrett sat down on the chair across from hers.

"I saw your journal sitting there and it made me recall what you said in the alleyway back in London," he began. Haven was instantly brought back there in her mind. However, it wasn't their most recent of meetings when she tried fleeing from him before he forced her to stay and ended up carrying her to Leiston's townhouse. Now that she went over the eventful night, and how he had to restrain her, embarrassment washed over her. She dearly hoped the light from the fire helped to disguise her face that was quickly growing red.

"What did I say?" she dared to ask, anything to get her mind off her discomfort.

"It was when I was handing the journal back to you."

Oh! He means the time before he dragged me to the house, Haven swiftly realized her mistake. It was so long ago and so much had happened since.

"I told you what I found out...what the journal intended. That you were going to...to die. Then you replied, 'I know'." There. He'd said it.

"Oh yes, now I remember."

275

"So you know what the journal is? You know what is going to happen?"

"Yes," she replied nonchalantly. Her reaction was exactly the same as it was the night he referred to.

"Aren't you worried? It says the very day you are to die!" Garrett said it again; hoping to get through to Haven.

"I understand it well."

"Well, how come it doesn't upset you? How can we stop it from happening?" his voice rose in distress. Haven was taken back by his great concern over it, yet she remembered well how upset she truly was when first finding out about the curse.

"I was indeed quite troubled over it then. So much so, I very nearly took my own life." Garrett instantly thought of when he first laid eyes on her on the bridge.

"I was there as well," he blurted. Haven's eyes widened at this.

"Oh, my…yes you were!" The memory of how she slapped him with all her might, played over in her mind, causing her to blush all over again. "I am sorry for being so angry at you then." *It doesn't bode well every time we meet, it seems,* she thought.

"There must be some way to put a stop to the curse," Garrett leaned forward and rested his elbows on his knees, his gaze fixed on the journal.

"I tried everything. Burning it, tearing it up, nothing worked, except one thing."

"What is that?"

"Only a power stronger than death could deliver me from the curse," Heaven slowly repeated the very thing Hephzibah told her. She looked down at the Bible and relived the glorious night when Hephzibah opened her Bible and shared the truth with her. The night Haven almost took her life, was the same night she found deliverance and freedom.

The night I found what real life is, Haven smiled to herself.

"Wait, are you referring to what you hold?" Garrett pointed to the Bible. Haven nodded. "But how? How can a book help put a stop to a curse?"

"How can a journal be cursed in the first place?" Haven reasoned.

"Why do you keep the journal with you?" he asked.

"To remind me what I've been set free from." Her answer did nothing to satisfy his confusion but only made him frustrated. This was getting them nowhere.

"According to what is written in it, you are to die on September ninth…only weeks away. Surely there must be a way to stop it," Garrett stood.

"But I've already found—"

"Could I take the journal for a little while?"

"Very well."

"Thank you. Good evening," Garrett picked up the book then left.

Haven watched him leave. She marveled at how concerned he was about her situation. She couldn't remember a time when someone had ever been so concerned for her.

Other than Derek. And there is Hephzibah, she was swiftly reminded. *I thought Trenton did as well,* she sighed.

CHAPTER FORTY-NINE

he next morning, Haven finished getting dressed. As she walked to the vanity to fix her hair, something caught her eye from the nearby window. Her room was located near the front of the estate and overlooked the entrance. A footman stood on the gravel driveway, holding the reigns of a horse. Haven stepped up to the window and peered out. She watched Garrett approach the steed and mount it.

Where is he off to? She wondered. The footman handed Garrett the reigns. It wasn't until then that Haven saw what he held. It was her journal. He placed it in the inside pocket of his double-breasted coat and buttoned it closed. He spoke something to the footman then unexpectedly looked up and met Haven's inquiring gaze. Haven gasped for being caught watching from the window. Garrett grinned and tipped his hat to her. In her astonishment, she swiftly stepped away from the window. A hint of a smile formed on her face through her fluster.

The entire family and their guests were relaxing in the drawing room before the fire, enjoying each other's company.

"Alright children, I suppose it's about time for bed," Mary spoke up and looked at her brood.

"Could papa play a tune for us before we go?" Stephen Jr. asked.

"Well," Mary hesitated. The other children piped up at this. "Yes, please papa…please!" Haven chuckled at their eager and sweet request. She didn't know what they were referring to until Stephen conceded and stood up. He went over to a cabinet with glass doors and pulled out a violin. The children clapped with delight. After briefly tuning it, Stephen placed the instrument under his chin and began playing a cheerful hymn.

Haven glanced at Garrett. He was happily beaming as he watched the children get up and begin dancing to the music. Haven thought of earlier that day when she watched Garrett ride away with her journal. Her curiosity had remained ever since then.

Where did he go? What did he think when he saw me spying on him? Someone speaking her name interrupted her musings. She glanced up to find Garrett standing before her with his hand out to her.

"Miss Romiley, will you have this dance?" he grinned. His eyes seemed to sparkle in the firelight. Giggles broke out among the children at this. They were excited to have some adults join in the fun. Before she let herself get too bashful, Haven placed her hand in his.

"It would be an honor," she agreed.

Stephen had just finished the hymn when he saw the two stand. He decided to play a waltz next. Garrett and Haven danced around the room, along with the children. The rest, who remained sitting, clapped with the music. Scarlette caught sight of her uncle and begged him to dance with her. With some persuading, Leiston gingerly got up as well.

When the attention moved away from them, Garrett looked at Haven.

"I supposed you are wondering where I went today."

"Well, I…guess I was a bit curious, a time, or two," Haven replied. It wasn't even close to the truth of it. It was a deal more than twice.

"I went into town to do some research about the journal." Haven was grateful that he lowered his voice when he mentioned it.

How long before he realizes his efforts to be futile? She thought and nodded in return.

The music was slowing down as it neared the end. As it did, it seemed to have a lulling effect. Haven forgot all about the others in the room. She gazed into his eyes almost in a new light. She didn't notice that her foot caught the corner of the large Persian rug on the wooden floor until she lost her balance. A loud gasp escaped her as she began to fall forward when Garrett caught her waist. Only then, they both noticed the music had stopped and everyone's eyes were on them. To break the awkward silence, Garrett backed away from Haven and formally bowed. Haven followed suit and curtsied.

CHAPTER FIFTY

September 8, 1836

wo weeks went by. Haven and Garrett talked more and frequently went on walks together. During this time, Garrett continued his research much like Haven had done. She kept telling him it was pointless, and so far, everything Garrett attempted, proved to be a waste of time. He was growing more desperate and almost panicked with each passing day. Haven's dreaded date was fast approaching. It loomed over him, increasing with each time he failed. The more time he spent with Haven, the more terrible he felt. He didn't want to lose her. What he still couldn't understand was how calm she was. She was at peace; a peace Garrett longed for. For the life of him, he couldn't grasp how she, someone who knew the very date she was destined to die, yet she held more tranquility than he. Garrett pondered this fact at every waking moment, and this morning was no different.

He got out of bed and went directly to the table in his room. The night before, he tried yet another means to destroy the book. Every time the journal reappeared, it would be sitting on the same table. Garrett sighed heavily when he laid eyes on it once more.

"Blasted book!" he mumbled to himself in frustration. He rashly wiped his hand across the table, sending the journal flying to the floor. Garrett was so consumed with his plight; he altogether forgot there was another person in the room. Leiston rolled over on his bed.

"What's going on?" he moaned in a groggy voice.

"Nothing. Sorry," Garrett went over and picked the book up. He then left the bedroom. He had to get some air.

He was in no mood to speak to anyone so he briskly marched passed the dining room to go outside. As he did, he noticed no noises were coming from it. Usually, at this time of the morning, there was laughter and much talking. He retraced a few steps and peered inside the room. Not one person was sitting at the long mahogany table. There was only a maid, dusting the mantle of the fireplace.

"Excuse me, where is everyone?" Garrett asked.

"It's such a glorious morning, they all decided to have their breakfast outside on the veranda," the maid informed. Garrett turned to look at the French doors behind him at the other end of the hall. He made up his mind against going out there as well. He was much too grumpy to make small talk. All he wanted to do was get away by himself to think.

He started to continue on his way when the maid spoke up. "They are waiting for you, sir."

"Alright," Garrett sighed. He thought as much.

He shortly arrived on the veranda. Mary and Stephen, along with their children, were sitting at a white wicker table under an umbrella. It was indeed a beautiful sunny day. Garrett approached, and by the look of things, they were nearly finished eating.

"Good morning," Stephen greeted.

"Morning," Garrett replied, halfheartedly.

"Mother, may I be excused to play?" Scarlette tugged at her mother's sleeve.

"Me too!" Stephen Jr. chimed in excitedly.

"Yes, yes." The two quickly got up from the table and ran off towards the meadow. "Don't play near the creek without your father!" Mary called after them.

"We know!" both children shouted back.

"Did you sleep well?" Stephen turned to glance at Garrett, who remained standing.

"Well enough."

"Won't you join us?" Mary offered.

"No thank you. I believe I'll go for a walk," with that, Garrett was off. He took the path, adjacent to the direction the children ran off too. He walked far enough until the house faded into the distance before he pulled out the journal.

"It appears you're on a serious mission." Garrett jumped in surprise when someone suddenly spoke. He spun around and saw Haven sitting on a bench on the side of the path in the shade.

"Oh, it's you!" he sighed. Haven smiled at him and shut her Bible, placing it beside her. She wasn't standoffish toward him anymore. Garrett was quite pleased to see she felt comfortable around him.

"Going anywhere in particular?" Haven asked and gazed at the journal he held.

"Uh, yes," he lifted it up. "I just need time to think." Haven immediately noticed the strain in his voice. She wanted to tell him, he need not worry so, yet she had already tried it countless times. "Care to walk with me?" Garrett asked. She eagerly nodded and they were on they're way. She had grown to enjoy their frequent walks.

They talked about several things before Garrett brought up the journal.

"I tried my last attempt to destroy this last night," he sighed hopelessly.

"And to no avail," Haven concluded. Garrett nodded at this. "There must be another way."

"There is," Haven urged. Every time she endeavored to tell him about it, he always came up with some other reason or idea.

"Forgive me if I don't fully accept the notion that your faith alone can stand against the journal's power," Haven quickly recalled Hephzibah's words to her when she brought up the very same point.

"It takes something stronger than death to get free from the curse," she repeated Hephzibah's words.

"And you are willing to risk your life on what you believe?" Garrett berated, nearly incredulous.

"At first I wasn't sure at all. At the time, there was nowhere else to turn to," Haven admitted. "There was nothing else I could do other than believe."

"At first?"

"Yes. But when I began reading the Bible and what He did for me...I didn't just believe because I was told about God. I experienced it for myself. He took the curse, meant for me, so I could be free. There is now in my mind, not a shadow of doubt. I found peace," Haven ardently explained.

"Peace?" Garrett huffed, scoffing at what she'd said.

"Yes. Why is it so difficult for you to believe what I'm telling you?"

"It's just…I haven't had peace since I can remember. And the peace I thought was mine, turned out to be a lie. I can't—" He stiffened, stopping himself midsentence. It surprised him how close he got to blurting the truth he'd managed to keep hidden for so long. He realized now, more than ever, how at ease he felt around Miss Romiley. It astonished him.

They continued walking side by side, in silence. Haven couldn't take it anymore. She had to find out what troubled Garrett so much that he refused to listen.

"What are you so afraid of?" her unexpected question baffled Garrett.

"Nothing," he exclaimed before he had time to think. They fell quiet again, other than the sound of their footsteps on the path. A considerable amount of time passed before Garrett became completely honest. He felt compelled to open up, for he knew so much of Haven's situation from reading her journal.

"Being wrong," he admitted quietly.

"Once you believe, I assure you, you will find out for yourself that God is the only truth…and then the truth shall make you free."

"It's probably always come easy for you in life…your fancy lifestyle and lot in life. I bet the only hardship you've ever had was this journal," Garrett's accusing tone was apparent. If truth be told, he was angry at Haven for spouting off scripture at him. His defenses immediately rose up.

Haven came to a halt.

"You think you know everything about me and my life? Why? From reading my journal? You have no idea!" She was furious and had to blink back angry tears.

"I didn't mean to sound...." Haven didn't wait for him to finish before she marched away to return to the house. "I'm sorry!" Garrett started after her. Then, from out of nowhere, a chilling and alarming scream echoed through the sky. Haven stopped short and spun around to glance at Garrett, who looked equally as alarmed.

"Help! Someone help!" the hysterical cry came from behind them, so they both ran towards it. The shouting sounded closer until Scarlette suddenly appeared when they reached a small clearing.

"Stephen...," she referred to her younger brother. "A branch fell on him. Hurry!" Before they could even ask what happened, Scarlette ranted breathlessly.

"Where is he?" Garrett asked, trying to understand her.

"The creek! He's in the creek," Scarlette wept fiercely. This was all he needed to hear. Garrett took off running down the path toward the creek with Haven close behind.

"Go and fetch your parents!" he shouted to the child.

"Dear Lord, let him be alright...Lord, please help," Haven prayed as she did her best to keep up with Garrett. Her skirts made it difficult to trudge through the brush. It seemed to take forever to arrive. By the time the creek came into view, she heard a splash. Garrett was already in the water past his knees, desperately searching for the boy. Sure enough, there was a large fallen tree that hung over the edge of the shore. The tree looked like it had been dead for a long time.

"Found him!" Garrett yelled. Haven gasped as she realized what had truly happened.

"My Lord," she placed her hand over her mouth as she watched Garrett bend over to grab ahold of a heavy branch. It was still partially connected to the dead tree and very large. He grunted and the veins in his neck were visible from the strenuous effort. It took Garrett everything in him to pull it out of the water, off of the small, child's body. He picked the boy out of the water and carried him to shore. Tears blurred Haven's vision when she took in Stephen Jr's poor little limbs hanging lifelessly in Garrett's arms. Once there, Garrett gently placed him on the ground and ripped open the front of the boy's shirt. It was as if Garrett knew exactly what to do.

Haven watched in wonder as he lowered his ear to the boy's bare chest. Haven gazed down at the child's face, yet all she could see was Derek. She was instantly taken back to the horrific day that Derek drowned. She grew more upset with every passing second and it became harder and harder to breathe. It was the worst day of her entire life.

"We're too late," Haven choked before she realized she said it out loud. Garrett glanced up at her to see she was nearly hysterical.

"Maybe not. I need to get him back to the house immediately. Can you help me and go ahead? I need a bellow."

"It's too late!" Haven mumbled and shook her head. Her feet seemed glued to the ground. Garrett didn't waste any time. He quickly picked up Stephen Jr. and went on without her.

He had only gone a few feet when the boy's father and a footman rode up to them.

"I need a bellow, now! There's not much time," Garrett ordered in all seriousness. "We have to get him back to the house."

"That will take too long," Stephen interrupted in haste and looked at the footman. "Get a bellow from the servant's quarters," he commanded. The man hurried his steed along.

"The servant's quarters are located right on the other side of the path...closer than the house," Stephen jumped off his horse and knelt beside his son after Garrett laid him down.

Stephen quickly took off his jacket and bunched it up to put under Stephen Jr.'s head.

Haven very slowly approached the grave scene. The footman returned and handed off the bellow. Garrett immediately went to work. He gently placed the end of the bellow into the child's mouth and slowly opened and closed it.

"My poor little boy!" Mary came running just then and fell to her son's side. Stephen took her in his arms and they both prayed quietly but fervently. Garrett went on opening and closing the bellow, strong and sure. The solemn group fell deathly still. A low gurgling noise suddenly came from Stephen Jr. When Garrett heard it, he removed the bellow from his mouth just as the boy started to cough up water. He was alive!

"Mama?" the child spoke hoarsely.

"Thank you, Lord!" Mary cried and carefully embraced him. Garrett leaned back on his heels and wiped his brow with great relief.

"Thank you for bringing him back to us," Stephen patted him on the back, tears brimming in his eyes. Garrett nodded in return and they all got to their feet. He watched Stephen pick up his son before the family started back to the house. "Are you alright?" Garrett turned around to ask Haven but she wasn't there.

Haven ran and ran as if she was endeavoring to escape her past. She couldn't bear to stand there and watch the boy die in his parent's arms.

I thought I was free...free from everything that happened before.... Her chest burned as she wept. She was soon forced to come to a stop. She fell against a tree, entirely out of breath.

"Lord, I need You. Help the dear Kinsey family in their loss...help me," she panted. There was a large tree trunk on the ground nearby, so Haven went over to sit on it and wipe her tears. Despite the sunny day, she felt surrounded by dark clouds. Among everything else, she felt like a failure.

What kind of example am I? I'm supposed to be a believer and look how I acted. What would Hephzibah say? What would she have done in my place? What will Garrett think? I couldn't help him with the poor boy. A new round of emotions swept over Haven. Just then a twig snapped. She swiftly glanced up and saw Garrett coming toward her.

"The boy is alive. He's all right." Garrett wanted nothing more than to comfort her, yet his news didn't seem to bring her any relief. There was something else clearly going on. Was the journal's curse finally settling over her? "How did you know what to do…to save him?" Now it was Garrett's turn to grow uneasy. Was he ready to share what he'd kept secret for so long?

"I attended medical school to become a doctor," he blurted before he had time to think against it.

"You did?" Haven's eyes widened in utter shock. Until Garrett cleaned himself up, she would have never believed it. He was a scraggly, filthy, man who appeared to be homeless.

"It was a good thing you were there," Haven got up and turned her back to him so he wouldn't see her cry. Garrett covered the distance between them and put his hand on her shoulder.

"Everything is alright now," he whispered.

"Someone I loved drowned," her voice quivered as she relived it all over again. "I was going to marry him." She covered her face and sobbed. She felt Garrett put his arm around her for comfort before she leaned against him and cried on his shoulder for some time. Garrett's caring gesture did console her. Haven felt secure in his embrace, something she hadn't truly felt since Derek.

Garrett didn't pull away until Haven calmed and stopped weeping. She dried her tears before either of them spoke.

"I would offer you a handkerchief but mine is wet from

the brook," he said. Haven quickly looked up and found him smiling with amusement. The abrupt change in the mood made her chuckle. She thought his attempts to cheer her up very sweet.

"There's so much about you I don't know. Did you finish college?"

"I didn't complete my training." Garrett hesitated at first for more than ever, he was compelled to reveal his past. "My father is the only reason I went. I never really did enjoy it. It's a long story really." Haven moved back to the fallen tree trunk and sat down. She gave him a knowing look, telling him to go on.

"I've never shared this with anyone. I uh...found out that my parents aren't truly my parents. When I demanded to know the truth, my mother finally told me everything. My entire life has been a lie. I was burdened down by knowing I was expected to carry on with my father's practice. I grew up thinking I was the son of a poor doctor when really, I'm an heir to nobility and wealth."

"Oh my, I imagine that is quite a shock to hear."

"I drove my parents away with my anger," Garrett also took a seat on the trunk, a few feet from Haven.

"Where are they now?"

"I don't know. I've been hiding almost ever since."

"Hiding?" Haven asked in confusion.

"I'm not a good man," Garrett painfully admitted.

"Yes you are. Today you saved a child from death. You're nothing less than a hero."

"I'm no hero," Garrett shot to his feet and started to pace in agitation. "Because of my selfishness and anger over finding out the truth about my family, I killed a man. I promise you, it was a mistake. But nonetheless, the mistake cost a man his life and possibly my father's practice," he ranted. He expected Haven to say so many things but she didn't. She merely listened. It was now her turn to comfort him.

"You won't know for sure until you go to them and make things right." Haven's heart ached. She would never be able to do what she suggested.

"They don't want to have anything to do with me. I assure you."

"I was at odds with my family when I left them. I would give anything to go to them. I lost my chance forever…for they died."

"Every one of them?" Garrett asked. Haven nodded.

"They were on a ship bound to America but it never arrived." The day she found out seemed like an entirely different lifetime ago.

"How about your true family…do they know where you are?"

"As far as they know, I lived only a few minutes after being born. They have no idea I exist. I dare say, they would never believe me, a stranger who goes to them and claims to be their son."

"I suppose," Haven sighed. Now that they had shared their past with one another, the level of closeness in their relationship grew anew. Haven felt she could share her heart.

She stood and approached him.

"There is One who can help you as He did me. God brought me a peace like none other. Certainly, I find myself waver…like today. But He is with me, during those times. He can give you the peace you seek, as well as the guidance you need," she explained gently, trying not to push him. She put her hand on his reassuringly. Garrett gazed into her blue eyes, brought out by the bright color of her muslin dress. Her porcelain complexion and full lips were radiant in the sunlight. She was so beautiful, he couldn't help himself. Garrett gingerly reached up and pushed away a stray hair on her face as he lowered toward her. His lips nearly brushed against hers when Haven turned away. She stepped back abruptly.

"I…I'm sorry. I was too forward," he confessed in hushed tones.

"No, I…." Havenstarted in indecision but then took a few more steps back. She gathered her skirts in one hand and fled without another word. Garrett helplessly watched her disappear into the trees.

Haven quickly went to the bench to retrieve her Bible. When she neared the house, she couldn't make herself go inside. There were too many people. She had to get away to think. She had to make a decision swiftly for Garrett might try to find her. Just then one of the large barns, located a considerable distance away from the house, caught her eye.

No one would ever look for me there!

Haven hurried to the barn and peeked inside. *Thank goodness…no one is here,* she sighed. Haven marched to the ladder and climbed into the hayloft. The sun shined through a round window and cast a yellowish light over the hay.

She went to a bale and knelt down before it.

"Lord, what's happening? The feelings I have for Garrett are so strong. But he doesn't believe in You. What should I do?" she prayed a while more before opening her Bible.

CHAPTER FIFTY-ONE

s it just me or is Trenton getting worse?"
Bernice sat down next to the other ladies at the
long vanity in the women's dressing room of
the theater.

"Indeed…with each performance, he loses his temper
more and more," another actress agreed.

"Well that's because he doesn't have his precious angel,"

Lindsay put in with a snide tone. "If you ask me, I'm glad she's gone."

"Of course you are," Wren finally spoke up on the end. "You've always been jealous of Haven's talent as well as the attention Trenton paid her." Lindsay only snorted at this.

A knock sounded on the door. At first, the ladies presumed it to be Trenton. However, he never knocked.

"There's someone here to see you, Wren," an attendant came in and announced.

"Me?" Wren questioned.

"Aye, they're in one of the middle boxes on the second tier." Wren got up and followed him.

She walked through the velvet curtain into the box. There was an older couple still seated.

"Can I help you?"

"Oh, hello, my dear," they both stood up and greeted. The older woman shook Wren's hand. "I'm Adelaide, and this is my husband, Bertram." Wren was confused. She had never laid eyes on them before.

"Wonderful performance tonight," Bertram stated.

"Yes, but that's not the only reason why we came, nor why we need to speak with you," Adelaide looked behind Wren to make sure the attendant left.

"Yes?"

"Our nephew, Stephen Kinsey...he lives in Dolbury. Anyway, they have some guests staying with them, whom you know," Adelaide gave her a knowing look.

"Haven!" It finally hit Wren and she gasped. She instantly lowered her voice. "Is she alright?"

"Yes, she is. She wanted us to tell you where she is in hopes that you could get there. We thought it would be better not to give you something with an address written on it. As long as you know the town and our nephew's name, you can ask for directions once you reach Dolbury. Practically everyone knows them for it's a fairly small town."

"Thank you."

"If you agree to leave now, you could come with us, and we can help you get to Dolbury," Adelaide went on.

"A…alright. I just need to fetch my things from the dressing room."

"We will wait for you in the lobby." Wren's heart pounded. Every day, since Haven left the theater for good, she regretted not leaving with her. Her fears were too great. This was her chance!

She rushed back to the dressing room without gaining anyone's attention. When she reached it, everyone was already gone.

Most likely getting in the carriages to bring them back to the townhouse. Wren rushed over to where her things still lay. After throwing a few items in a bag, she started for the side door when she heard someone enter from the stage entrance. Her breath caught in her throat as Trenton walked in.

"Oh…uh, sorry to have kept the ladies waiting," she tried to calm herself.

"It's fine," Trenton said, his voice unusually monotone.

What should I do? What should I say? Wren panicked. She pretended to grab a few more things from the vanity counter.

Trenton moved to the other side of the room and leaned against the exit with his hands in his pockets, just staring at her. Wren's hands shook in fear.

"I'm ready now," she turned to face him. How could she get away now?

"Where are you planning to go?" Trenton asked.

"What do you mean? To the carriage of course."

"I overheard something in the hall, near the boxes." Wren froze. Trenton moved closer. "I thought I heard you say something about Haven," he stepped closer. "About where she might be," he whispered in her ear. Wren shivered. "I'm only going to ask this once," he looked at her sternly. "Where is Haven?" his voice lowered.

"I don't know what you're—" Wren began but Trenton grabbed her wrist and twisted it roughly. Wren winced loudly as she dropped the bag she held.

"Don't you dare lie to me!" he said through clenched teeth. "You tell me where she is or I'll kill you," he twisted further.

"Alright!" Wren cried out in pain. "She's in Dolbury!" She sighed with relief when he released her. Wren rubbed her wrist as tears burned her eyes. Trenton then ruthlessly took ahold of her black hair.

"You and I are going to take a little ride right now," Trenton shoved Wren forward against the side door.

CHAPTER FIFTY-TWO

arrett didn't see Haven for the remainder of the day. He hoped she would come to dinner so he could get a chance to speak to her. He greatly regretted what he'd done and wanted to apologize.

The family rejoiced over Stephen Jr.'s quick recovery. Other than a few scratches and bruises, he was fine. Mary had the cook prepare all of his favorite foods for a special dinner. They also praised God for Garrett, for bringing their son back to them. Garrett enjoyed all of it, but there was only one thing on his mind. He decided to leave the merriment early. He walked to the top of the stairs and looked down the hall to his left where Haven's room was. He stopped, wondering if he should knock on her door, but eventually went to his own room.

Garrett lay down on his bed and stared at the ceiling, going over everything that had taken place. All he wanted to do was to talk to Haven. He tossed and turned until he sat up in frustration. Leiston hadn't come to bed yet so Garrett was free to be as loud as he wished. He got up and went to the desk near the window, where he'd left the journal. September ninth was ever etched in his mind for that was the day Haven was going to die. Every night, Garrett would cross off the day on the calendar that sat on the desk. He picked up a quill pen, dipped it in the inkwell, then slashed a line through that day in the moonlight.

"Tomorrow is the day," he stated. A sorrowful knot formed in his stomach. Garrett regretted his actions all the more when he realized this was the last night. He wanted so badly to spend all the time he could with her.

Garrett spent the rest of the night willing himself to come up with a last desperate attempt to stop the ever pursuing curse.

CHAPTER FIFTY-THREE

September 9, 1836

 arrett dreaded the morning. He must have fallen asleep for he startled awake. He instantly looked out the window and was surprised to see the sun was up. He glanced to the other side of the room and saw Leiston was already gone.

What time is it? Garrett jumped out of bed and rushed to the desk to look at the small clock. *Ten o'clock. How did I sleep so long?*

Garrett swiftly dressed and nearly ran to the dining room. He met Mary along the way.

"There you are! The other men left hours ago."

"Left? Where?" he anxiously asked.

"Fox hunting. They discussed it last night during dinner," Mary informed and eyed him curiously. Garrett partially recalled them doing so, yet his mind had been quite preoccupied.

"Where is Haven...I mean, Miss Romiley?"

"Still in her room, I suppose. I haven't seen her." With that, Mary went on her way. Garrett watched her leave.

Instead of going to the dining room, he retraced his steps back up the stairs. He marched up to the door of Haven's room and knocked. There was no answer. He tried several more times but still nothing.

Where is she?

"Morning, sir," a maid meekly greeted and walked by. She was no doubt a bit disturbed seeing one of the gentlemen guests banging on the ladies door furiously.

"Morning. Could you do a favor for me and see if Miss Romiley is well? She's not coming to the door."

"Aye," she agreed and moved to the door. She gave a quick knock then slowly opened it and went inside. Garrett restlessly waited until she came out.

"She's not in her room, sir."

"Really? That's strange...perhaps she went for a walk."

He was now on a mission. He left the house and began his search for Haven. Garrett frantically walked all around the different paths surrounding the estate where he and Haven had gone before. She was nowhere to be found.

"Where could she be?" he finally stopped and asked himself. Part of him wanted to get everyone together and start a search party, yet what would he say? They would surely ask questions. He couldn't reveal to them the absurd circumstances concerning the cursed journal. Furthermore, Haven often secluded herself to pray and read the Bible. Was this merely the case?

The date written in the journal cannot be ignored! I have to find her! What if Trenton captured her? What if she's hurt? Garrett feared all the possibilities. *Perhaps I should ride into town and have a quick look around.* He couldn't just sit there and do nothing. Garrett rushed back to the estate. Thankfully, the servants already had a horse ready, presuming he would go hunting with the others.

He anxiously rode to the quaint town of Dolbury. He pulled back on the reigns, slowing his steed down to scan the area for anything suspicious. The only thing he spotted that seemed a little out of place was a dark enclosed carriage parked in front of the mercantile. Garrett intently watched it to see who emerged from it. He didn't have to wait very long, for the door opened and a well-dressed woman with black, upswept hair, stepped out. She took in her surroundings as if she'd never been there before then went inside the mercantile. There was really nothing more to do than to head back to Caragin. Garrett turned the horse around and rode away just as someone else climbed out of the carriage.

Trenton looked around at what he thought to be a pathetic little town. He spotted a man on a horse riding down the street.

This is a waste of time, Why would Haven come to a tiny town such as this? Trenton thought and started to climb back into the carriage. At that moment, he heard something. The same man stopped his steed and spoke to someone standing outside of the livery. Something about him drew Trenton's attention. He'd never seen him before. The instant he spoke to the other man, Trenton knew precisely who it was.

How can it be? I ordered my men to kill him. He looks nothing like the homeless retch!

Trenton intently watched Garrett until he hurried his horse along. An uncontrollable urgency rose up in him.

"It is him!" he mumbled through clenched teeth. "I'm sure of it."

As quickly as Wren walked into the store, she emerged.

"They wouldn't tell me where Mr. Kinsey—" Wren began but Trenton interrupted.

"Hurry up! We have to go…now," he barked. Wren's pace slowed in confusion. Apparently, she wasn't quick enough for Trenton rushed up to her and grabbed her arm.

"Get inside now…so we don't lose him!"

"Who?" Wren gasped.

"Driver, follow that horse!" he pointed to Garrett, who had rounded the corner and hurried his horse along.

Will Haven be there when I return? Where could she be? What should I do if she's not there? Garrett's troubling thoughts flew by him, as did the scenery. His concern and urgency made him push his horse all the harder to get back to Caragin. He tried to stay focused on a plan of some sort, yet the fear of losing Haven to the curse's power was so great. He had to stop it somehow but he dreaded it was too late.

He briefly glanced to his right to look at something in the distance when he realized he was being followed. Garrett strained to look behind to get another look as a knot formed in his stomach. It was the same dark carriage and it was following him at a fierce speed. It was all too clear who was chasing him. He kicked his heels into the sides of his steed to go faster. He could easily keep ahead of the carriage, yet if he kept going, he would surely lead Trenton right to Haven. Garrett knew Trenton wouldn't give up trying to get Haven back.

Why did I bring her here? I was so daft to think he would stop in his search for her. You know what Trenton is capable of! His thoughts screamed. He had to do something to prevent him from finding her. Garrett saw a crossroads swiftly coming towards him when a desperate idea seemed to present itself. Instead of continuing straight, which led to Caragin, he directed the horse left, away from it. Sure enough, the carriage turned as well. Garrett kept leading them further away from Caragin.

"I knew those two idiots couldn't be trusted to get rid of him," Trenton ranted.

"I gave them explicit orders!" Malcolm spoke up.

"We'll never catch up to him at this rate!" Trenton jeered in frustration. He was starting to catch on that Garrett was taking them in circles. This would get them nowhere.

"There's only one way to stop him," Malcolm met Trenton's gaze. "I'll shoot his horse." Wren's eyes widened with fear when she heard this. All this time, she silently prayed Garrett would get away. She helplessly watched Malcolm pull out a pistol. He leaned out of the window and took his time to try and steady himself as best he could in the shaky carriage. He closed his one eye to aim when Wren lunged forward and shoved him. The gun went off and pierced the sky with a deafening bang!

Haven suddenly sat up and gasped. She glanced around in confusion, trying to get her bearings. She had been sleeping soundly and forgot where she was. Haven reached up to push her hair away from her eyes when she found a piece of straw. It was a mess and had all but fallen from the hairpins.

Oh I remember now…I fell asleep in the barn. Haven moved her gaze upward toward the small window in the hayloft. *It must be late!* She got up and shook off the straw from her dress. She reached down to pick up her Bible when something seemed to hit her deep in the chest. An uneasy feeling seemed to flutter with each breath she took. There was something terribly wrong.

"Lord, what is it?" she whispered. Whatever it was, Haven had to find out straight away.

She rushed to the main house and plowed right into the housekeeper.

"Oh, my! What's the hurry, Miss Romiley?" the older woman gasped loudly.

"Where is everyone?" Haven asked, greatly concerned.

"The men went fox hunting and I believe Mrs. Kinsey is with the children."

"They did say they were going to go hunting, didn't they. How far from the estate does it usually take them?"

"Pretty far sometimes. I dare say we won't see them until dark."

"Oh, I see," Haven sighed. What was it then? A hunting accident of some kind? The housekeeper saw the uneasiness on her face.

"Is something wrong?"

"I don't know." Without saying anything more, Haven turned to leave. She walked down the remainder of the hall and to the back door that led to the veranda.

"Lord, what is it? Did I merely have a bad dream or something?" The minute she went outside, Haven began to pray. She had to find out what was going on. She prayed for safety over the men and anyone else that came to mind, yet she felt no relief.

"Stupid girl!" Trenton shouted and struck the side of Wren's face, causing her to fall back into her seat. Trenton then looked out the window, as did the others. To Wren's horror, Garrett and his horse were no longer on the gravel road.

The carriage slowed to a stop when they came upon them. Garrett lied face down in the grassy ditch. He'd been shot in the back. His horse, however, stood in the field, agitated.

"I should have you shot as well," Trenton growled at Wren. "Now we lost our leverage…and a way to get to Haven!"

"Wait, look!" Malcolm pointed to the horse. Trenton looked and saw the steed start walking in a certain direction. "Perhaps it will lead us to Miss Romiley after all."

"Good. Maybe it's not a complete loss," Trenton angrily eyed Wren again. "Driver, follow that horse."

"Yes, sir."

"What about him?" Malcolm motioned to Garrett's lifeless body.

"Leave him."

CHAPTER FIFTY-FOUR

irds were singing in the distance and there was a faint breeze. Garrett willed his eyes to open but his eyelids seemed so heavy. He fought and struggled until finally he opened them and saw the clear blue sky through the tall grass. That's when a piercing pain wracked his body. The agony was so great he could barely breathe. It shot through his body each time he inhaled. What was even worse was the misery of not knowing how long he'd been there and what was happening to Haven.

"I've got to save her!" he winced and tried to turn himself over onto his back. He nearly shouted from the excruciation. "I must save her," he moaned. He rested for a few minutes, before trying to move again. He reached for a handful of coarse grass, his hand covered in blood, and pulled himself until he fell onto his back. This time he did yell out. His head pounded and he felt as if he would pass out. He desperately wanted to get up and go to Haven. He had been so concerned with Haven's safety and well-being, he'd never thought about his own.

I'm going to die. What will happen to Haven then? Garrett willed himself to stay awake; his troubling thoughts were swiftly getting blurry. He laid helpless, breathing heavily and gazing at the sky.

"Lord," he cried out with everything in him, yet it was but a raspy whisper. "I've never prayed to you…please help me. Help Haven…help me as You have helped her." Every time he blinked, it was more difficult to open them. The sky grew blurry, as did everything else around him. He gradually slipped into unconsciousness, or so he thought. Things never went dark. The complete opposite happened and everything turned white, the brightest light he had ever known. Garrett then heard a faint sound of music. It was a sort of symphony and it echoed on the wind. The music enveloped him in perfect peace, as did the warmth from the light. Garrett's eyes could hardly adjust to the brightness. He shielded his gaze when it fell upon a figure of a man, walking toward him on the field. He came up to him until he stood over Garrett and looked down at him. Garrett could only make out the outline of the man, for it was as if the sun radiated directly from him. The only thing he could see clearly was the man's eyes. They drew him in. There was something about them that was strangely familiar.

The man reached out his hand toward Garrett's shoulder and touched him. He then shut his eyes and Garrett saw pain flash across his face. When he opened them and looked down at Garrett, a hint of sadness was found in his eyes. He stepped back from him and for the first time, Garrett could see more of the man. He wore white clothing and had black hair and beard. His skin was tanned as if he worked under the sun often. The man put forth his hand again, but this time he held it out for him to take. Without allowing the impossibility of being able to get up hinder him, Garrett took hold of it. With a strong grip, the man pulled him to his feet with ease. Garrett glanced down at his legs, amazed to be standing on his own. He then realized the white aura once surrounding him, disappeared and with it, the comforting music.

What just happened? Garrett tried to process the situation but was left sorely confused. One thing was clear; this was no longer a vision of an unconsciousness state. He was fully awake and coherent.

Was it only a dream? he asked himself. *But I'm standing! It's impossible.* The pain that, just a few seconds ago, wracked his body so he could hardly breathe, only ached now. All of a sudden, Garrett heard a distant voice, as if on the edge of thunder.

"'Surely He has borne your griefs and pains in His own body on the tree.'" Garrett hurriedly looked around for who was speaking to him. He almost missed it but sure enough, far in the distance was the same man. He was slowly walking away from him in the very same field, from which he came.

"'By whose stripes, you were healed.'"

He wasn't sure if he was merely seeing things, but there appeared to be a dark red stain on his back. It was easily seen in contrast to his white clothing. The blood seeping through his clothes was the very spot where Garrett's gunshot wound was. He blinked and the man vanished. Garrett looked around him to find he was all alone.

'By whose stripes, you were healed.' The words seemed to

ring in his ears. He didn't quite know what it meant, yet he felt different. It was as if he stood outside of himself at times.

Now that he was on his feet, the problem at hand came back to him.

"Haven," he muttered. *I've got to get to her!* The urgency he had before when he cried out to God, rose up in him in full force. *But how?* He was stranded in the middle of nowhere without a horse. Garrett scanned the area and spotted a single farm about half a mile away. It was on the other side of the same field the man had walked across and in the same direction. Surely it was a sign. Very carefully, Garrett took a step in the direction of the farm, then another, and another. He marveled that, though he was in some pain, he was indeed walking. It was nothing in comparison to before.

By the time Garrett reached the house, he was considerably sore and out of breath from the exertion. He briefly leaned against the rail of the stairs to catch his breath before clumsily climbing the stairs to the front door. He pounded on the door several times. No one came.

"Hello? Is anyone there?" he shouted then turned toward the barn. "Hello?" It appeared no one was home. Since this was an emergency, Garrett didn't hesitate to try the door. To his relief, it wasn't locked.

"Anyone home?" he opened the door a little and tried one last attempt to announce his presence. The house was completely still, so Garrett stepped inside. He planned to get a few things before helping himself to a horse in the barn. At least he dearly hoped he would find a horse there.

The first place Garrett sought was the kitchen. He stumbled through the house and found it. Once there, he opened all the cabinets and finally found the iodine. He picked up the dark bottle with bloodied and shaky hand. It was quite a struggle but he eventually managed to remove his jacket and vest. Next, he tore the front of his white shirt, sending buttons flying onto the floor. He pulled the cork out of the bottle with his teeth and braced himself for what he was about to do. Garrett poured the black liquid over his shoulder and back, causing him to shudder and shout in pain from the fiercely biting sting. It shot through him like lightning. There…the terrible task of warding off infection was completed. As daunting as it was, Garrett knew it had to be done. The training he'd received before leaving medical school proved to be helpful. The next matter hanging over him would be to find the bullet, lodged deep inside his back. That would have to be done later. Saving Haven was the only thing Garrett cared about.

On his way back to the front door, something caught his eye. He slowed to a stop when he saw a gun cabinet.

I had better go prepared, Garrett thought as he moved closer to it and opened it. He picked up a pistol and a box of bullets. The next thing to do was to go to the barn. Garrett was more than relieved to find a single horse in the stall.

CHAPTER FIFTY-FIVE

*H*aven prayed and prayed but instead of feeling better, she grew more uneasy as time went on. Although she desperately needed direction, the fear in her was too great and blocking it somehow, much like storm clouds blocking the sun's rays.

She had been so consumed with her thoughts; she didn't realize how far she walked until she came to the end of Caragin's tree line. She gazed out over the rolling hills before her.

"Lord, how do I get my peace back? Lead me...lead me in what to do," she whispered earnestly. She longed for Hephzibah. *She would know what to do.* Haven blinked back anxious tears. *What about Mary?* Haven thought as she recalled the active faith she'd witnessed ever since meeting the Kinsey family. *Yes! Mary...perhaps she'll know how to pray or what can be done.*

Haven turned to leave when something came over the ridge. She squinted intently to see better when she realized it was a horse. A knot formed in her stomach for there was no one riding it. Forgetting her plan, Haven ran to it. The horse didn't try to resist or flee when she reached out to take the reins. A million questions poured through her mind. Was it one of Caragin's steeds? Where did it come from? Where was its owner?

Haven inspected the saddle closely to see if there were any engravings on the saddle and to look inside the saddlebag. Her heart skipped a beat when she removed her hand from the saddle and found blood on it.

"Oh no!" Tears sprung to her eyes in fear. The only conclusion had to be a terrible hunting accident. She opened the saddlebag. To her horror, she pulled out the journal. "What now?" Haven tried to push away her fear to think of a plan. Her thoughts were cut short for someone grabbed her from behind. The journal fell from her grasp and to the ground as she was carried away. He took her in the direction the horse had just come from.

"Let go of me! What do you want?" Haven asked. It was futile to scream for no one would hear her so far away from the house. Along the way, she managed to get a swift glance at the man. He had a husky build and balding slightly. Though she couldn't be certain, he looked somewhat familiar. The man ignored her. Once they made it over the ridge, Haven saw a carriage parked on an old road, with two men standing outside of it. They got closer when Haven recognized them. It was Malcolm Barstow. It wasn't until she saw Trenton that she shivered. She greatly dreaded the day she would ever see the horrible man again. All of a sudden, she realized who held her. It was Trenton's carriage driver. She had seen him many times yet never really took notice.

"Hello dearest," Trenton greeted calmly, almost eerily, and smiled wickedly. He opened the carriage door before the driver threw her inside. Both Trenton and his assistant, Malcolm got in after her and shut the door.

"Haven!" Wren shrieked and immediately helped her to the seat across from her.

"Wren?" Haven gasped and took in Wren's tear-streaked face. "What are you doing here?" Wren didn't answer but fearfully glanced at Trenton.

"I brought you to this little reunion to—" he began.

"Where is Garrett? What have you done with him?" Haven quickly interrupted. Trenton, still calm, sat back and smiled.

"Why don't you ask your friend here?" he motioned in Wren's direction. Haven met Wren's gaze as tears filled her eyes.

"What? What happened? Don't tell me it's what I fear," Haven asked.

"I promise you…I was only trying to stop them," Wren choked, so Trenton went on to explain.

"Because of her, your…bloke is dead."

"What? No!"

"Shot in the back," Trenton spoke each word spitefully.

"No!" Haven buried her face in her hands and wept.

"I'm so sorry," Wren cried.

"Driver, take us to the coast. Make sure we remain unseen."

CHAPTER FIFTY-SIX

I have to get there in time! I must hurry! Garrett rode to Caragin as fast as he possibly could. It was tough going for with each gallop, pain rattled his body. He wrapped his arm around his midsection to try to ease his discomfort. It still was not anything like it was before he experienced the bright encounter.

He came to a crossroads when the horse almost threw him off as if spooked by something.

"Whoa!" Garrett gasped and hung onto the reins tightly. He couldn't understand what could have scared him. There wasn't anything near them. He swiftly got the animal under control and gently kicked its sides to continue but the horse tried to go down the other road instead of straight ahead to Caragin. Garrett steered him ahead again, yet he stubbornly wanted to go down the other one. Something seemed to draw him to it as if beckoning him.

Why should I go that way when Caragin is this way? He endeavored to move the horse along one more time but it still wouldn't budge.

"What do you want with me anyway?" Haven asked and wiped her eyes. Trenton wasn't moved by any sympathy whatsoever.

"It's only part of our agreement."

"Just let me go…and Wren."

"I won't do it."

"You don't own us!" Haven snapped. Trenton gazed at her intently. He realized she didn't fear him like she used to, and he didn't like it one bit. He didn't say anything more, knowing what had to be done.

The carriage stopped when they reached the coast. Malcolm got out and held the door for Trenton. Trenton was pleased when he saw that the coast rose high above the sea with a very steep cliff. The wind howled and they could hear the waves crash against the jagged rocks.

"Bring both of them," he ordered.

"Come on," Malcolm took hold of Wren's arm when she hesitated and pulled her out. He then shoved her forward toward Trenton. Haven meekly got out, saw the driver jump down from his high seat, and come up behind her. He didn't touch her but only stood guard. She took in the cliff and saw Trenton holding Wren in front of him. Wren vulnerably met her gaze with a fearful expression.

"Alright Haven," Trenton stated loudly. "I'll give you only one chance...one chance to choose. Either come back to the theater with me and marry me, or she dies," he briefly glanced down at Wren.

"Trenton," Haven could hardly believe his queer reasoning. She soon realized he was very serious. "Please don't do this," she cried, horrified.

"Make your choice."

"Don't go with him!" Wren shouted.

"Hush!" Trenton shook her so she would stop.

"Trenton, stop this!"

"Choose right now!" he yelled louder than ever. "You are nothing without me. Your gentleman friend is dead! You have nothing...nowhere else to turn to"

"I'm sorry," her voice wavered, making Trenton all the more furious.

"You don't think I'll do it, do you?" The crazed look in his eyes made Haven cringe with fright. Trenton recklessly dragged Wren to his left and threw her over the cliff right before her eyes.

"No!" Haven could not comprehend what just happened. It was so quick. Wren was gone. Her dear friend's scream rang loudly in her ears. Haven fell to her knees in sorrow.

Both Malcolm and the driver were surprised as well at Trenton's cruel action.

"After all I've done for you...taking you off the streets, giving you everything, making you famous...and this is how you repay me?" Trenton took a step toward her. "We have an agreement." Haven looked up at him through her tears.

"You are a monster! I will never go with you," she spewed. Trenton pulled a pistol from his pocket and raised it up, pointing it at her.

"Kill me if you wish, but I will never go with you!" Haven wept and no longer cared what became of her. Trenton pulled back the hammer when they heard a noise. Haven quickly turned around. Garrett was atop a horse and charging toward them at a fierce speed.

"Leave her alone!" It all happened so quickly, all at once. Garrett pulled the trigger of his gun. It hit Trenton in the chest, sending him stumbling backwards. His footing gave way under him and he fell over the side of the cliff, but not before shooting at Garrett. The bullet narrowly missed him but hit his horse. Since he was going so fast, Garrett flew forward when the steed crumbled beneath him.

Garrett woke up from blacking out for a brief moment. When he came to, he was lying on his back. All was quiet. He sat up as fast as he could and saw Malcolm rush to the carriage.

"Let's get out of here!" he commanded the driver then they both swiftly drove away. Garrett glanced at the horse, which lay unmoving. Only a few feet from it, was Haven.

"Haven!" Garrett gasped in horror. He scrambled to her side as his medical training took over. Haven's eyes were closed. She was breathing, but very faintly. He carefully lifted her head when he found blood. It was coming from the back of her head profusely.

The horse must have rolled over her! Fear washed over him for he saw the ground underneath her. It was solid stone, covered in a small puddle of Haven's blood.

"Dear Lord, what have I done?" His gaze was fixed on Haven's ashen colored face as tears welled in his eyes. "I'm so sorry," Garrett, still on his knees, gently gathered her into his arms. A very quiet moan escaped her lips and she slowly opened her eyes.

"Haven!" Garrett stated in astonishment.

"You're alive," she said, barely above a whisper. Garrett knew all too well how grave Haven's condition was. He choked up for he knew she didn't have much time.

"I'm so sorry...for everything."

"Don't fret. There is nothing to fear," she reached up and touched the side of his face lovingly. The affectionate act only grieved him further.

She doesn't know the extent of her injuries...surely she wouldn't be so calm if only she knew. Haven's unshakable demeanor deeply challenged him.

"Why do you cry so?" Haven asked. Garrett didn't have the heart to tell her.

"I...found peace," he admitted. He was quite shocked at what he said. Even in the midst of this terrible tragedy, there was an inner peace kindled in him that he'd never experienced before. He couldn't understand it. Haven sighed with relief at his confession. She opened her mouth to speak when her lungs strained for air. This was the first time Garrett saw evident pain on her face. It hurt him to see it. Her eyes fluttered.

"Haven, no. Don't slip away. Fight...fight to stay awake." Haven struggled to open her eyes but was fading quickly.

With a power and adrenaline not his own, Garrett scooped up her limp body in his arms and got to his feet. With the carriage gone and his own horse dead, there was no other choice than to start walking to Caragin.

"By whose stripes, you were healed. By whose stripes, you were healed," Garrett quietly repeated the divine words with each step he took. He marveled how he was able to keep going. When it would start getting difficult, he would repeat the phrase and could continue on. Though he didn't really even know what the words meant, they somehow gave him the strength he so desperately needed.

Every few minutes, he would look down to make sure Haven was still awake.

"Stay with me. We're almost there. Don't leave me. Stay awake," he urged.

It seemed like an eternity before Caragin came into view. He was more than relieved at the sight of it. He just crossed the threshold of the front gate when he stumbled a little. His strength was swiftly beginning to fade.

"We're almost there! Just a little further," Garrett huffed, now trying to convince himself to keep going.

"Mama, mama!" Stephen Jr. ran into the drawing room. Mary was sitting beside Scarlette, helping her with some needlework.

"What is it dear?" she halfheartedly replied but didn't turn to look at him.

"There's a man!"

"Alright."

"He's holding a girl. Mama!" he called louder, not liking to be ignored. In desperation, he scampered up to his mother and tugged at her sleeve. "Mama, there's a man holding a girl!"

"What are you talking about?" Scarlette asked.

"Dear, I'm busy right now. You go and play."

"But there's a man…he's coming." His ardent persistence finally gained Mary's attention and she looked at her son.

"What man? Where?" She was surprised at how upset he was.

"Come on!" he grasped her arm until she got up to follow him.

He led her down the stairs and to the front door. Mary no more than opened it when she gasped. She spotted Garrett straight away. He was holding Haven and stumbling forward with much difficulty. His face was grey. Something was terribly wrong.

"Charles!" Mary cried out for the butler. "Come quick!" She flew down the driveway. As she got closer, she saw Haven's bloodstained hair as well as the front of Garrett's shirt.

"Garrett, what has happened?" Mary asked. It sounded muffled and distant to him as if he was underwater. Sweat rolled down his brow. He was lightheaded and felt his strength leaving him. His back started bleeding again. Haven was slipping out of his grasp.

"Garrett!" Mary almost reached him when his legs gave way and he fell to his knees. She made it just in time to catch Haven's head before Garrett collapsed completely.

The last thing he remembered before losing consciousness was several footmen and the butler arriving and standing over him. He glanced at Haven's face when all went black.

CHAPTER FIFTY-SEVEN

September 12, 1836

 ays passed before Garrett opened his eyes. He looked around his room at Caragin. Leiston was sitting sideways on his bed, leaning against the wall sleeping.

Was everything that happened merely a nightmare? His memory was a bit clouded. He very quickly found out when he tried to sit up and pain went through him as a gasp escaped his lips. There were tight bandages wrapped around his chest, shoulder, and back.

"You're awake," Leiston heard him and woke up. He quickly got up and approached.

"Where is Haven?" Garrett groaned and lay back against the pillow.

"She's in her room, still unconscious."

"She's alive," Garrett said, mostly to himself in sheer amazement. His education told him, while she might be alive, she most likely will never wake up after enduring such a wound on the back of her head. Garrett took a deep breath before endeavoring to sit up again.

"Where are you going?" Leiston asked.

"I have to see her."

"You should really rest. The doctor said—"

"I have to see her," he huffed. "But I need help." Leiston sighed.

"You always have a way of convincing me to go along with things," he bent over to help Garrett stand to his feet.

Garrett conquered the task of getting dressed then slowly walked to Haven's room. He found the door already open. Mary, a maid, and the doctor were inside when he walked in. The doctor was just finishing up changing the bandages on Haven's head.

"Keep close watch over her. I'll be back in the morning. Fetch me if there's any change," he solemnly instructed before walking passed Garrett to leave, but not before looking at him. "Make sure you take it easy as well," he admonished.

"Yes sir," Garrett dutifully replied. Leiston, who had followed Garrett, eyed him as if saying he told him so. He then left to seek the doctor out.

"How is she?" Garrett limped toward the bed.

"Well…we are all praying very hard," Mary forced a weak

smile.

"I'll sit with her for a while," he eagerly offered.

"I'll check on both of you in a little bit," Mary patted his hand reassuringly.

"Thank you."

Once alone, Garrett sat down in the chair closest to Haven's side. He gingerly took her hand, almost constantly pushing away the guilt he felt. It was his fault that she was hurt.

"I'm so sorry for everything," he whispered. He stayed at her side steadfastly for hours, holding her hand the entire time. All he did was pray as best as he knew how. He was growing a little tired when there was a quiet knock at the open door.

"How are you doing?" Mary asked quietly.

"Fine. There's been no change yet," he stated, his voice hopeful.

"Do you want me to take over?"

"If it's all the same to you, I'd like to stay."

"Yes, of course." There was nothing more to say so she started to leave.

"What day is it?" Garrett had all but forgotten until just then.

"September the twelfth."

Three days have passed? "Thank you," he said and Mary went on her way.

Garrett carefully leaned forward and took both of Haven's hands.

"Haven, three days have passed since the day...and you're still alive. You did it. You broke the curse when it was impossible. You pulled through its power. I believe you can do it again. You can come through this as well. Come back to me...I love you," he poured out his heart to her, his gaze fixed on her pale face. He then lifted her hand to his lips and kissed it. When nothing happened, Garrett leaned back against the chair. As he sat there, deep in thought, he recalled all the things Haven told him about God. She was more sure than anything that she had been delivered from the journal's curse and it was God alone who did it.

"I want an assurance like hers," Garrett mumbled to himself. His own experience, when he was at the brink of death, came to him. It was all so real. He wished there was some way he could know for sure.

Another hour went by when he saw Haven's beloved Bible sitting on the nightstand. Nearly every time he saw her, she had the book with her. Garrett reached out and ran his hand across the cover before picking it up. He looked at a few pages then let it fall open on his lap but he didn't read it. Instead, he laid his head back against the back of the chair with a long sigh.

The day wore on until the sun set and it grew dark. To keep himself awake, Garrett finally gazed down at the open Bible and began to read.

"He is despised and rejected of men; a man of sorrows, and acquainted with grief: and we hid as it were our faces from him; he was despised, and we esteemed him not. Surely he hath borne our griefs, and carried our sorrows: yet we did esteem him stricken, smitten of God, and afflicted. But he was wounded for our transgressions, he was bruised for our iniquities: the chastisement of our peace was upon him; and with his stripes we are healed."

Garrett quickly leaned forward to look more closely at the words.

Am I reading this correctly? His brow furrowed for these were the very same words spoken to him when he cried out for help.

"With his stripes we are healed." He reread the wonderful words again in wonder. It was real. The experience out in the field wasn't a delusion from loss of blood or any other reason. After further reading of the chapter, Garrett discovered the person whom the verses referred to was the Son of God. Garrett gasped in shock. Did he truly come face to face with Jesus that day?

He slid off the chair and to his knees.

"I believe," he whispered ardently. "Lord, I believe." The Bible was still open in his hands. Tears sprang to his eyes. It felt like the very presence of God Himself filled the room. Garrett had never felt something as warm and wonderful as this. Nothing but love surrounded him like a fog. He layed the Bible aside and moved forward to lean on the bed. He then took ahold of Haven's limp hand.

"Just as you gave me the strength that day to rise up from death and go to Haven's aid, please heal her. Give her vigor, restore her to health...'By His stripes, she is healed.'" He quoted the verse again and again. He did this for an incomprehensible amount of time until he slowly drifted off to sleep.

The morning light streamed through the window and onto the foot of the bed. Garrett was fast asleep yet his hand still lay over Haven's. The next thing he knew, he felt his hand squeezed. He opened his eyes, looked up and saw it was Haven. Her hand squeezed his again.

"Haven," he whispered and moved his gaze to her face as her eyes slowly fluttered open. "Haven! You're back!" Garrett gasped. Haven looked at him. She immediately saw a

difference in his eyes. She then glanced down to see his hand
holding hers.

PART

III

"We had the sentence of death in ourselves, that we should not trust in ourselves, but in God which raiseth the dead: Who delivered us from so great a death, and doth deliver: in whom we trust that he will yet deliver us."

2 Corinthians 1:9-10

CHAPTER FIFTY-EIGHT

March 20, 1837

 ive months passed and in that time, Haven recovered quickly. In all the medical training Garrett had received, he knew all too well it was nothing less than miraculous that she recovered and so quickly. They informed the

authorities in Dolbury everything Trenton had done. They in turn, notified the London police and the investigation began there, as well as their pursuit of Malcolm Barstow.

Another miracle was the one in Garrett. He was indeed a new person. After much prayer and discussion, Garrett decided it was high time that he return to London, to make things right with his adoptive parents. Also, to regretfully come clean about what he'd done. It weighed heavily on him and regardless of what the circumstances might be, he wanted to make things right. He no longer feared anything that might await him there.

The carriage drove through the bustling city. Garrett and Haven dropped Leiston off at his townhouse then traveled to the east side of London to where the Blakeslee's resided. They barely spoke since Leiston left. Garrett was deep in thought. The carriage stopped outside of the house all too soon for him. He peered out of the window. As far as he could tell, the clinic located at the front of the house looked exactly the same and still open for patients. Garrett pictured it so many times but his troubling thoughts caused him to see it closed and rundown. He figured because of his careless actions that caused a man's death, the British Medical Association closed the clinic and revoked his father's medical license. What he saw now wasn't anything like what he thought.

His musings came to a halt when Haven, who sat beside him, took his hand. He turned from the window to her.

"This is the right thing to do," she reassured him lovingly. Her smile melted his worried expression.

"In my heart, I agree. It's just that…what I said the last time I saw them was so…so—"

"All of that is in the past now. You are a changed man."

"Yes," Garrett replied yet his voice was filled with doubt. "Shall we pray before we go in?" he asked. Haven nodded then they bowed their heads.

Garrett knocked on the side door, which was the family's personal entrance, separate from the clinic. He felt a little foolish knocking at his own home. It had been so long. He dearly hoped his parent's reaction in seeing him wouldn't be like anything he had pictured in his mind so many times. All he could see was them slamming the door in his face after all he'd done.

He held his breath when his mother, Merril came to the door. She took in his face and tears immediately came to her eyes.

"Oh Garrett!" she gasped and lunged forward to embrace him.

"Hello mother," he choked.

"I thought I would never see you again!" Merril cried and eventually pulled away from him. Haven took Garrett's arm when she finished wiping her own tears away.

"Mother, this is my wife, Haven." Merril covered her mouth in shock. Haven extended her hand toward Merril. The older woman didn't take it. Instead, she gently hugged her as well.

"What a wonderful and beautiful surprise. Come in, come in," she then showed them inside.

He couldn't wait a moment longer. As soon as they sat down at the table, Garrett took Merril's hand.

"I must apologize to you. What I said…and everything

I've done...." he stopped when he saw his mother look behind him. He turned to see his father walk in from the clinic side of the house. Garrett's heart sank when he saw Stanford's bewildered expression. This was the part he dreaded since deciding to make things right.

Garrett stood to his feet and forced himself to face him.

"Father, I...." *Did he know? Surely he did. Did he lose his medical license?* His thoughts reeled as he tried to find the right words. "I'm sorry for everything. I've made so many mistakes."

"Please don't say another word," Stanford stopped him. Garrett panicked. This was just as he feared. "I'm glad you're back, son." Garrett was more than astonished when his father pulled him in to hug him briefly. A new round of emotion washed over everyone.

Garrett soon introduced Haven to his father. Merril served tea then he began to explain everything that had happened.

"With everything you both did for me, this is how I repay you. I regret it more than anything." He finally got everything out, everything that had hung over him for so long. Both Merril and Stanford saw the change in him. There was no anger or resentment in him. There was hope and light on his countenance. It roused something in them, causing them to want to know more.

"While we did find out what took place, you should know Miss Arlington never pressed any charges against you. She knew how upset and sorry you were, not to mention the kindness you showed her in the first place. Her father had been very ill for a long time," Merril said to try and comfort him.

"She is right. No one expected him to live as long as he did. It was only a matter of time," Stanford explained.

"I still cost him his life...all because of my recklessness and anger. So no one came after you and the clinic?"

"No." Garrett now felt like a fool. He'd been hiding for two and a half years, all for nothing.

They visited for hours before Garrett and Haven said their goodnights and got in their hired carriage to leave. They got inside and Garrett no more than shut the door when he covered his face with his hand. Everything seemed to hit him all at once. Haven looked up from her lap and found him nearly weeping.

"Dear, what's wrong?" she gasped and put her arms around him. He couldn't speak for some time. Haven began to cry with him at seeing how upset he was. She imagined the weight of regret over him, was reconciled at long last. Haven was so happy he faced the unknown and conquered his doubts. As much as she was overjoyed for him, a small pang of sadness touched her heart. She would never have a chance to do the same with her family. She greatly regretted the way she left the ship that day and the last thing she'd said to her mother.

"I'm fine...really. I'm just relieved. It's over!" Garrett sighed heavily. All the terrible things he thought had happened to them, never did.

"It's all over, except one thing," Haven stated as her husband finally met her gaze in question. "It's quite obvious from what you're parents told you before you left. Your true family is here...right in London," she went on in all urgency. Garrett only nodded, deep in thought. "Don't you see? God wants to restore that as well."

"It's just...how will they possibly believe me and the absurd story? They are highly regarded and a member of nobility as well. I'm just...."

"Their son," Haven finished with confidence.

"But what would I say?"

"Just speak the truth. God will take care of the rest."

"Alright," Garrett eventually nodded in agreement. "We'll go to parliament tomorrow morning. Depending on when they're in session, we might have to wait for a break…less than a preferred setting for such news as I have to tell them."

"I dare say, there is no perfect setting. Nevertheless, this is surely a divine appointment," Haven said.

CHAPTER FIFTY-NINE

March 21, 1837

 s they readied upstairs the next morning, Haven overheard Leiston answer the front door.

"Can I help you?" he asked when he opened it and saw a young woman.

"Does Miss Romiley reside here?"

"Uh, yes for the time being. Just a moment please," he turned to fetch Haven just as she came down the stairs. If truth be told, she was quite curious.

"Someone is looking for you."

She went to the door and saw the woman was Lindsay Adair. It was the very last person she ever thought would be calling.

"Hello Lindsay, what brings you here?"

"These are for you," she handed Haven a small trunk.

"What is it?"

"Some things that were found in Trenton's office during the investigation…things Trenton was keeping from you…and all of us." Haven was surprised for there wasn't the usual air of snobbery about Lindsay's presence. She was different and softer towards her. "There's a few letters and a large amount of money owed to you. The authorities were going to bring it but I wanted to bring it myself."

"Thank you," Haven took the trunk.

"I…I'm sorry for everything. I heard what happened to you…and Wren. I'm glad you're doing well," Lindsay glanced down, partially in embarrassment over the way she had treated her. This astonished Haven more than anything.

"Thank you, Lindsay. It means a lot. What's to become of the theater and the other actors and actresses?"

"The theater will be handed over to new management and everyone will stay on as before. You can certainly return as well if you wish," she looked back up at her.

That's sweet of you to say. As of right now, I'm not sure what I'll do yet. Won't you stay for a cup of tea?"

"No thank you. I must get back."

"Thank you again." Haven shocked Lindsay by giving her a quick hug.

Garrett hardly said a word while they ate a quick breakfast. He nervously pushed his food around on his plate until Haven spoke up.

"Shall we go?" she felt uneasy for him, as did Leiston.

"Make sure you tell me everything tonight," Leiston stood when they did and walked out with them to make his way to college. The hired hackney carriage arrived right on time then Haven and Garrett were on their way.

They rode in silence through the busy marketplace, toward parliament. All of a sudden, the carriage jolted forward, lurching to a quick stop. Haven was caught off guard and nearly fell to the carriage floor but Garrett caught her arm to steady her.

"What was that?" She asked. Just then they heard the driver shout in anger.

"Oi! What do you think you're doin' running in front of me! Get out of my way!" Both Haven and Garrett glanced out of the side window to see what all the commotion was. A grubby man stumbled to the curb and turned back to look at the driver.

"Sorry!" he raised his hand. The minute she saw the man's long black hair, thin build, and crooked teeth, Haven gasped.

"Jessikiah!"

"What?" Garrett asked in confusion.

"I know him!" she exclaimed. *Out of all the people in London, and I see him here of all places?* She marveled.

Jessekiah started to scurry up the street. Concern instantly arose in Haven for he appeared to be frightened and bewildered like he was lost. There was apparently something terribly wrong.

The carriage started again and they continued on their way.

"Wait, stop!" Haven spoke up.

"Stop the carriage," Garrett shouted to the driver. Haven didn't wait for it to completely stop before she opened the door and jumped out.

"Jessekiah!" she called after the young man. When he heard someone say his name, he slowed to a stop. He was completely taken back when he turned around and saw a young woman in a fancy apparel and large hat.

"Jessekiah, please wait," Haven huffed, out of breath.

"Miss?" He was perplexed until she got closer and he saw her light blonde hair and face. "Miss, vat are you doink here?"

"I was in the carriage that stopped back there. Is everything alright?" Just then she noticed another man, with dark Romani features, approach them.

"Oh, I'm sorry. I didn't mean to run in front of you. Ziss man," Jessekiah pointed to him. "Let me know my dya— mother, I mean…she had a very bad fall and doesn't have much time levt."

Sabina…dying? Haven was instantly brought back to the day Sabina gave her the dreaded journal. *She knowingly gave it to me. The beginning of so many troubles and sorrow.* Part of her thought the horrible old woman was finally getting what she deserved. She quickly pushed the resentful thoughts aside and then recalled what she said to Garrett.

"This is a divine appointment. God is restoring what happened!" Her heart was immediately compelled to go, yet her mind told her not to.

"I'm goink there now before it's too late," Jessekiah shifted from foot to foot anxiously. "I haven't seen her since...the day ve both left." Guilt flashed across his face.

"Might I go with you?" Haven almost forced herself to ask. At that moment, Garrett came up behind her and put his hand on her shoulder. "I know, you can ride with us in the carriage!" she stated when the idea struck her.

"A...alright," Jessekiah glanced passed her at the angry carriage driver.

On the way to the gypsy camp, Jessekiah informed that he had been working in the market, building furniture and doing quite well at it. The other man with him said Sabina had been growing weaker the last few weeks then just a few days earlier, fell down the front steps of her wagon. She hit her head and broke her leg as well. She now had a fever from infection and was fading quickly.

They arrived at the Romani camp and rushed to Sabina's bright yellow wagon. Haven felt so strangely coming back to the wagon. Because there wasn't much room, only she and Jessekiah went inside. She solemnly followed him to the bunk in the back of the wagon. A woman sat with Sabina, holding a cold compress to her forehead.

"How is she?" Jessekiah quietly asked the woman. Before she could reply, Sabina abruptly spoke up on the bed.

"My chiavala," her voice was low and raspy. Jessekiah took the other woman's spot on a wooden stool at his mother's side.

"My son, you've finally returned." Haven cringed as she recalled how Sabina verbally abused and manipulated him. Sabina took his hand. She then glanced up and caught sight of Haven. When she did, her eyes widened as she pushed back against the pillow, pulling at her blankets.

"Za! Za!" she gasped as if she was seeing a ghost. At first, Haven was confused by the fear in the old woman but she swiftly realized why. Sabina surely presumed Haven to be dead from the curse's power months ago.

"Vy is she here? This rakli is a spirit..a spirit!" Sabina wailed and moaned.

"Dya, calm down. It's not good for you."

Why did I come? This wasn't a good idea, Haven thought. Sabina refused to calm down until she had a violent coughing fit that left her gasping for air. She was forced to quiet down. As Haven witnessed how sick and helpless Sabina truly was, something happened in her. More than anything else, there was hopelessness about the woman's face. Haven spotted it for it was the same hopelessness she felt the night she nearly took her own life. A strong compassion began to bubble up in her for the gypsy woman. Any animosity she had previously felt, vanished, and in its place, a love so great, it wasn't her own.

"It's goink to be alright," Jessekiah tried to console her. Sabina wasn't at all comforted by her son but became more fitful than ever. Haven noticed how the pitiful sight upset Jessekiah. She could only imagine that he was feeling guilty, thinking it was his fault Sabina was dying. She also witnessed how Sabina wasn't making any effort in trying to make things easier on her son, but quite the opposite.

Haven approached and put her hand on Jessekiah's shoulder. He turned to look at her.

"Let me try," she boldly whispered. He sighed with relief and moved aside to let Haven sit by his mother. The instant

Sabina saw her draw near, she grew panicked and listlessness all over again. It was as if she was petrified at Haven's very presence.

"Za...za!" Sabina spewed in Romani.

"Sabina," Haven tried to take her hand but the older woman pulled away before she could touch her. "Why are you so afraid of me?"

"You are a rakli spirit! Surely a spirit to haunt me!" Haven realized the woman had probably never seen a curse fail before. She now knew what to say.

"I'm not dead. I've come because I care about you," Haven said in a quiet, comforting tone. Sabina met her gaze for the first time in utter shock. "And you know what else? I forgive you." Sabina's breath caught in her throat.

"You are alive. How?"

"I found a power, stronger than death, to deliver me from the curse," Haven thought against bringing up the past. There was no time. "You can have the same power."

"No...there's nothink that can save me from all I've done," Sabina argued. Haven was both surprised and relieved that Sabina regretted her spiteful actions.

"I thought the same as you do now until God overwhelmed me with His love. He sent His Son to this earth to take our place. The punishment and curse meant for us, He took instead so we could be free," Haven reverently but hopefully explained. Sabina looked into her eyes when Haven saw a glimmer of hope in her.

"How do I get it?"

"You only have to ask. I'll help you." Another coughing spell took over. Sabina took ahold of Haven's hand tightly. She seemed to tremble when she thought it was her last. She eventually made it through and now lay, exhausted and completely worn out. Haven fervently prayed it wasn't too late.

"Only darkness lies before me," Sabina stated strangely. It sent a shiver through Haven at the abruptness.

"Pray with me, before it's too late." Urgency rose up in her, so she leaned forward and held Sabina's hand up to her. Sabina nodded, knowing all too well she didn't have much time left.

"Me too" Jessekiah suddenly spoke and placed his hand over theirs. Haven led the mother and son through a simple salvation prayer. There wasn't a dry eye amongst them by the time they said amen. Haven presumed Sabina would quickly grow peaceful much like she had done after praying the same prayer with Hephzibah, yet it wasn't the case. Sabina began to sob louder and louder.

"I have a terrible secret...I have to tell you. You come and forgive me...after all ze horrible thinks I've done. You don't know that I lied to you about your family."

"Wait, what do you mean?" Haven asked and quickly glanced at Jessekiah but found he was just as confused as she was.

"I lied," Sabina groaned with regret. I told you zat you're family went down on de ship zay were on...but it isn't true. I only said it to try and keep you wit us...for Jessekiah," she cried. Jessekiah's face grew red at her last statement. His mother didn't know Haven was now a married woman.

Haven tried to comprehend what Sabina had just confessed. Her family was alive? After all this time of thinking they were dead and grieving for them? Anger threatened to come over her yet the hope stirred in her was greater. Just the previous day she wished she could have made things right with her family. Haven suddenly pictured reuniting with her parents and sister.

Where are they now? Have they been looking for her? All the more questions piled over her.

"I'm so sorry, my dear chey," Sabina's cry brought Haven back to the present.

"I forgive you," she blurted before she knew what she was saying. *Are you daft? How can you forgive her?* Her mind seemed to scream.

"Chiavala, I'm sorry for everythink I've done to you," Sabina took Jessekiah's hand. She was indeed a new person! He raised her hand to his face.

"I forgive you, dya. You can be at peace," he choked. When she heard it, Sabina layed back and sighed heavily. Visual peace swept over her as all anxiety left. Now that things were made right, she closed her eyes and smiled.

"I see it...a great light and golden shores," she breathed, then was gone. Haven and Jessekiah watched in wonder at the glorious look on Sabina's face. Her son slowly bent over and kissed her forehead.

"Goodbye, dya," his voice was husky with emotion. "Thank you," was all he could say to Haven when their eyes met.

"You will be reunited with her again in glory," Haven wiped her eyes.

"What will you do now? Will you be alright?"

"Yes. I will now," he smiled.

CHAPTER SIXTY

 arrett slowly paced beside the carriage at the gypsy camp, patiently waiting for them. A half an hour passed when Haven emerged from the wagon. She solemnly approached him.

"How did it go?" he asked. Haven was nearly to him when she rushed the rest of the way and fell into him and began to weep.

"She's gone. She accepted Christ right before," she managed to say between sobs. Garrett held her closely.

When all her tears had been spent, she pulled away just enough to glance up at him.

"My family is alive!" she cried with joy.

"What? How?"

"Sabina lied about it."

"Sorry to interrupt, but parliament is going to be out of session soon," the driver informed when he pulled out his pocket watch and saw the time.

"Oh, Garrett! We must hurry, so we don't miss them! I'll tell you about it on the way," Haven said and they hurried into the carriage. The driver went as fast as he could but it was extremely busy at the present hour.

Once there, Garrett and Haven rushed into the public entrance at Westminster Palace, which they soon found to be a maze.

"Excuse me, are they still in session?" Garrett stopped a well-dressed man and asked.

"They just finished up and everyone left. Sorry, old boy." Garrett met Haven's disappointed gaze.

"Well, we will just have to come back tomorrow," he said. The man who had informed them overheard.

"Who might you be looking for?"

"Reid Lennox, Marquess of Kerrich."

"Ah yes. I spoke to him just this morning. The session of parliament that he is involved in is actually over. They adjourned just today. He and his wife are boarding a ship back to Ireland this very afternoon."

"Do you know what ship?" Garrett asked hastily.

"If memory serves me right, I believe he said the Florentine."

"Let's go!" Garrett said to Haven and they quickly turned

to leave.

"You're most likely too late!" the man shouted after them.

"Driver, please take us to the port of London and to the ship called the Florentine straight away!"

"Yes, sir."

"Let us not be too late," Haven prayed once they were off. Garrett rested his head on his hand as he starred out of the carriage window, watching the passing buildings.

They arrived at the port at long last. Fog drifted in from the river, for the air was cold on the crisp spring day. Garrett intently peered out and took in the enormity of it. Nearly one hundred ships lined the port, along with countless wagons, piled high with cargo, crates, and trunks, not to mention the many people working to load and unload the ships. How would they ever find the ship they were seeking?

"Lord, please help us...guide us," Haven prayed again under her breath.

"You there." The couple heard the driver shout to a nearby sailor. "Where can I find the Florentine?"

"Why, you're nearly lookin' right at it. It's that one right there, with the blue and gold flag," he pointed at the third ship from them.

Without waiting to hear another word, Garrett opened the carriage door and climbed out.

"I'll meet you there!" he shouted behind him to Haven as he broke into a run toward the ship. He saw that the sailors on it were letting down the sails, surely preparing to set sail at any moment. He would have run onto the gangplank and to the deck, if not for two sailors, who carried a large trunk, right in his way. From the looks of it, it was the very last trunk.

"I'm looking for someone on this ship."

"Well, you are too late. After we carry this, we're settin' sail," one grumpy man barked.

"You don't understand…it's of great importance. It will only take—"

"We don't care what it's about. We're leavin' so bug off!" Once they set the trunk down, the man immediately pulled the gangplank in so Garrett couldn't come aboard.

He helplessly watched them go for the large ropes tied to the docks.

This can't be it…to be this close only to miss them!

At that moment, he saw a very wealthy dressed, refined woman walk across the deck. The fur collar of her thick coat and extravagant hat made her clearly stand out from the grubby sailors working on deck. It was no doubt Garrett's true mother.

"Lady Kerrich!" Garrett desperately shouted. The woman instantly stopped and looked toward him. She was about to step closer to the rail when a man, wearing a top hat and long black coat, came up behind her.

"Eibhleann, our room in the hull is this way," he informed.

It seemed so foreign for Garrett to see them as his father and mother. They were in an entirely higher class than he could only imagine. It intimidated and made everything in him want to retreat and forget the notion of revealing the truth. At that moment, Haven's words came back to him.

"Don't you see? This is a divine appointment."

Garrett looked at the couple before him. If what Haven said was true, this was his one and only chance to do something about it. There was nothing to lose.

"Lady Kerrich, please…I have something to tell you." Eibhleann turned back to look at him.

"Dear, someone is callin' me name," she told her husband, Reid.

"What? Who?" Reid asked when a crewmember almost plowed into him. "Eibhleann, we must go below, so we don't get in the way while we set sail."

"I suppose you're right."

When Garrett saw them about to leave, he got even more desperate.

"Do you remember March 1815?" This clearly gained their attention. Reid took charge and went to the rail.

"I'm sorry, we can't help you. As you can see, we're setting sail," he said in his business tone of voice. "It's probably just someone who knows us and wants money or something," he lowered his voice and explained to his wife. He gently put his arm around Eibhleann and they began to walk away.

"Wait, please!" Garrett shouted all the louder. "On March 20, 1815, you had a son…a son that died."

"Reid," Eibhleann came to a halt. The mentioning of the painful night caused a knot to form in her stomach. They both slowly returned to the starboard side.

"Who are you?" Reid asked. Garrett took in everything going on around him and all the people. The enormity of what he was about to say fell over him. This was his chance. It could change his life forever, that is if they believed what he said to be true.

"This isn't the preferred setting…for something of this…importance," he stumbled over his words to find the right way to say it. He looked at Reid and Eibhleann standing there waiting for him to speak. They were his true parents. Surely, they would want to know him as much as he wished to know them.

"Your son lives," he finally blurted. Eibhleann gasped.

"How do you know all of this?" Reid asked, skeptically.

"It's him…I know it," Eibhleann stated quietly with confidence.

"Sail ho!" Just then a sailor shouted from the crow's nest.

"Wait, stop this ship!" Reid shouted.

CHAPTER SIXTY-ONE

 ate that night, well past midnight, the Lennox's private carriage dropped Garrett and Haven off at Leiston's small townhouse. They tried to be quiet when they let themselves in and to their room. Neither of them was tired in the least. After Reid and Eibhleann got off the ship, they went with them to their very large townhouse. Once there, Reid had some footmen fetch their luggage from the Florentine and it set sail

without them. The truth was finally told, on both sides. It was a warm and tearful reunion. The Lennox's firstborn son was restored at long last. They all thanked God for bringing them together. Garrett and Haven planned to return to the townhouse the next morning to discuss the future and to make plans.

"God is so good!" Haven exclaimed yet again. They felt so happy it seemed as if they floated home. They tried getting ready to go to bed but they kept stopping to go over all the miracles that had taken place.

"What God did to restore me to my family, He will do for yours as well," Garrett reassured.

"Yes," she replied, though halfheartedly. There were so many possibilities as to where they could be. There was so much she didn't know. Did they continue on their way to America or did they return home and were in England somewhere? Where did she even begin her search?

Garrett got into bed but still wasn't at all tired. Haven was about to join him when she saw the small trunk sitting on the dresser, where she'd put it after Lindsay delivered it that morning.

"Oh, I forgot to see what's in it," she walked over to it and opened the lid. Sitting on the very top was a thick envelope. She picked it up and found a large amount of money inside.

"Oh my!" she gasped. "Well, we have plenty of money to travel to America if need be…when the time comes." She set the envelope aside then went back to the trunk.

Why was Trenton hiding these from me? She questioned when she found several letters addressed to her. She read the return addresses of each one until she came across one that caught her attention.

"What is it?" Garrett sat up when she froze. Haven didn't answer but ripped the envelope open and began to read. Within seconds, she raised her trembling hand to her mouth; tears blurred her vision. She unintentionally crumpled the precious letter in her other hand and fell to her knees. Garrett swiftly jumped out of bed and went to her side.

"What is it?"

"It's from my mother!" Haven choked. "She saw my name in all the newspapers last year when I became famous. They're in America!" she exclaimed and fell against her husband's strong embrace. "They probably think I hate them because I never wrote back. But now I know where they are!"

"God has done a quick work!" Garrett stated in wonder at everything that had happened in only a matter of days.

"I'm overwhelmed by all of this," she sobbed.

"We are supposed to go to my parent's townhouse tomorrow morning to talk about future plans. I'm going to tell them before we talk of traveling to Ireland, we have something of most importance we need to attend to first."

"But you can't put off your family. They have such high hopes for you. Besides, to make such a trip to America would take months!"

"It will be just fine. They will wait months. They've already waited over twenty-one years. I've been restored to my family. Now it's your turn. It's a divine appointment as you once told me," Garrett smiled, "Especially with the money you just received. My parents will feel the same...I know it. We will just explain the entire thing to them."

"Oh, Garrett! You are wonderful. To see my family again...it's my heart's desire," Haven cried as they embraced each other again until Garrett leaned down to kiss her.

EPILOGUE

July 2, 1837

"Ma'am," the maid walked into the drawing room. "Someone is here to see you."

"Who is it?"

"Don't know ma'am, but they said it's very important," she informed

"Send them in."

The maid scurried away then came back with the two visitors following close behind.

"Hello mother." The woman froze, for she knew the voice well. She looked up and saw who it was.

"Haven!"

THE END

PSALM 107

"Hungry and thirsty, their soul fainted in them.

Then they cried unto the LORD in their trouble, and he delivered them out of their distresses.

And he led them forth by the right way, that they might go to a city of habitation.

Oh that men would praise the LORD for his goodness, and for his wonderful works to the children of men!

For he satisfieth the longing soul, and filleth the hungry soul with goodness......

Then they cried unto the LORD in their trouble, and he saved them out of their distresses.

He brought them out of darkness and the shadow of death, and brake their bands in sunder.

Oh that men would praise the LORD for his goodness, and for his wonderful works to the children of men!"

Jessica Benson

Kelly Aul lives in rural Minnesota. She works part-time as a
Pharmacy Technician and is in full-time ministry with her family at
Love of God Family Church in Fergus Falls, Minnesota, pastored by
her parents. Kelly edits and produces all of the media, from weekly
television programs to short films, websites, and social media, along
with creating flyers, newsletters, and books. She is enthralled with
19th-century European history, but her greatest passion is reaching
people with the Good News of Jesus Christ. She is in pastoral
training and helps head up the children's, teens, and other
life-changing ministries.

Jesus said, except a man be born again, he cannot see the kingdom of God. (John 3:3) Being born again or the New Birth is not: confirmation, church membership, water baptism, being moral, doing good deeds.

Ephesians 2:8-9 "For by grace are ye saved through faith; and that not of yourselves: it is the gift of God: not of works, lest any man should boast."

You have to simply admit you are just what the Bible says – a lost sinner. Then you come and accept what Christ has purchased for you – a gift! (Romans 10:9-10)

Please pray this prayer to receive Jesus as your Savior.

Dear Heavenly Father, I believe in my heart that Jesus Christ is the Son of God, that He was crucified, died, and rose from the dead.

I ask you, Lord Jesus, to be Lord of my life. Thank you for saving me and coming into my heart, for forgiving me and redeeming me from all sin.

It's important to find a church where they teach the Word of God by studying right from the Bible, and to renew your mind by reading the Bible every day.

— Maggie Aul, Senior Pastor
Love of God Family Church
www.LoveofGodFamilyChurch.com

Purebooks

I'm excited to announce PUREBOOKS Publishing. The PUREBOOKS imprint on the covers of my books means, the content is appropriate for all ages.

Before I ever started writing, I found myself frustrated when reading Christian Historical Fiction. I wanted to feel safe, reading only Christian books but was having a harder time finding them. I decided to write books filled with adventure, suspense, and romance, and all the while not compromise my Biblical convictions.

This PUREBOOKS emblem will ensure this is a safe read that will draw readers of all ages in, while keeping a pure heart.

"Blessed are the pure in heart for they shall see God." Matthew 5:8

❖ Pronunciation of Eibhleann ~ Avelynn

❖ Please visit the Official Author Website
www.KellyAul.com

❖ Like on Facebook
facebook.com/KellyAulNovels

Never Forsaken ~ Book One

She knows nothing of the tragedy that haunts her family's past.

Audrey has had enough of the emptiness of society and prays for something more. Unbeknown to her, someone is watching her every move just waiting for the right moment. It's only when Audrey faces death that her faith proves true at all costs in the midst of the storm. A new beginning is finally able to transpire when all is revealed and love is found in the most unlikely place.

AUDREY'S SUNRISE BOOK PREVIEW
Check out the video!
http://youtu.be/mrgABZLImjc

Never Forsaken ~ Book Two

She is held captive within herself with no chance of being rescued.

One decision changed their family forever. One choice tore them apart. Their every thought is now consumed with regret.

When everything she holds dear is taken away, her faith dwindles to nothing. She has no choice but to resign herself to the sorrowful fact that her once childlike faith in God, was nothing more than that...childish.

It isn't long before something else discovers her vulnerable state. She doesn't know what it is until it's too late. There is no one to turn to and the dreadful grips of fear, that haunts her every move, is hers alone to endure.

Try as she might to hide away her past completely, her persistent dreams won't let her forget. She's tempted to give in to the black shadows and simply give up.

She soon finds herself desperately searching for the one place she never wanted to see again. It is where she comes upon a treasure. Something that holds her only rescue from the dark presence pursuing her, as she finds hope in the midst of darkness.

IN THE MIDST OF DARKNESS BOOK PREVIEW
Check out the video!

https://youtu.be/0FeHG-E06OQ

Never Forsaken ~ Book Three

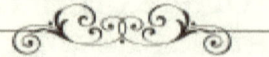

She must hold onto a hope when everything around her is falling away.

Brenna had lost everything dear to her. She had little else to do but come to the end of herself. At her darkest moment, an unexpected lifeline was shown her. Will she be able to hold fast to it as overwhelming challenges come upon her? Fear tempted to rise up in her. She couldn't help but wonder if the trying matter would awaken everything she had finally been able to rid herself from.

When a challenge far beyond her wildest dreams befalls her, Brenna truly sees she must let go of her mere efforts and cling to God completely. The power of love and faith she discovers is unshakable.

HOLDING FAITH BOOK PREVIEW
Check out the video!

http://youtu.be/0LShVcjJOVY

Never Forsaken ~ Book Four

He found a love so great, it was stronger than death itself.

When the one person Reid looked up to the most was stolen from him, a single promise gave him the determination needed to go on. Reid continually fights against every possible hindrance and rejection from high society. A relationship that should have brought joy, was built upon nothing more than secrets and deception. The love he'd sought after had betrayed him. Reid didn't know who he could trust, other than himself. That is until the unthinkable happens and leaves him completely helpless. Reid was forced to examine his life and it was then that he was shown a love so vast, he realized this unconditional love only comes from God. Little did her know what would be required of him. To lay down his life for another. A brother's hatred, a son's promise, and the Father's everlasting love would change the course of a rejected people forever.

EVERLASTING BOOK PREVIEW
Check out the video!

https://youtu.be/VATXE3_yQpw

The
SECRET
—— to Low Cost ——
SELF-PUBLISHING

Have you written a novel, a notebook filled with poems, or a children's book? Now what? Do I send it to a publisher? How? Do I Self publish? Where do I start? How much will it cost me? How much will I make?

There's a ton of self publishing help out there. What's different about this? KEEPING IT VERY LOW COST TO YOU.

How? Here's the secret. By doing everything yourself. From formatting, to the cover. That is what I want to show you how to do.

The most expensive thing you will have to purchase if your ISBN number. It's around $125. (a one time fee per book) The rest is well below that!

In these videos, I will give you easy, step by step information for everything you need to get your book published. Everything I know coming from someone who had no idea where to even start to 11 years and 5 published novels later. I want to help you!

You can purchase the entire set or each episode. Learn the things you want at your own pace

These instructional DVDs are available online:

facebook.com/KellyAulNovels

www.kellyaul.com